CRIMES OF THE YEAR 2000

CRIMES OF THE YEAR 2000

RAY CUMMINGS

INTRODUCTION BY
MONTE HERRIDGE

ILLUSTRATIONS BY
SAMUEL CAHAN
FRANK R. PAUL

POPULAR PUBLICATIONS · 2023

TABLE OF CONTENTS

INTRODUCTION BY
MONTE HERRIDGE

RAY CUMMINGS SEEMS to be better known for his science fiction stories than for his work in other genres. However, he wrote many stories for the detective and mystery pulps. This series marks a combination of these two genres in which he worked. The first story in the series was titled with the series title and also included a foreword, which was intended to explain the series premise:

> In presenting this series of crime stories, I have tried not to be fantastic. Imagine now that you are your grandson, with a future copy of this same magazine in your hands. You would not think these tales fantastic. The scientific devices, the mode of life pictured here (or at least something fairly comparable) would mirror your normal daily existence. And if, as you read, the stories project you in fancy forward to that time you yourself doubtless will live to see, my purpose will have been accomplished.
>
> RAY CUMMINGS

This foreword would naturally not have been necessary if the stories had been published in a science fiction magazine, but was felt to be needed in a magazine which ordinarily would not consider publishing this kind of story. There is no reason known for this series being published in *Detective Fiction Weekly*. The series is one of a short run, consisting of eight stories in 1935 and the ninth story in 1937.

Georg Trant and Jac Lombard are the primary characters in this series. They are members of the Shadow Squad of New York's Bureau of Criminal Investigations, working out of offices in the Shadow Squad Building in New York City. The cases they work on are not limited to the city but cover the entire country. Jac Lombard describes himself as being twenty-five years of age in 2000, and born in New York. His partner is about the same age. Lombard describes both of them; Trant was "a blond, easy going good-natured giant, the perfect contrast to me, for I am small, dark and swift-moving. And somewhat short of temper." (The Case of the Frightened Death) Shadow Squad members always work in pairs, and by 2003 they had been partners for seven years. They identify themselves to others by use of insignia tattooed on their arms. The regular police department uses the Police Alarm Squad to handle emergencies.

The Crime Prevention Bureau gives them assignments in criminal matters to investigate. One of their prime concerns was the prevention of crimes, not merely investigating after a crime (though that was also part of their job). The Crime Prevention Bureau is shown most clearly in the first story. The two investigators work under the Chief of City Night Desk 4, Captain Macfarlane. Macfarlane is "a fat little fellow, with a shining bald head and a ruddy cherubic moon-face." He sat at a large flat-top desk covered by several instruments. Each City Night Desk was responsible for the work of five pairs of investigators.

The series works in numerous technological advances that exist in the period. Some, like the miniature wax recording disk, are way off reality. One touch is right on target: there are cameras covering many areas of the city that are monitored when needed from the City Desks. This is something coming into use in some areas at this time. The stories also use the typical futuristic aircars, which we still have not seen come about. Regional aerial power stations broadcast power for the aircars. Other technological items include a heat ray gun, a mechanical scent sniffer for tracking (called an olfactory classifier or a bloodhound machine—in lieu of a dog), television broadcasting (called netcasting here), video equipped telephones, stratospheric airplanes, and other minor things.

The first story in the series is just known as "Crimes of the Year 2000," without the kind of specific title later stories had. On the third through the eighth stories, the series title is shown on the contents page, but the specific story title is shown in the description underneath this. The specific title is also shown at the beginning of the stories. This beginning story spent more space than the later stories in setting the scene for the series. The date is given as June 20, 2000. The first story involved the hunt for a most wanted master criminal known as 2XZ4 and attempted to discover the upcoming crime he was planning. 2XZ4 had planned a large precious metals robbery and the story relates the prevention of the crime and the conflict with the criminals. The bloodhound machine plays an important part in this story.

In the second story, the title on the contents page is "Crimes of the Year 2000"; however it is known from the contents page description blurb as "Studio Crime." But on the first page of the story itself the author gives it the title "The Television Alibi" (7/20/35). This case is involved with a live television broadcast from a small studio set in the Arizona desert. The date for this case is given as being June 25, 1999.

"Death in the Fog Tower" (8/3/35) starts on March 10, 2000, though most of the action in the story does not occur until a week later on March 17. Large airplanes are just going into service that will take away the freight business from the railroads. There is an unknown force threatening this new type of transportation, and the two investigators try to find out exactly what is going on. These giant airplanes are described as triple-winged, and use broadcast power like aircars.

"The Bandits of Pontoon 9" (8/17/35) takes place over and on the Pacific Ocean, as the two investigators become involved in a chase of kidnappers and terrorists. The story begins with the two on board a trans-Pacific airplane en route from Japan to San Francisco. The giant airplanes are designed to fly in the stratosphere, and can fly at eighty thousand feet. Their wings are two hundred feet long, and the planes are pressurized and temperature controlled. When two passengers on the airplane are kidnapped by Japanese criminals, the two Shadow Squad men are assigned to the case. The criminals take an escape vehicle from the airplane and land on Pontoon 9. The Pontoon of the title is one of a series of emergency landing fields in the shape of giant rafts. They are placed every two hundred miles across the 40th parallel across the Pacific. The ones to the West of a certain line belong to the Japanese, to the East of the line they are American.

In the story "Wreck of the Sub-sea Freighter" (9/14/35), the two investigators find that there is a connection in the events there to the events of the previous story. In this story the two investigators are involved with Spanish revolutionaries and arms smuggling. Cummings tells a little about the future history in this story. He mentions that after the war in 1967, international laws prohibited the movement of weapons from one country to another. The weapons mentioned in this story cover biological disease bombs, giant ray beam projectors, darkness bombs, and light bombs for blinding people. The sub-sea freighters of the story are actually submarines.

The sixth story, "The Man Who Died Twice" (9/28/35) involved prevention of a crime connected with one of the many people in suspended animation. At this time, people could go into suspended animation for a period of time, and arrange to be awakened to take up their lives again. Their estates were legally arranged to be held in trust for them. This story is dated September 14–15, 2000.

In "The Mystery of the Metal Murderer" (10/26/35), they investigate a crime rumored to have been committed by a domestic house robot. The date for this story is October 14, 2000, and involves a number of murders. The illustration for this story is a poor one. The man is dressed in 1930s era clothes, and the robot is a large, clunky, boxy looking thing that certainly couldn't be a domestic house robot. The illustrations for the series show a marked lack of imagination, and do not convey a sense of future times. The only exception to this is the more science fiction-like illustration for the last story, which shows a futuristic cityscape.

The story "Death in the Fire Pit" (11/30/35) takes place at a Federal government coin mint in Pennsylvania in September, 2000. The investigators find evidence of counterfeiting of coins, and a mysterious death of a mint employee. The fire pit of the title refers to an abandoned coal mine nearby, which has been burning for many years. The climactic struggle with the criminals takes place there.

The last story in the series is "The Case of the Frightened Death" (7/24/37), which was published more than a year after the previous story. The date of the story is stated to be August 4, 2003. This story involves someone using a sort of panic ray to terrorize the city populace. The ray is strong enough in its effects to cause the deaths of many of those people. Others suffer a severe nervous shock. The two investigators chase leads and the criminal all over, before finally ending his reign of terrorizing.

The series is interesting, and part of the interest of the stories is its difference from the kinds of stories usually found in this magazine. The series stories are full of action, and do not get bogged down by overly depending upon the science fiction aspect of the adventures.

CRIMES OF THE YEAR 2000

A Look into the Future at Amazing Crimes and Marvelous Devices for Detection

1

THE NIGHT OF June 20th, 2000, when the power failed and we so unexpectedly trapped 2XZ4—America's most famous murderer-at-large—will be a red star always in New York's criminal records.

You remember, of course, the main newscasted facts of the night when the power failed. But by chance it was my lot to be intimately concerned with that brief and sensational series of events; and I set them down here exactly as they occurred, with the hope that the details (hitherto untold) may be of interest.

I am a New York S.S. Man—plain-clothesman of the Shadow Squad of New York's Bureau of Criminal Investigations. I was twenty-five years old last year, when this affair transpired. I am government-educated; a New Yorker by birth, of American-born stock through six generations, though originally my father's family came from Italy. My name is Jac Lombard.

On the evening of June 20th, 2000, at about 11 P.M. I reported for work-assignment to my immediate superior, Captain Macfarlan, Chief of City Night Desk 4. I found him there with Georg Trant, a fellow of about my own age. Trant was, and still is, my partner. We S.S. men work in pairs, sticking together under all circumstances.

Mac's office was dim. He was bending over the multi-

*We leaped over the
little rail and had him
loose in a moment.*

plicity of instruments on his big, flat-top desk. A fat little
fellow, with a shining bald head and a ruddy, cherubic
moon-face. But he didn't look cherubic now. Every line of
him was tense.

Behind him, big blond Trant stood motionless. As I
entered, advancing noiselessly on the padded floor, Trant
gave me barely a nod. I sat down. Then I stood up beside
him.

"What's in the air?" I whispered tensely.

"He's worried over Kenna. Sent him out alone a while
ago. His partner's sick," Trant whispered.

There wasn't a single instrument alive on the desk. Mac
just sat staring, waiting. The place was so silent that Mac's
little electric clock thudded with a racing, excited, beat.
It is anything but easy, if you're a conscientious man like
Mac, to run one of these City Night Desks. You have a

maximum of ten operators—five partners. You send them out, and at the desk you sit through the night, responsible for their lives, for almost their every action. The desk is the nerve-center—the brain.

I gathered that Kenna was overdue in reporting.

THEN SUDDENLY ONE of the little loud speakers buzzed. The tiny, wirelessed voice of Kenna whispered, "Sorry, Mac. Couldn't get a minute before now...."

The words blurred; Mac bent down lower to the speaker-disc. Then I heard Kenna say:

"It's tonight—Latitude 40° 15' 10" N., Longitude 73° 44' 50" W. I'll call you again shortly. If I can only get closer to them! My Eavesdropper lost them just now."

He clicked off. Mac sat back, relaxed and relieved. And he told us now what it was all about, so far as he knew, which wasn't much. Kenna hadn't come to the desk tonight. On his way in he had radiphoned that he'd stumbled onto something. That was Kenna's style—by nature he was a browser. Something that concerned the present whereabouts of 2XZ4.

That was startling, of course. 2XZ4—the man wanted for a score of crimes, from murder up to treasonable plotting. 2XZ4 had never been arrested, never been typed. But we had his olfactory classification; the Bloodhound Machine, as the newscasters luridly call it, had contacted his trail several times, so that the scent of him was mathematically known.

Much good that did us! No one knew where he was now; nor what was his name, his nationality, nor what he looked like. Indeed we knew nothing about him at all, except his scent, which gave him the index-symbol 2XZ4. And now, when Kenna announced that he had by chance tuned his electric Eavesdropper upon two men—overheard a snatch that seemed to indicate that they were in contact with 2XZ4—well, Mac told him to go right ahead and tail them.

"Where is Kenna now?" I demanded.

Mac glanced at one of the dials on his desk, which had swung when Kenna's incoming call was received.

"Twenty-two thousand feet N.N.E. of here," Mac said. "These damned direction-finders are only approximate at best. He said he was in a sub-level corridor, getting pretty close to the river."

We knew the general locality. Mac's office was on top of the eighty-level Police Building, central in Lower Manhattan. Kenna was some four miles north-north-east of us.... I think about ten or fifteen minutes went by. Mac was discussing a tame routine job on which he was planning to dispatch Trant and me.

Then suddenly Kenna's little red danger bulb on Mac's desk was illumined. For an instant Trant and Mac and I stared at it, stricken breathless. Very seldom had I ever seen one of the red bulbs glowing. It was an ugly, frightening sight. It meant that the hidden chest-band which held the tiny microphone under Kenna's shirt, was being ripped away. Kenna was being attacked!

And suddenly Kenna's voice sounded: "Got me! Don't give a general alarm—that would ruin everything. Send two partners quietly. Try to get more information. It's something big. It concerns Palisades Aerial Power. Warn Paul Green—it's tonight—2XZ4 is—I'm located at—"

His labored, incoherent whisper broke; and then the whole apparatus went dead. Mac swung around. His red face had gone pale; his usually mild blue eyes were blazing. He had lost a man.

"You heard him," he said. "They've killed him, I guess. But I'll respect his words. No general alarm. Go after him, you two. If you find him—if he's alive—drop everything. Get medical help first."

Trant and I sprang to fling on our instrument equipment, and to record what few details were available. 2XZ4 in some plot. Something about to happen tonight. A mysterious latitude and longitude which we knew was in the Atlantic Ocean somewhere off the Jersey coast. And the thing also concerned the Palisades Aerial Power House.

We were only a few minutes getting ready. Mac had called General Air Police; warned them of something unknown impending off the Jersey coast, so that an aerial patrol would be there…. Then he called Palisades Power House. It was a routine air-call with visual connection. On the mirror-grid we saw the florid face of Paul Green, for years chief of the power house. All the broadcasted aërial power, from which aircraft traversing this district were operated, was under the night supervision of this Paul Green.

"What's in the air?" Green demanded. "You look harassed, Mac."

Mac told him only that we had a vague tip. Some criminal activity, directed possibly against the power house. Green was a phlegmatic sort of fellow. The little image of him on the grid showed that he was smiling skeptically. Behind him we could see the outlines of the main power broadcasting room, lurid with blue electric flashes.

Mac said, "I'll be sending you two or four routine guards presently."

"Right," said Green.

They disconnected. Trant and I took a look at the mute and motionless dial indicator which recorded poor Kenna's last position.

Mac said, "Well, good luck, boys. Keep connecting me."

He flung himself back in his chair. We hurried out, closing the door; and I recall how grimly he stared after us. There is a thrill in prowling abroad. I wouldn't want to be the man who has to sit and wait.

2

WE TOOK THE moving sidewalk of the Hudson River ramp; and on the top level slid northward at thirty miles an hour. It was a warm, starry night. There were quite a few pedestrians strolling here. We leaned unobtrusively against the rail, in appearance just a couple of nondescript young men in dark clothes who might have their minds on selecting a pair of girls from the strollers. The gleaming, moonlit river was dotted with pleasure planes landing and taking off; and the sky overhead, especially in the lower lanes, was fairly crowded with air traffic.

Within a few minutes we switched to the Eighty-sixth Street crosstown ramp, sped eastward between the rows of towering apartment buildings, over the Central Playground, and into the midtown East District by the other river.

Trant already had connected Mac. The chief had been trying to calculate on a city Street Level Map just where Kenna had been. That dial-reading of direction and distance embraced a considerable territory.

"He said he was in a sub-level corridor," Mac reminded us.

That was not very definite, either. The river section here, particularly in the two or three sub-surface streets, had of recent years become a disreputable slum. We found ourselves presently walking north in the second sub-level corridor about a block from the river. It was exclusively a pedestrian street—not much more than a vaulted arcade. There were dingy shops here, and cubby dwellings of the cheapest sort. Most of them, at eleven-thirty at night, were dark. Occasionally there was a little restaurant, blue with cigarette smoke, its entertainers visible through the window as an allure to the street pedestrians.

The corridor was dim. Only an occasional ceiling tubelight cast its blue-white sheen over the intersection of the narrow cross corridors and the infrequent inclines leading to the surface street, or down to a lower level. The whole place was shabby, disgraceful to a modern city like ours. Yet perhaps there was sense to it—vice concentrating itself here, comparatively undisturbed by police supervision, on the theory that the more wholesome parts of the city might be free of contamination. A cesspool, necessary to sanitation. I am only an S.S. man; I cannot argue civic welfare.

The few pedestrians along here were shabby, furtively slouching and at many corners women lurked. We pulled our caps low and strode ahead. Somewhere in the general neighborhood Kenna had been operating. There was a way by which, dead or alive, he could lead us to him—if only we could get within the eight-hundred-foot magnetic range.

We were trying to do just that. Trant was using our tiny compass inductor now. That is one big advantage of partners—we each carried only half of the multiplicity of small instruments of our equipment. Except, of course, we both had a radio-telephone connecting us with Mac. It was, of course, on a secret split-wave. Both of us had the thumbnail-size disc fastened to the alarm-band around our chests. The alarm-band is accursedly sensitive with its trouble warning—altogether too sensitive, as a matter of fact, which we were soon to have demonstrated to us very forcibly.

Then we got within Kenna's magnetic range. Trant gave a low, triumphant chuckle. "Good boy! Dying or not, he kept his wits. I've got it, Jac! Coming in strong. Tell Mac."

Kenna, dying or not, had switched the current into his electro-magnet. The highly magnetized needle of Trant's compass inductor was feeling the magnet-pull, as the needle of an old-fashioned compass swings to magnetic north.

We stood in the dim street-corridor. We were in the middle of a block. The inductor indicator pointed diagonally at the dark show window of a small tobacconist shop, a shabby cellar wall with tenement dwellings overhead and all about us.

We tried not to look suspicious to anyone who might be watching us. I called Mac with chin down to my chest, as though I were peering at the display of tobaccos in the window. The tiny plug in one of my ears gave Mac's voice:

"You think Kenna might be in that house?"

"We don't know."

"How strong is the signal?" Mac demanded.

Trant calculated that Kenna might be five hundred feet away from us.

"Then he's not in that house," Mac decided. "I don't believe it's that big. I'll look it up on the large-scale map. And you try your Eavesdropper."

The electric Eavesdropper roared with a torrent of

sound—the magnification of all the myriad blended city noises near us. But I couldn't isolate anything significant.

Then Mac came back to the connection. "An alley in the other street," his voice murmured. "Stay with me—I'll direct you. And watch yourselves—"

We shut off all instruments save my connection with Mac. Trant drew his Banning heat-gun; held it under his jacket. We went up to the next cross corridor; turned left; doubled back into another vaulted street. The block was seemingly deserted; dim and shadowed.

Mac's voice whispered, "Just ahead, on your left—a narrow alley between those two protruding walls. See it?" **HIS HUGE WALL** map showed it; but all we could see was a decrepit building wall projecting a few feet into the street, with a black gash. The gash proved to be a six-foot wide canyon alley, which apparently ran into the next parallel street. It was wholly unlighted. We stood cautiously at the entrance, peering into the darkness. There was just a faint glow marking its other end. Was Kenna in here? Or in one of the adjacent buildings? Dead? Or captured?

To me the empty, silent darkness of that alley seemed full of a myriad menacing possibilities. The devices of modern detective science work both ways. It's ironic, but true, that although our scientific instruments are in many cases little known to the public, we could be sure that the criminals possessed them all.

Mac quite evidently didn't like the aspect of this alley. His voice murmured, "Wait! Let's try—"

But Trant, like the brash fool he always is, had already started forward. Don't misunderstand me; I like Trant. He's my partner—as fine a partner as anybody could want—

except that he's too accursedly courageous. Big, lazy, and smiling—I guess, like Mercutio, he'd smile with a mortal wound, and smile as he died. I'm his exact opposite. I'm rather small and dark—bad-tempered, he says; grim and over-cautious.

He turned and murmured, "To the devil with your instruments. Shut Mac off. Come on."

He was already quite a bit ahead of me; and I disconnected Mac with a hurried explanation and went forward.

"Nothing here," Trant murmured.

"Maybe not," I whispered.

We stood midway of the alley length. There was plenty of dark doorways. I could imagine men might be lurking in any of them, watching us. Kenna had come along here, maybe, following somebody who was joining some secret rendezvous in one of these shabby cellars? I wanted to try the Eavesdropper again, or see what the magnetic reading of Kenna's location might be now.

But Trant whispered, "Devil with it—quicker to look for ourselves!"

We poked along, peering into the vestibule doorways. Trant even had the brashness to use his small actinic flash-torch.

And then we came upon Kenna—his crumpled body lying in the shadows up against the alley wall. We bent over him and saw at once that he was undoubtedly dead. His white shirt showed the little round burned hole, seared bloodless by the heat, when the Banning heat-flash had stabbed through him.

I stared at Trant. "They were here. They rifled him."

"Yes, I see it."

"Took some of his weapons," I whispered. "Ripped his shirt—see it? That's when Mac got the red signal."

They had evidently wanted to learn Kenna's identity. A hurried search, and then they had fled.

"If only he could have told us who they were," Trant murmured.

I was feeling up Kenna's forearm, under his sleeve. A wild chance....

"If they didn't smash his phono-disc," I said. "If only he stayed alive long enough—"

The tiny phonographic recorder on his forearm was intact. I switched his battery current into it. Trant and I crouched breathless. The wax disc revolved under the needle and diaphragm; Kenna's laboring, dying voice murmured microscopically at us!

"Got me—they've gone—it concerns 2XZ4—and it's at Palisades Power Station about midnight tonight. The—the incoming Great Circle Flyer—you had better—"

The microscopic gasp and rattle as he choked and died were gruesome, horrible. It was almost as though he were dying here now.... The little phono-disc ground and scratched emptily to its end.

Trant snatched at me. "Power station—midnight tonight? But it's eleven-fifty now, Jac! I'll tell Mac—the incoming Great Circle Flyer—"

I jumped erect. "Let's get out of here first! If they—"

It must have been a premonition. Certainly we had no warning. The darkness of the alley was abruptly stabbed with a sizzling Banning heat-flash. It missed me by inches. I heard Trant rip out an oath, saw him rise up, stagger and go down. Dead? I think I have never had such a sickening sensation of horror as in those few seconds. I saw a distant running figure; I stabbed after it, but the hissing blue flash went far wide.

"Jac!"

Amazing relief! Trant was not dead. The flash had seared his shoulder, burned his jacket and shirt; stunned him so that he stumbled and fell over Kenna's body. He rose up now, still dizzy, with his arms flailing wildly. It was a queer coincidence. Unfortunate mischance. I was aware that his flailing fist struck me smartly in the chest, but I thought nothing of it then.

I gripped him; steadied him. "You're all right?" I asked.

"Hell, yes. Almost—got me." The heat-bolt—so brief, but so utterly intense—had burned his shoulder only a little; but had shocked his whole nervous system. He was trembling as though palsied; but I saw that he was grinning. He stammered:

"That fellow got away?"

"Yes. Only one. He ran—"

"Then you call Mac," Trant insisted. "Tell him—"

"We've got to get out of here first," I insisted.

3

THE FUGITIVE HAD ducked like a rat out of the distant alley end. We ran that way. Trant staggered at first, but in a moment he had recovered. The corridor street beyond the alley showed no alarm. There were a few distant pedestrians, and a nearby cross corridor on which vehicular traffic was passing. No sign of the running fugitive.

We stopped to peer into a lighted window. I tried to call Mac, and then we discovered the unfortunate mischance. The portable wireless apparatus, as I said, is damnably sensitive to trouble. When Trant stumbled and fell over Kenna's body he had smashed his sender—and his flailing fist, a moment later, had smashed mine.

Mac had gotten the red alarm-signal from both of us! I can imagine how Mac felt. Three of his men killed on one job. And it had shocked Mac so that he threw caution to the winds. The whole tradition of the S.S. Division is secrecy; but Mac now turned in a general neighborhood alarm. Down at the corner, where the vehicles were passing, a street siren set up its sharp electrical whine. An actinic alarm light bathed the whole street in this vicinity with its dazzling white glare. The alley had no such equipment, but it would be lighted by the reflected glow. The nearest police and news lens-eye on their fixed street posts would all be transmitting the scene to headquarters.

The street sprang into a sudden turmoil; people peering and shouting from windows, pedestrians miraculously gathering, the vehicular traffic getting itself into a snarl. Within another minute a score of the roaming routine police and traffic officers would be here.

Trant clutched at me.

"Good Lord, Jac—we mustn't get caught in this! Ten minutes from now, in that Power Station—"

By S.S. training, by instinct and all common sense, the worst thing we could do was to get tangled in this police-routine turmoil. Those ten precious minutes would be gone.

Trant shoved me through the gathering crowd. "We can get to the Power Station in ten minutes and phone ahead to Green from the taxi. That's the quickest way—"

For once I agreed with him. We spotted a little pedestrian incline up to the surface street. Already it had a uniformed police guard. We showed our credentials and told him to report to Mac at once that we were unhurt. Then we ran up from the alarm-glare to the comparative darkness of the surface street, and hailed the first passing taxi.

"Westchester-Hudson Power Station," Trant said as we leaped aboard. "An' make it fast, fella. S.S. business—you get into the air the quickest you know how. We want the Power Station roof landing."

The taxi-pilot nodded, with an awed look at us. With reckless abandon we outsped the rolling traffic up an ascending ramp onto a take-off incline. And within a minute were in the air, gliding swiftly up into the open starlight.

"Pilot, open this audiphone," Trant ordered.

The taxi's instrument opened for Trant; he called Aerial Central.

"Westchester-Hudson Power Station," he told the Central Operator. "S.S. man calling, asking visual connection."

Within a few seconds the taxi's mirror-grid glowed with the image of the power house wireless operator. I knew him—a little hunchback fellow named Iturbi. A mid-European. He had been night operator in charge of the power house for several years. He said:

"What's in the air?" He had an image of the interior of our taxi but he didn't know Trant. "Who are you? S.S. man?" he said. Then he saw me leaning over Trant's shoulder. He said, "Oh, Jac Lombard!"

Trant said, "Everything all right with you there?"

"Why, of course. We had some warning—"

"Macfarlan of City Night Desk 4 should have sent you an extra guard," Trant said. "By now they ought to be there."

"They're here. Four of them. They're upstairs with Green now. Only Green and one assistant up there—we're running low-manned tonight. But it's all right."

Trant told him it wasn't all right; that something might go wrong there any minute; to warn Mac's men of that, and tell them we were on our way up—we'd be there in a few minutes, landing on the roof stage.

"Correct," Iturbi said; and reached to disconnect. Just as his image faded, it seemed that I saw on his face a very queer look. It startled me. And certainly it startled Trant. Instantly he plugged back for the Central Operator.

"Give me Westchester Aërial Power again," he demanded sharply.

AND THEN WE got another shock. An out-of-order signal from Iturbi. The main switchboard of Westchester Power was out of order! Audiphone emergency men would be rushed there to re-establish service. Then we tried Paul Green's personal instrument. "No answer" signal. No answer—and Iturbi had just told us that Mac's men were upstairs with Green and Green's assistant! Six men up there by this instrument—and not one of them to answer it?

Trant and I gazed at one another. Very queer this. There was now no time to call Mac. Already our little taxiplane had sped over the terraced buildings of the Yonkers district. The gleaming Hudson lay to our left. And in half a minute the small, square building of the power house, on its isolated little hilltop with incongruous woods and gardens around it, lay beneath us.

The broadcasting mechanisms, for all their giant capacity, were small and easily manned. The quadrangular metal building was no more than fifty feet square and only two stories high. The power came by wire from the huge turbine stations of the Adirondacks. There was nothing here but the converters, the power tubes and the senders, flinging into the ether the wireless waves of energy to be tapped by every craft subscribing to this wave length.

We knew, by what Iturbi had said, that there would be in the power house now only Green and his assistant in the broadcasting room of the upper floor. Mac's four guards were supposed to be there with them; and Iturbi himself would be at the switchboard downstairs. And an attendant on the flat-roof landing stage. The little roof lay almost under us now as we spiraled down toward it. But no attendant with his welcoming light-signal was visible. The roof lay dim, seemingly deserted.

Our pilot gave us a look of startled inquiry.

"Drop down," Trent commanded grimly. "Charge the fare to City Night Desk 4. You land us—quietly—and you make away."

The taxi's helicopter propeller came out. We dropped silently, swiftly, almost vertically down to the empty roof top. The taxi rose again and sped away as we leaped from it. It had barely touched the roof surface.

I was familiar with the place and Trant was not. I went ahead of him, on a run for the stairs. The little building was shrouded with trees set close beside it on the hilltop. As we ran across the roof there was the sound of a departing surface vehicle on the road down the hill, and an instant later it seemed that we heard the intensified motor-thrum as it took to the air and increased its speed.

We dashed down the stairs to the upper story. There was only a dimly lighted corridor, and the main broadcasting room, where Green and his assistant and Mac's men should have been gathered. An amazing scene greeted us as we burst through the swinging doors. The big square room was luridly illuminated, mainly by the deep orange glow from the giant six-foot power vacuum tubes—a dozen of them ranged in series and occupying the space along one wall.

The broadcaster was in normal operation, hissing and spitting as it sent the transformed power up to the main aerial stretched above the roof. The transformers throbbed and whined; the huge emergency switch was closed, as it should have been; its giant, naked electrodes, fenced in for safety by a low metal guardrail, glistened with a coppery gleam, giving no hint of the amazing voltage passing through them.

All were working normally, but momentarily unattended now.... No one here? We stood stricken for an instant in that doorway, gazing at the tragic scene. The dead bodies of many men lay strewn amid the overturned furniture of Paul Green's railed-in little office space, which occupied the center of the room. Five men, all dead, lying in attitudes which bore mute witness to the brief fight they had waged against a surprise attack. Mac's two partner-pairs, and Green's young assistant. All of them stabbed with the Banning flash. Not long ago, for the acrid smell of it still lingered here.

A room of death. Our gaze encompassed these details far quicker than I can record them. There was a sixth man— and he was alive. In the chair before his desk, inside the small railed enclosure, Paul Green was sitting. A crude cloth gag was tied around his face; a heavy wire lashed his ankles and bound his arms behind him. His face was as pale as the white cloth gag which hid most of it. At our sudden entrance his eyes swung to us mutely imploring, and he twisted and writhed against the wire that bound him immovably in his seat.

We leaped over the little rail and had him loose in a moment. He seemed uninjured. Trembling, confused by the shock, he fell against me. I saw that the tail of his loose office jacket was burned where a Banning stab had barely missed his body.

"They got away—just a few minutes ago," he gasped. "A

dozen masked men—leaped upon us—no warning. They must have killed Iturbi and the roof attendant. We had no chance—your men wounded one or two, but they all got away."

4

IT WAS A few minutes past midnight now. The first impulse Trant and I had was to call Mac. Trant said, "This audiphone here—"

The audiphone instrument on Green's desk seemed uninjured. It was the one we had called from the taxi, and got the "No answer" response.

"Your main-waves board downstairs is smashed," I told Green.

I remembered that queer look Iturbi had given us when we called him from the taxi. Had he been attacked just at that instant?

Green was lying back in his chair, still trembling and panting. "You can—call from here," he gasped. "I guess it's still working—it's been buzzing, but I couldn't answer it."

Trant reached for the instrument. I said:

"The incoming Great Circle Flyer!"

The huge mail flyer from Europe was due just about now. And I had a sudden flash of realization. That mysterious latitude and longitude which Kenna had given us; that point off the Jersey Coast would be just about where the incoming flyer was now.

"Incoming flyer?" Green stammered. "Why, what—"

He got no further. Trant was in the act of calling Mac when in the room with us there came a sudden flash. A hiss; a queerly muffled puff. It startled us so that Trant slammed down the instrument and we both leaped to our feet. The flash was over by the wall, fifteen or twenty feet from us, and within a second or two there came the tinkling of breaking glass—a dozen staccato reports.

The giant power tubes, one after the other smashed and went black, as the thin glass enclosing the six-foot vacuums burst inward.

A time-bomb! The escaping criminals had set it here, and now it had ignited, wrecking the power tubes. The ignition wires burned with a swift red flash.

The whole thing was over in a few seconds. And as the disorganized electrical power rushed for an outlet, automatically it threw the big safety switch. The handle visibly moved; the switch opened. For just an instant the berserk electrons streamed in a luminous flow across the two-foot space between the switch-terminals. Then the whole apparatus died—went dark and quiescent.

The aerial power for the entire metropolitan district was off!

"Why—why what is that?" Green gasped.

Trant jumped for the audiophone. Called Mac. Got him. I did not hear Trant's hurried explanation. I was busy trying to help Green, who seemed to have fallen into a sudden panic. Then across the room I suddenly noticed two more dead bodies—the roof attendant and Iturbi. A yellow flame from the burning filaments of one of the broken power tubes showed them plainly.

Queer. The attendant must have been murdered on the roof, and Iturbi murdered downstairs. Yet the criminals had carried them in here so that the discovery of the bodies would not be made until someone entered this particular room.

But that was not the queer part. That Iturbi should be among the victims was queer. Vaguely I had thought him one of the murderers.

"Jac, look! Look here!"

Trant was vehemently beckoning me to the desk.

"Jac, look! I got Mac. Told him everything. The Great Circle Flyer is bringing platinum from the Bank of England tonight. There's your motive for this damned thing. Four million platinum dollars—what a prize for these bandits! And Mac's connected us with a police plane off the Jersey coast. Take a look!"

The mirror-grid on Green's desk was glowing with the colored image of the scene from one of the planes of the aerial patrol, which had been lurking above a cloudbank in the sub-stratosphere off the Jersey coast. And the patrol was now swooping down.

Amazing, silent drama out there over the calm, fitfully moonlit ocean! Swift culmination of this brief affair.... The aerial power had failed. Local craft everywhere were seeking hasty forced landings....

From a height of perhaps ten thousand feet we gazed down. Winging low out from the coast was a dark little taxiplane. It flew with incredible speed—evidently a modern racer disguised as a taxi. Doubtless it was the one which had taken off from the power house just before we arrived. The high-lurking patrol spotted it. A search-glare stabbed down—and a moment later a giant heat-bolt caught the taxiplane, so that it burst into flame, fell like a whirling torch, and was extinguished by the sea.

SO MANY THINGS happening almost simultaneously! The big Great Circle Liner had been brought down by the failure of the power. It was settling now quietly to the placid ocean, making ready to taxi ashore. But a sub-sea vessel was lurking here—a freighter engined for speed, an armed bandit craft manned by these criminals. It lurked at a few fathoms depth. Doubtless it had been unaware of the hovering patrol hiding so high—unaware of them until just now, when they began swooping down upon the criminals.

The bandit sub-sea vessel never had time to rise and attack its victim. The patrol search-glare, flinging vertically down from so great a height, disclosed its presence. We saw now, on our mirror-grid, the huge white patch of glare on the ocean surface; and at a few fathoms depth, the oblong blob which was the lurking bandit submarine.

The patrol ship dropped a sub-surface bomb. It sent up a glistening silver geyser, but it missed....

The bandit vessel tried to make off. It swung and sank lower, but in a moment another bomb caught it. The geyser of silvery water was dotted with fragments of metal. Air-bubbles came up in a torrent. The torn hulk sank too low for the light to reveal.

For a moment longer we gazed at the silent anticlimax of the drama—bodies coming up, whirling in the maelstrom of wreckage. Trant was absorbed. I turned away from the mirror. I don't know what instinct actuated me, but my mind suddenly left that moonlit scene off the Jersey coast.

It is a strange fact that the cleverest criminal, at a crisis of his career, will often do something extremely stupid. I thought of that now; and for no reason at all I was suddenly struck afresh with the queerness of this affair here at the power house. These marauding criminals had ruthlessly murdered so many men; they had set a time-bomb to shut off the power exactly at the moment when the Great Circle Flyer would be forced to descend near their lurking sub-sea ship.

How had they been able to calculate that exact instant? But more queer still, why had they gagged and bound Paul Green when they had so ruthlessly killed everyone else? Paul Green had official knowledge of the flyer's exact location; but why, after the bandits had forced the information from him—why hadn't they killed him?

It was an intuition, which I translated into action almost without waiting to reason it out. Trant was still engrossed with the mirror-grid—the triumphant ending to the affair. But as I saw it, it was not quite ended yet. Green was close to me, lying back in his chair. It seemed suddenly that his face bore a very strange expression as he became aware of the events out on that moonlit ocean....

I turned swiftly and whipped out the little classifier— the Bloodhound Machine.

I thought that Green was not watching me, but at once he gasped:

"What—you doing?"

I did not answer, but jumped suddenly and pressed the vacuum cup of the classifier against his shoulder. The dial indicators swung wildly, and instantly settled.

2XZ4!

Green twisted; mumbled, "You—you—"

A clever criminal, perfectly stupid with every detail of this, his last crime. He staggered to his feet. There had been nothing physically wrong with him. It had all been pretense. But he was shaking now with horror. And he mumbled:

"Why—that's a lie—that damned thing—"

I dropped it and snatched my Banning gun. "Don't move! I'll drill you! We've got him, Georg! He's 2XZ4!"

But we didn't have him. He ignored my weapon. He let out a wild, irrational laugh, turned abruptly, and vaulted the railing. I withheld my fire for that moment. He rushed, still with that eerie screaming, not for the door, but for the broken power tubes. A bound took him over the guardrail of the open power switch.

Trant shouted a warning—then we both stood transfixed. Green's leap brought him staggering against the open terminals. But it was intentional, for he seized one of the terminals with each hand.

For a few seconds he hung, galvanized, with feet lifted from the floor. The high-voltage current surged through him, leaped from him like a crackling aura, burned and shriveled him. A few seconds, yet to us it seemed an eternity. Then his charred, twisted body broke at the wrist and fell away. The snapping terminals went dark. There was only the little smoking heap on the floor to mark the end of the criminal we had sought for so many years.

THE TELEVISION ALIBI

The Detective and the Dancer Were Alone in the Arizona Desert—Yet They Were Eye-Witnesses of a Strange Crime Thousands of Miles Away

1

AS A MEMBER of New York's Shadow Squad—tough, hard and generally ill-natured, or at least so my fellows tell me—I don't suppose it's very fitting for me to sermonize. I have no such intention. But I am thinking that the case which I call "The Television Alibi" illustrates the point that fundamental rightness of action has a providential tendency to be rewarded. The case may be of interest here. I was involved in it last summer—in June of 1999, to be exact.

My partner, Georg Trant, assigned with me under Macfarlan of City Night Desk 4, was on his vacation. According to routine, therefore, I had a partial-vacation; "rest-work," they term it. This television case was a routine job on which supposedly I could work alone, without stress or danger. There were a few moments in it, however, when I could have been killed very easily.

It was an unusual case for me, from many angles. Chiefly, it introduced me to the most beautiful and appealing girl I have ever seen. And it tempted me to let a criminal escape. I very nearly did that—and for Jac Lombard, tough, hard, ill-natured S.S. man, that certainly was a new experience! Trant, the only person so far to whom I have told the full details, has ever since regarded me with ironic admiration—amazed, he says, that I am human enough to be tempted.

The affair occurred on June 25th, 1999. I was supposed to have a rest-day, but Macfarlan summoned me.

"Assignment from the Crime Prevention Bureau," he announced. "A perfectly decent young fellow seems liable to commit murder."

He tossed me the memorandum. It involved three people, two of them very well known: Elena Denizon, famous television dancer; Willard Jared, President of the American Television Company; and one George King, a young law student.

The old triangle—two men in love with one girl. The men had had several quarrels, and made threats, perhaps under the heat of too much alcoholite. At any rate, the thing got enough publicity so that the Crime Prevention Desk took it up, and turned it over to Mac.

"Easy job," Mac told me. "A nice relaxing trip to Arizona—Elena Denizon's studio-home. You'll find the boy there with her, probably."

"I think I'll see this Jared first," I said.

"Suit yourself," Mac agreed. "Connect me when you like—I won't worry over you."

I had no trouble getting an interview with Jared. It's Contempt of Law to stall off the investigation of a suspected impending crime. I called Jared on his private wave, and he admitted me at once, though naturally he wasn't very cordial.

I found him just what I had anticipated—a man of forty-five or fifty, flabby and toad-like. He was immaculately dressed, heavily jeweled. His fat face, with small fish-like eyes, was dominated by a big old-fashioned rolling mustache, obviously dyed black. His office and residence was an exotically-furnished tower apartment above the New York City broadcasting studio of his company. It was a somewhat notorious tower—unsavory for the gay parties which Jared held with young women, many of whom he attracted there, no doubt, with promises of a great television career.

He sat now, eyeing me coldly across his desk. He said distastefully:

"Jac Lombard? Shadow Squad?"

I told him the purpose of my visit. I said, "The Crime Prevention Bureau wants a report. It is quite confidential, of course. If you are legally engaged to marry this Elena Denizon, we will protect you from any interference."

"She filed public refusal of my claim," he said.

I knew that, of course. "And this George King has claimed her?"

His cold stare clung to me. He said, "If I don't get her, that boy won't get her either."

NOW I HAVE had considerable experience with lawbreakers. I'm telepathic enough to know when there is menace radiating from a man. But this was something different—in his eyes I saw a wild, smoldering look, as though on this subject of Elena Denizon he might be demented. Sex psychologists may argue the psychosis of it any way they like. I saw it here.

He repeated slowly, "She can't marry that boy. I won't let that happen."

I drew back slightly. It may seem idiotic to admit it, but I dropped my hand to the Banning gun in my pocket. I said:

"Then my report must show that you are the aggressor."

Thick, dark color suffused his fat cheeks. He said, "Your report be hanged. Aggressor? You—you—I don't want to talk any more about this. I don't want to see the accursed boy again."

"But you do see him. You quarrel with him—"

"He comes to see me."

I stood up to terminate the interview. I said, "I'll talk to him about it. I think the bureau will take legal action to bar him. He must realize that if anything happened to you he will be blamed."

His eyes gleamed at that. I added, "You have exchanged threats. You have threatened him, just now, to me."

He stood up with me. He interrupted, "There is no law to make me talk any more about this, is there?"

"Plenty," I said. "But I have no authority, yet, to force you."

I left him then and took the Sunset, a low-altitude flyer. It was about a three-hour trip to Arizona. I had late supper on board; hired a local plane in Phoenix and flew to the rambling one-story home of Elena Denizon, set isolated in all that was left of the once great Arizona desert, two thousand miles from the image-casting laboratory in New York.

Queer whimsy of this girl! But though she was only eighteen, already she was famous enough to get away with it. She hated the city; claimed that her art needed this isolation. And like a hermit, for the summer months she lived here, absolutely alone save for the Indian woman who came by day to do her work.

The television company of necessity had yielded to her whim. Her home here was equipped with a dance floor and the necessary television mechanisms hooked with the laboratory in New York.

I found a landing field and hangar out on the open cactus-strewn desert; and a twenty-foot high metal barrier wall—with an electrified barrage, so the huge warning-sign told me.

At the gate I buzzed for admittance. The lens-eye glowed, carrying my image to her. And presently her voice said:

"Who are you?"

I told her; and I displayed my identifying signature, tattooed on my forearm.

Her voice said pleasantly, "The art of wax-disguise is not difficult. And anyway, you know it won't be Contempt of Law if I refuse to see you now, because I am alone here."

Her saying it didn't prove that George King wasn't here with her. I smiled. I said, "That's true. I made bad connections. I've been four or five hours getting here. I didn't mean to be so late."

Her light laugh rippled at me. "You don't look formidable. I have no old-fashioned conventionality. You may come in."

I dismissed the taxi. The barrage gate slid aside, and closed with a click after me as I passed through. The desert outside was a blank stretch of sand, with undulated waves like a frozen sea, pale in the glittering starlight. But inside I found a fairy garden. Rose-colored tube-lights from hidden sources illumined its winding paths—a glowing garden, a little bower of ferns and vivid flowers which surrounded the bungalow.

The front door slid aside. Elena Denizon, most famous dancer of the air, was before me.

2

SHE SAT UNDER a spot of light before her cosmetic table mirror. At my entrance, she turned and surveyed me.

"From the Crime Prevention Bureau?" she said, smilingly. "Sit down, please. You won't mind—I'm busy just now. I go on the air presently."

I sat on a stiff little chair near her. She powdered her legs with blue-white talc-dust; adjusted the vivid red costume scarf around her breast and hips, and uncoiled the black waves of her hair. She added lightly:

"I do assure your bureau that I am not planning any crime."

She was enough of an actress, of course, so that whatever her emotions, I knew she would not display them. Was George King here? I had no way of guessing. My gaze swept the small dressing room. To one side a big archway opened to the dance floor. It was dim in there now; I could just distinguish the television senders; the waxen and canvas props and scenery, and the banks of lights.

The girl was quietly finishing the coloring of her face, and for a moment I sat silent, regarding her. Glamorous little figure, indeed! Trant insists that right from the beginning I was hypnotized by her, so that no longer was I an S.S. man, but more like a country lout spellbound by meeting an actress.

Maybe so. She sat, save for that red costume scarf, like Lady Godiva enveloped by the long, thick mass of her black hair. Her face was of course familiar to me—I had seen the dancing image of her many times. It was an exceedingly beautiful face, with the stamp of intellectuality upon it. But in the dance, with the surge of music and the hum of the transmitter flinging the image of her around the world, her eyes dark as a moonless night, her mouth red like a scarlet flower—her face then would carry a pagan look, as though this were no girl of the year 1999, but a princess of Barbary, voluptuous as Venus.

Yet chaste as Diana. The public seemed to know that. It was part of the charm which Elena Denizon carried with her dancing to all the far-flung corners of the amuse-ment-seeking world.

I said at last, "It wasn't you I came to see, Miss Denizon. I hoped George King would be here."

That startled her, though of course she had anticipated it. She was adjusting heavy jeweled bands on her ankles and tipping the burnished nails of her toes with carmine. She sat up abruptly and faced me… I think it was perhaps the involuntary gesture of her hand to the cosmetic table—at all events, I saw for the first time the muzzle of a little golden Banning gun, partly hidden by the cosmetic jars.

But her hand did not touch the gun; she seemed only bracing herself against the table. She said sharply:

"George King?"

I nodded. "The bureau is worried over him."

I gazed vaguely around the apartment. She said:

"But he is not here. I have not seen him—for some time."

"Do you know where he is?"

We stared at the mirror-
grid, which now showed
the garden gate.

She shook her head. Hostility was stamped on her now. For all the apparent frankness of her smile, I was aware of it.

"He's in New York, I suppose," she said.

Her hand back on the table came forward as she leaned toward me. She added earnestly: "You represent the law, Mr. Lombard. I want you to be assured of just one thing— George King has nothing to hide. There is no crime—no impending crime. He and I always will deal quite frankly with you."

I stared at her, judging her. The house was very silent, with the silence of the outer spread of desert crowding it.

Then there came a sharp buzz, which in the silence startled me as though it had been the hiss of a Banning heat-stab. On a bracket beside the cosmetic table one of the commercial message-mirrors began glowing. Franks, her technician manager, was calling from the broadcasting studio in New York. His voice sounded:

"Elena?"

She said, "You'll excuse me, Mr. Lombard?" She drew down the bracket and gave audible connection.

"You, Franks?"

"Twenty-five minutes only. Are you ready?"

"I will be, of course."

I could see in the mirror-grid over her shoulder the image of Franks' thin face, with the semi-circle of orchestra players partly assembled behind him. He looked strangely worried. He said:

"Elena, you don't let me see you. If you—"

"Oh, I don't mind." She gestured for me to move away from the visual angle of the instrument; then she gave visual connection.

"Lovely as always, Elena," he said.

She smiled. "Did you call me to tell me that?"

"Elena, you—nothing has bothered you tonight?"

THAT STRUCK ME into alertness. A side-angle duplicate of the mirror showed me Franks' image, though he could not see me. His anxious gaze was roving Elena and the angle of the room behind her.... The sudden premonition came to me that this already might be more than an affair for the Crime Prevention Desk....

Franks was saying, "If I live to the age of a pensioned

I jumped and drew the wounded man before the television window.

tower-timekeeper, I'll never get used to having you off there alone on that desert."

"You would not like my dancing if I shut myself up in your metal city," she said sweetly.

He smiled back at her, but his eyes still were worried. "Have your own way, Elena. You will, anyhow."

"Because I am a woman?"

"And an artist, which is worse. Be ready on the second, Elena."

"Of course."

They disconnected. She turned and smiled at me. But

she was disturbed by the call, that was obvious. I could almost imagine her thinking. Why was he so worried?

Certainly I was thinking it. She began weaving a garland of glittering bangles into her hair.

"I do not mind your staying here to see me dance, if you wish," she said. "But George King must be in New York."

As though in answer, there came the sharp buzz of the signal from the entrance gate of the garden. Someone demanding admittance. Whatever startled premonition came to her, I could see the color draining from her face and throat. The questioning gaze she flung at me seemed to hold an agony of vague terror.

We stood at the mirror-grid, which now showed the garden gate and the starlit desert behind it. A little private airplane was resting there.

Elena gasped, "George—"

It was George King. A tall, slim figure with the starlight glistening on his shiny white flying suit and black helmet, he stood clinging to the gate, drooping. His voice gasped:

"Elena! Elena, dear, let me in! Quick!"

I saw his face, white and strained. Blood smears were on it, and the shoulder of his flying suit was wet with blood.

3

I STOOD ASIDE in the shadows of the room while she ran to meet him in the doorway, with outstretched arms.

"Georg! You're hurt—why—why—"

He gasped, "It's—nothing. Just bleeding—"

He stumbled as they crossed the threshold—a handsome boy, just twenty, my information from the bureau had told me. His blood-smeared face was chalk white; his lips pallid.

"I didn't—want a doctor," he gasped. "I just wanted to get to you, Elena. It's nothing—just a stab in the shoulder."

He sank from her arms into a chair. He looked as though he were on the verge of fainting from loss of blood. I said:

"We'd better get that jacket off him."

I saw that all the blood seemed to be from a wound in his shoulder. He had smeared it on his hands, and then to his face.

He sat up weakly at the sound of my voice. "Who's that?"

I said: "I'm from the Crime Prevention Bureau. Don't you bother about me. Get that jacket off."

He flung the girl a confused glance. Then he seemed dazed. He sank back, letting us strip off his blood-soaked garments. It was a nasty cut from a knife. His shirts underneath the flying jacket were slashed. But it was only a superficial flesh wound. The bleeding had stopped now. There was no danger save from a possible infection.

I helped the girl bathe the wound in an antiseptic. At my weapon belt I had a little first-aid projector of the healing, germ-killing violet-ray, so I said:

"You'll need surgical treatment for this pretty soon, but this is helpful for now."

He lay relaxed, watching us as we worked on him. He said suddenly:

"S.S. man from the Crime Prevention Bureau? Well, I have nothing to hide. I—you go on the air soon, don't you, Elena?"

"Yes," she said. Again it seemed that they exchanged glances.

"I guess I'm all right now. Just weak and dizzy—losing blood, and the pain. You—just let me rest here while you dance. I'll tell this S.S. man—"

"You don't have to," I said. "Not now."

"But he wants to," Elena said quickly. "Don't you understand? We have nothing to hide."

Brave speech indeed. She was no actress now. She regarded me defiantly. She said, "Go on—ask him anything you like. You're the Law—that's your privilege."

I shook my head. "Later—"

"No, now," she insisted. "I'm going to ask you to leave in a minute. You'd better take your chance while you've got it. We don't want you here—"

I smiled. "All right," I said. "King, if you want to explain this, now seems to be your chance. Were you in New York tonight?"

His eyes avoided both the girl and me. He said, "Yes, I was."

"And you saw Willard Jared, didn't you?"

It seemed that all the silence of the desert was crowding us. There was only the boy's labored, panting breath.

I added, "I saw him myself in the late afternoon. You went to see him soon after that, didn't you?"

"Yes," he said at last.

"In his tower studio?"

"Yes."

It shocked Elena. I realized now that she knew no more of this than I. And her fears must have swept her, so that for the moment she forgot what impression her words might make upon me. She burst out:

"Georg! You did go to New York! You did see Jared, and I asked you not to!"

"Well, what if I did?" he flared. "I didn't go looking for trouble. I told him so. I told him—"

She bent forward over him.

"Georg, look at me. You went and saw Jared. Did he— did he do this to you?"

"Yes," he said abruptly. And suddenly he drew her down to him. "Elena, I love you. I want—"

"Wait, Georg! Tell me—you didn't do anything to harm Jared? He's—all right, isn't he? Tell me that. Tell me he's— not hurt in any way?"

"No, he's not. Of—of course he's not. Elena, I do love you. Not for all the world would I get your name publicly into this. You had nothing to do with it. I shouldn't have gone. I know that now. I'm sorry. But no one saw me there. No one saw me leave, or enter. And I wasn't with him very long. He struck at me—I tell you no one knew I was there. I called him on his private wave, and he said come on up and I went, in the outside lift. Oh, it wasn't anything. I didn't do anything to him."

Relief swept her—relief at what he said, whether she believed it or not.

"I suppose he quarreled with you?" she prompted.

"YES. I TOLD him he'd have to stop annoying you. I'll tell you what happened exactly. You and this S.S. man. You can put this in your report to the Crime Prevention Bureau," he added to me. "But you leave Elena's name out of it.... Elena, listen: I told him that you were going to marry me— that you'd already filed public refusal of his claim. I told him that I filed claim for you yesterday—which you know I did—and when the hundred days are up, I told him that then you'd accept me. And he said—he said—"

There was a pause.

"He said—" she prompted.

"He said that if—if he didn't get you I wouldn't either. He went—all white. I never saw a man so white. I reminded him he was fifty and you were eighteen. Ridiculous! I told him so, and then he went white and he struck at me with a knife."

"What knife?"

"It was lying on his desk between us. A thing like an ornament. I jumped and took it away from him. But it cut me—slashed my shirt and into my shoulder. I knocked him back in his chair and for a minute I held him. I never saw a man so white with rage. He couldn't speak. He—he looked at me as though he were witless. I guess he is— issuing air-casts the way he has about how he loves you."

"Then what, Georg? You held him in his chair?"

"Yes. Then I let go of him. I told him again that he'd better keep away from you. I didn't do anything to him. I didn't even hurt him. When I let go of him he jumped for the knife again. I—I just got out. Ran. That's all, Elena. That's all I did." He saw her looking at me. He rose up a little in his chair and said: "You can report it to the Crime Prevention Bureau and the devil take you. But you keep Elena's name—"

"What time was it?" I said.

"When I left him? About four and a half hours ago. Just about that. I took my airplane and flew straight here. There's a fair wind from the northeast at the twenty-thousand foot level."

The girl swung on me. "Are you satisfied? You can go now and file your report. We don't want you here."

She stood before me, grimly imperious. There was only the terror in her eyes....

I've no possible idea what I would have done. Young King was lying back in his chair. His eyes were closed; he seemed to have used all his strength. The buzzer sounded again. King did not open his eyes. He had fainted, though we did not know it then.

I said, "What's that? Someone at your gate?"

"No, it's an incoming call. I'll take it."

We received the image and a voice; but she gave only her voice. "I am Elena Denizon...."

The little image-grid again showed the face of Franks, with the New York studio room behind him. His voice gave the routine call—seven minutes before her appearance; and then he began talking. It wasn't important. Urging her to give him visual connection. Talking banalities, almost as though he were flirting with her. I stood, unnoticed beside her. Franks couldn't see us. He had only audible connection... I stared at that small image of the New York broadcasting studio. Behind Franks, two uniformed men of the New York City police were standing over against the wall. We could see them plainly. And then I saw and recognized the figure of Rankin, Midtown Police Chief.

Franks was saying, "Elena, don't be silly. Let me see you."

"In the dance," she parried. "Can't you wait five minutes, Franks?"

Then suddenly my heart was pounding. The image showed the door to the stairs of Jared's tower apartment over the studio. The door was opening. I heard Elena catch her breath with a little agonized gasp. And Franks heard it.

"What's the matter, Elena?"

"Nothing," she murmured. "What—what is that behind you?"

They were carrying in a stretcher with a white form on it. A white face showed over the covering of white sheet... I understood now. Rankin was letting the girl see this, to surprise her, to find out if she had any guilty knowledge.

Somebody said, "Won't need a more complete autopsy. We've got all the evidence now. That fellow King did it."

It was Willard Jared lying there under that sheet. Jared—dead. Murdered.

4

NOW MY PARTNER Trant tells me the Shadow Squad is forever disgraced because I was caught standing witless and let a girl disarm me. However that may be, it certainly did happen. I was vaguely aware that Elena reached and snapped off the audiphone. The image faded. And all in that second the shocked and agonized girl wavered backward. I thought she was going to fall. She backed into her cosmetic table and as I reached to steady her, suddenly she stiffened.

"Stand back! Don't touch me. Put up your arms or I'll drill through you!"

The muzzle of her little golden Banning gun came at me, leveled at my chest. Above it I saw her face, with dark eyes blazing.

You never can tell what a girl is liable to do. Her crooked finger was on the sensitive button of the trigger; the safety lever was up; my life hung on the merest grain of pressure of her twitching finger. I own that it gave me a shock. I took a step backward, with upraised arms. And I murmured:

"Careful, there—that trigger is delicate."

She eyed me as though there were nothing else in the world but my face. She said tensely: "Drop your weapon-belt."

Docilely I unloosed it; dropped it to the floor.

"Kick it away."

I kicked it; and abruptly she reached with her left hand under my upraised arms. No skilled criminal ever denuded me of weapons more quickly. She tossed my Banning gun across the room; in the silence it fell with a clatter.

And again she had backed out of reach, still eyeing me with that blazing gaze.

I said quietly, "Don't get excited. I'll do whatever you say."

It seemed that a shudder swept over her. She gasped:

"Oh, Georg—we've got to kill this man. You've got to escape, Georg—"

She did not look from my face. Out of the tail of my eye I could see the slumped figure of King in the chair. No answer came from him. I said suddenly:

"Good Lord, he's dead!"

That got her. The little golden muzzle wavered aside as she turned toward the chair with an involuntary, agonized gasp. And in that second I sprang and seized her wrist. The gun-bolt fired. The hissing stab of heat shot over my shoulder and seared the ceiling. There was no strength in her hand. A twisting jerk gave me the weapon as I jumped sidewise.

"Georg—Georg, dear—" She went past me. Flung herself to the floor by the chair. "Georg—don't die, Georg!"

He was recovering consciousness. He murmured, "Elena, what happened? Why, I guess I fainted—"

Sobbing wildly she drew him to her, caressing him. The audiophone was buzzing. Weapon in hand, I reached for it. Never have I heard so despairing a sob as that which came from the girl. On the arm of the big chair she sat now with

King's face pressed against her breast—his face so pallid against that crimson scarf.

I shut off the buzzer and gave audible connection. It was Police Chief Rankin. He gave me both audible and visible. The mirror glowed with the image of his square, grim face.

He said, "Denizon studio? Where is Miss Denizon?"

"She's here," I said. "This is Jac Lombard—S.S., City Night Desk 4. What's in the air, Chief?"

I shot a glance at the chair. Elena was staring at me, breathless. She and young King were beyond the audiphone's visual range. I gave Rankin my image. He said, "Well! Jac Lombard!"

"Hello, Chief. Mac sent me here. Miss Denizon was startled just now. Is Willard Jared really dead?"

I was trying to figure the thing out. Something told me to go easy on what I said or did.

"Murdered," Rankin said. "Obvious who did it. We're after George King. Simple enough case. Jared died with his audiphone transmitter in hand. He called for help and just as he died, he gasped out to the local wave-sorter the name of the man who stabbed him. Young George King."

There was a faint gasp from the chair in the shadows. I made a gesture to silence it. Rankin did not hear the gasp. He went on grimly:

"And we've got chemical proof. Blood on the body and on the desk and the chair. Blood which isn't Jared's blood. This fellow King is native of New York and so the Bartel record of his blood is on file here. We've identified it as George King's blood. A chair was overturned—the desk ornaments scattered. They evidently had a fight. Both of them wounded, and Jared was stabbed to death."

Mingled with Rankin's grim words, across the background of my mind a stream of conjectures was flowing. A queer phrase of Willard Jared's came back to me, "If I don't get her, the boy never will!" What did he mean by that? And I recalled his wild, irrational look as he had said it… The answer to this thing began dawning on me….

Rankin was saying, "You'd better call Mac for orders. We'll use you and Trant to track down this fellow King—"

I said abruptly, "George King is here."

THE IMAGE OF the police chief showed his jaw drop with startled surprise as he stared at me. And from the chair, Elena Denizon leaped and stood trembling, gazing wildly. Young King had staggered to his feet. He looked as though he were about to run, but my menacing weapon stopped him.

Rankin said, "George King is there now?"

"Yes. He came a little while ago. Flew his airplane from New York."

Behind Rankin in the New York studio a distant voice called:

"Lights! Lights for Miss Denizon! Two minutes!"

Through the open arcade near me, the great bank of tube-lights over the dance floor was illumined. The room in there was a dazzling blue-white glare. The reflection of it showed me the chair where young King now was sitting weakly upright, staring around him in confusion. And Elena standing nearby. Amazing, the instinct of the artist—the power it had over her. From the radio-speaker above the dance floor she heard now the thrum of the tuning instruments of the studio orchestra. The lights were bathing her. It was almost time for her appearance before the world—that vast unseen audience waiting now to see her dance.

And imperatively that obligation thrust aside her personal anguish. She stood trembling, smoothing her costume scarf. And she was mustering a stage-smile through the blank despair on her face.

Rankin was saying, "George King is there?" His grimness was gone. He added, "Well, I'm certainly relieved, Lombard. Show him to me, will you?"

And I was certainly relieved. I had figured it correctly. I jumped and drew King before the mirror, holding him there in spite of himself. And Rankin said:

"Why, hello, King! I sure am glad you're there! Why, it's a perfect alibi! Jared has only been dead thirty minutes. By his own dying words to the wave-sorter he was stabbed less than forty minutes ago. No physical way you could get from New York to Arizona in forty minutes! He must have committed suicide. He tried it once before."

Thirty minutes ago! That was about when Franks had called and looked worried. I had had the hunch then of something like this. Jared had committed suicide, to blame it on King! I had seen that suicidal mania in Jared's eyes!

Rankin added, "Jove, it's lucky you showed yourself, young fellow. A little later tonight and the Southwest High Altitude Liner would have killed your chances of an alibi."

Elena had given a half hysterical sob of joy. I don't know whether, even now, she realizes that I gave the boy up to Rankin in order to save him. But I sort of hope she does....

King stood sagging against me, murmuring, "Didn't kill him? Of course I didn't kill him—"

"Ready, Miss Denizon?" The New York director's voice

blared from the dance floor speaker. "Take your place. Thirty seconds to go."

The orchestra leader was tapping warningly with his baton. Elena sprang at young King, pulled him from me. Her face was radiant—the impending dance, and the knowledge that King was innocent. She led him back to his chair, stooped and kissed him fervently.

The orchestra began playing. The New York director's voice said:

"Miss Denizon! Entrance!"

"Georg! Georg, dear, let me go! Don't hold me now! Sit there and watch me. I'll kiss you all you want when I get through!"

She swayed out under the banks of tube-lights to the rhythm of the dance.

DEATH IN THE FOG TOWER

*When the Murderer Clicked the Strange
Machine an Icy Invisible Hand Tightened
About Jac Lombard's Throat*

1

THE AFFAIR WHICH I have labeled "Death in the Fog Tower" never attained a national publicity. It solved the murder of two prominent people. But the potentialities of the crime—that part of the murderer's daring plot which never came to fruition—none of that was made public.

Important things sometimes hang upon small details. If we of the Shadow Squad had been less skillful, or less lucky perhaps, in unmasking this murderous plotter—well, conceivably the whole future of the new airmail parcel post service might have been altered.

The forerunner of the brief series of incidents which terminated so dramatically in that fog tower of the Midland Airways Fast Freight, came about a week previous. It meant nothing to us at the time; but I mention it first, because it was, of course, the prologue—the murderer's opening move.

It was the night of March 10th, the year 2000. Midland Airways, a British-American Company capitalized at some eight million platinum dollars, had sprung into amazing prominence, you will remember, by proving the practicability of carrying freight by air. After a series of test flights with its new, heavy duty aeroplanes, Midland Airways gave up its passenger carrying service.

Fast freight. It was a new blow at the railroads. On

March 1st, 2000, the Central Pacific Railroad System lost its government parcel post contract. Midland Airways hereafter would carry the government freight. And private shippers began following government example.

Midland Airways was an instant success. The giant triple-winged 'planes, using broadcasted power from coast to coast so that they were unburdened by fuel, transported a truly amazing pay load of the lighter types of freight; perishable food, largely, which needed the swiftest possible transportation.

I name only the familiar facts which had a direct bearing upon the diabolic plot in the solving of which we were so soon engrossed. Midland Airways began its freight service on March 10th. It chanced that the Atlantic seaboard area was enveloped by a most extraordinarily heavy fog. And that night of March 10th one of the big Midland Airways 'planes very nearly came to disaster. A fog tower instrument man, who was guiding the East bound 'plane, east of Harrisburg, Pennsylvania, was taken ill or collapsed in some way upon his radio beam sender, so that he disarranged his signals. The 'plane was flying blind in the fog, and it very nearly crashed before the tower operator recovered and guided it safely in.

The operator was discharged from service. He was a young fellow—an Italian-American named Arturo Giorni. He was alone in the fog tower at the time, and his only defense was that he was frightened—too frightened to operate his instruments. And that, of course, didn't seem to mean anything. Giorni wasn't arrested. His heart was acting queerly; he still had all the evidence of extreme

*Through the glassite
tower walls I could see
the young operator.*

fright. He was sent to a New York hospital and kept under
police observation.

A near-accident isn't startling enough for the newscasters to blare about. You probably never even heard of
it. But the Crime Prevention Bureau listed it for possible
future reference and distributed its thousand-copy memo.
One of them came to my immediate superior, Macfarlan
of City Night Desk No. 4, and he passed it on to me and
Trant, my partner.

THIS, THOUGH WE didn't know it, was the prologue. A

week later—on March 17th, so Irish a day that Macfarlan was annoyed because he had to be at work—Trant and I were called to the desk. It was early evening. We found Macfarlan there with three influential visitors.

Mac introduced them: John J. Baker, president and controlling stock owner of the Central Pacific Railroad—a portly, gray-haired man of sixty-odd; Carrington Carter, his son-in-law, handsome, efficient looking type of young business executive, eastern traffic manager; and the president's young daughter, Editha, his only child and Carter's bride of a few months.

Ill-fated trio! We could not guess it then, but I recall that I was at once struck by the aspect of disaster which somehow was indefinably upon all three of them. The older man plainly showed the sleepless nights and mental stress of his business cares. No wonder—for Central Railways, with the loss of its freight business, was facing bankruptcy. To John Baker that would mean the loss of his vast personal fortune, which, most unwisely, for years he had been flinging into the company until now he was almost the sole owner. Carter was glum, and his young wife unmistakably was at a high pitch of nervous excitement.

Mac said, "This pair of my operators I will assign to you, Mr. Baker. This is Georg Trant and Jac Lombard." He added to us, "This young woman has some strange ideas. Tell them, Mrs. Carter."

Strange indeed. We have enough problems of science to cope with; but here was this young woman flinging at us something too futuristic to be real science. But she had impressed Mac—and I will say that as I listened to her now the thing sounded impressive to me.

It was brief enough. She was government-educated, and as a hobby she had taken up the study of telepathy. "Thought transference," as, of course, you know, has always been in the class of occult science—a thing dependent upon some mysterious psychic phenomena. But of recent years that has been slowly changing. Back at the beginning of the century Sir William Crookes, eminent British scientist, whose fluorescent tubes were the forerunner of all modern lighting systems, advanced the belief that thought is in itself a physical vibration—tiny rapid waves traveling, perhaps, at the speed of light.

I am only a Shadow Squad man, with a routine crime to narrate. I have no skill, nor desire to argue science.

We listened now to this Editha Carter....

"Perhaps I am only hysterical, as my husband suggests," she said earnestly.

Carter smiled, but it was a very uneasy smile. He said, "I do think she has frightened herself. We are having business troubles, of course, and that's depressing to her." His hand pushed back the wavy black hair from his damp forehead. There was no question but that he was really as perturbed as his wife.

"But I do not think I am frightening myself," she said vehemently. "I have proven so many times that my brain must be one of those which are capable of receiving and translating incoming vibrations of thought. Gentlemen, please don't smile at me...."

"Nobody's smiling at you," Mac said. "Go ahead, tell them."

For a week or two now she had been receiving some alien thought vibrations. Vague, disturbing thoughts, not to be identified; hardly translatable. But they were constant, and very strong. Something of menace.

"But it's more than that," she said emphatically. "Not woman's intuition. Not a premonition of evil. I tell you I can almost put them into words. Somebody is thinking and planning disaster to me and to my family." Her gesture embraced her father and husband. She smiled tremulously. "I am perfectly aware that someone is thinking of killing us."

In spite of myself the thing gave me a shudder. It bothered Mac too. He said gruffly, to Trant and me:

"That's about all there is to it. I'm assigning you two to protect Mr. Baker and his family."

They all three lived together in a small surface residence in the Hudson Heights district of upper New York City. Trant and I were to live there with them for a time, as family friends, beginning tonight. And with our Shadow Squad training and our instruments we would try and locate the source of this menace.

BUT THAT NEVER came to pass. The three of them left Mac's office presently and went home. Trant and I equipped ourselves with our instruments. Then, about 9.30 P.M. we flew by taxi to Trant's Westchester home and then to mine in Jersey, and with our necessary personal belongings in two small suitcases we flew to the Hudson Heights section of Manhattan Island.

It was a moonless, partly cloudy night, damp and raw, with a heavy mist, suggestive of a coming fog. The Baker home was a small but valuable property—a little triangle of ground on the Heights overlooking the river, with huge apartment residence buildings crowding it. Baker had clung to the old-fashioned style. In the midst of an acre or so of garden, surrounded by a fence, his small two story marble home lay secluded. There was no landing stage; our taxi dropped to a public ramp-platform a few blocks away, and we rolled through the unattended gate and into Baker's driveway.

Trant dismissed the taxi. We stood at the front door, pressing the buzzer, but there was no answer. A lens-eye in a bracket to one side was aimed at us. I fronted it so that those within the house could see my face clearly. But it remained dark and inert. No current came into it; there was no one in the house curious enough to verify us.

Trant and I gazed at each other. I said, "Shall we call Mac?" I reached for the tiny radiophone on my chest, hidden by my shirt, but Trant checked me.

"Let's find out more first. Something queer here."

The heavy door resisted us. We pounded on it. There should be three people inside, expecting us—old man Baker, his daughter, and his son-in-law. No servants. We knew that the eccentric millionaire employed only one middle-aged woman, and she went home to her family at night.

"No use," Trant panted. He had been trying to shove open the door with his shoulder. A hydro-torch would have melted the lock in a moment, but it was not part of our equipment. I drew my little Banning heat gun.

"Come on," Trant urged. "Let's try a window. You'll ruin your gun."

We found a window unlocked; clambered through. A photo-electric cellbeam of invisible light, broken by our passage over the window sill, set off an intruder alarm.

The shrilling call of the little siren momentarily screamed through the dim and silent interior.

But there was no human commotion. We burst at last into the library. It was the only room on the lower floor that was lighted. And what a stricken scene of strife and tragedy was here! Much of the padded alumite furniture was overturned—several chairs, a side table with its printed books and phono-cylinders; the radiograph and news-mirrors, overturned and smashed.

A desperate combat, quite evidently, had taken place here. And only a few moments ago. The smell of Banning heat flashes was in the air; the ceiling and walls were seared where two or three of the flashes had struck, and the drapes of an interior doorway were stabbed and smoking.

We saw it all with a swift, horrified glance. On the floor in the middle of the room lay a tubular torn section of blue silk—the sleeve of a man's shirt torn from him in this struggle. I recognized it as the shirt Carrington Carter had been wearing an hour ago in Mac's office. The cuff was here. I remembered, because our minds are trained for such details, that Carter bad worn these platinum cuff links.

Trant had already rushed past me to the center of the room. On the floor there two bodies were lying—old man Baker and his daughter. They lay, side by side, both in an attitude curiously stiff, with wide open eyes and an expression of frozen horror upon their dead faces.

2

TRANT AND I never were time wasters. You can't encounter the murdered bodies of two people unexpectedly without being shocked; but we were both well aware of the importance of every second in a thing like this; clues get cold very fast. I recall that Trant murmured a startled oath and, kneeling, whipped out several of his instruments.

And I called Mac on the split wave, two-way wireless through my tiny microphone. Mac listened almost wordless. Suddenly he said,

"No one lurking in that room? Watch yourselves!"

There could be, of course. I ripped at the drapes, snatched open a closet door... The intruder alarm had ceased its racket. The dark house was silent. I dimmed the library tube lights so that there was only a spot of illumination on the bodies where Trant was working. Banning gun in hand, I knelt by Trent. He was heedless of any possible attack upon us, but I kept alert. My split-wave was constantly connected with Desk No. 4. Mac murmured:

"I've ordered Alarm Men there. They'll arrive in a few minutes. Work fast. You haven't searched the house?"

"No," I said.

"Well, don't. They've evidently captured Carter—or killed him. They may still be in the house. You watch yourselves. I'll have the place surrounded in five minutes."

Trant said, "Both dead. Something queer about this. Not just an ordinary stabbing."

Both bodies showed an ugly stab wound over the heart. Quite evidently the weapon was a knife. But it was queer. The smell of the Banning gun heat flashes was here in the room; Carter, it seemed, must have put up a fight here, and only a few moments ago. But these bodies, though they were still warm, were stiff. Rigid muscles. An expression of horror, frozen on the faces. You can't look like that when you're stabbed in the heart.

Mac's voice murmured, "Seems obvious that they were paralyzed first. Don't you think so? A needle job...."

Undoubtedly, but we didn't take the time now to verify it. Trant was using his small olfactory classifier—the "bloodhound" machine, as the newscasters so luridly call it. Besides our own, he swiftly got four classifications. Three of them were immediately identified—the two murdered bodies and Carter, which was obvious from the fragment of shirt sleeve.

The fourth—the intruder perhaps—was far more dim. I gave its general index to Mac.

"I'll look it up," he said. "We may have some record matching it."

Or it could be the household domestic who had been in this room probably only a few hours ago.

"No knife?" Mac's voice demanded.

I found the knife in a hurry: there had been no particular attempt to hide it. The magnetic indicator located it readily. It was tossed under the upholstered cushion of an easy chair. I picked it up gingerly and placed it on the center table where the routine investigators with their larger instruments could tackle it.

This murderer was no dumb cellar sweeper. We only had to glance at the long, keen, bloodstained blade to realize that this knife wasn't going to yield anything. There'd be no fingerprints, obviously; and no scent of the hand which had held it. The handle was wrapped with a cloth, chemicalized with an evil-smelling liquid; insulation against the bloodhound machine. You didn't have to be a dog to detect that pungent, familiar odor.

WE HAD BEEN no more than two or three minutes, though it seems longer in the telling. Trant was kneeling on the floor by the easy chair where I had found the knife.

He said, "Jac, look at this—"

A half-burned celluline match sliver lay on the rug, with a fragment of paper ash near it. Trant applied the vacuum cup of the scent-classifier to the match. There was no reaction. That meant that the murderer probably had used this match, and also that he must have been wearing insulated gloves. He had stood here—after the murders doubtless— and burned a fragment of paper.

But the paper ash was very tiny. It suggested a half-inch square of paper. What murderer would stop to burn so small a piece? I had a flash of intuition: that accursed evil-smelling insulating liquid is non-inflammable. More than that, even its radiating odor kills combustion. Anybody knows that who has used—and smelt—a fire extinguishing spraygun. But the murderer, in his haste, might have forgotten it and tried to burn a larger piece of paper and failed. I searched among the upholstered cushions of the easy chair and found a crumpled ball of half-charred paper with a corner burned off. The murderer in his haste had tossed it here when he found that it wouldn't burn.

We smoothed it out. There was a scribbled notation on it—a weather report and forecast for tonight. Fog was coming, of a density and depth paralleling the one of a week ago. The notations concerned, obviously, flying conditions—there was a specification of several of the local traffic levels, with a predicted fog-density at various altitudes.

The paper was partly burned, charred and crumpled, but under the electro-magnifier what there was available of the writing came reasonably distinct.

We read it to Mac and it seemed fairly to galvanize him. "That all?" he demanded.

There was another memorandum; it had been made first—the flying forecast was scribbled partly on top of it.

"Harrisburg Stage 39, Eastbound, leaves 12.02 A.M.—flying time about 8 minutes tonight at 10,000 foot level. Allow 20% retardation for fog."

That didn't seem to mean much to us at the moment, but it did to Mac. He said, "Harrisburg Stage 39? I'm pretty sure that's the aerial field used by Midland Airways. Their eastbound freighter passes there, I think, at 12.02 A.M. I'll verify it. Hold the wave open. Don't shut me off."

I remembered that eastbound freighter now. A week ago; in a fog similar to that which probably was gathering tonight, this same Midland Freighter had very nearly come to grief. *"Flying time eight minutes."* That could very readily refer to the flying time of the freighter from Harrisburg to the fog tower in which Arturo Giorni had been stationed last week when he claimed he had become frightened and could not handle his instruments. That fog tower, I knew, was some thirty or forty miles this side of Harrisburg, perched on a lonely little mountaintop....

Trant was saying, "We might as well get out of here—the Alarm Squad will be coming."

Mac came on my still open line. "That's what it is," he said. "Something in the air concerning that Midland Freighter."

He gave us his orders. The Alarm Squad was gathering outside now. The house was surrounded. If the criminal—and Carter, dead or alive—were still about the premises they could not now escape.

WE LEFT THE library for the Alarm men to come with their routine investigation. It is never the role of the Shadow Squad to mix in that. We work apart. Our tradition is secrecy and speed. I am forced to admit, of course, that there is some professional rivalry. Mac, for instance, told us now to take that charred bit of paper with us, and to say nothing about it. I don't want to argue the ethics. I am an S.S. man; I have had many proofs of the fact that the bullish methods of the routine men often defeat their own purpose. In this case, for example, an Alarm Squad causing a tumult at Harrisburg and at that lonely fog tower—well, it would have been exactly the wrong procedure....

We padded noiselessly back through the dim and silent lower floor of the house and out the window through which we had entered. The little garden outside was dank and dark. No question about the gathering fog—it hung a dripping, gray-green shroud all about us.

We started down the garden path, and then moved aside into the shrubbery. Trant murmured:

"I'd better send them a flare. Mac's told them we're here, of course, but you never can tell about Alarm men."

We sent the little purple puff of light signal over us. Down by the front gate it was answered. And then the Alarm Squad rushed the house, surrounding it, entering its several doors and windows simultaneously. The interior lights sprang on. We could hear the tramping searchers.

Would they find Carter's body in one of the upper rooms? Had the criminals been lurking in the upper story? I did not think so, and as we stood listening there was no sign of fighting….

I had shut Mac off; now I called him again. "You fellows report back to the desk," he said.

Trant said, "What are they finding here in the house?"

"Not a thing," Mac chuckled. "You fellows found it all, apparently. Come on back—we'll figure it out."

We started down the path toward the front gate. The fog was solid around us. You couldn't see the gate. The nearby trees and shrubs were dim, ghostly shapes. Behind us, up at the house, there were spots of light, all blurred by the fog. But you could hear plenty. It's amazing what noise and turmoil an Alarm Squad makes. Shouting voices around the house, the tramp of footsteps, banging of doors and windows… The whole neighborhood here was alarmed now. Taxiplanes were landing nearby; people were gathering outside the guarded gates. Other arriving officials came thumping up the path; we slid like shadows unseen to the shrubbery, to let them pass, which was easier than arguing with them.

And as we crouched Trant suddenly gripped me, and whispered,

"That's queer! Listen!"

Despite the widespread turmoil I thought I heard the surreptitious sound of shrubbery crackling near us. Some-one hiding here, clumsily moving. You can't hear much with the unaided ear; and, worse, you get no real sense of direction. The vague sound instantly stopped. Then Trant and I, silently crouching, tuned our electrical eavesdrop-pers. With the distant roaring torrent eliminated, distinctly we heard the sound of a low panting breath. Someone was lurking near us, here in the fog-shrouded darkness. Labored, excited breathing. The direction was obvious. We moved between the dim shrubs; made a rush. There was only a dull sound of the scuffle we made—those Alarm men never heard it; they were too busy with their own noise.

Trant murmured, "Well—got you!"

We stood gripping a terrified young woman, who was crouching with a Banning gun in her hand.

3

SHE COWERED AS though we were about to kill her with some mysterious deadly weapon when Trant applied the little vacuum of the classifier to her forehead. There was no identification; the classification was a new one; this was not the unknown person who had been in that library where old man Baker and his daughter were murdered.

I said, "You haven't been in that house tonight?"

"No," she gasped. "No—I was here—only here. The police have come. What is—"

"We'll ask the questions," Trant said gruffly. "What are you doing out here? What's your name?"

She seemed to realize suddenly that we were the police. Sullenness fell on her. She stood trembling, her breast swiftly rising and falling with her excited breath. Trant held the small spreading blue beam of his hand torch upon her.

"What's your name?" I demanded. I snatched up the loose sleeves of her jacket. There was no name on her forearm. It wasn't painted over with an attempt at disguise—it simply had never been tattooed. That's the trouble with our Government Bureaus; they get good ideas, but don't carry them through. This girl was a foreigner—an Italian, and obviously she was one of the many thousands whom the Identification Bureau had so far failed to label.

Trant shook her. "What's your name?"

"Santa."

"Santa what?"

She fell again into defiant silence. I said:

"You've decided not to talk? That it?"

"Yes," she murmured. "You—you let me go. I have done nothing."

"Except crouch here in the bushes with a Banning gun while two people got murdered," Trant said.

"Somebody—keeled?"

She may have been a skilled actress, we had no means of judging, but it seemed that she was stricken with horror. "Somebody keeled?" she stammered again. "Who—"

"A man and his daughter," I said. "I guess you know who I mean—Mr. Baker and young Mrs. Carter."

Trant said, "Shall we take her in with us, or call Mac first?" Then, to the girl, "You'll talk plenty when we get the office instruments on you."

Her frightened gaze swung from Trant to me. She said, "Those policemen—have they caught somebody?"

"Only one got caught is you," Trant grinned. "That's rough on you, isn't it? All the rest got away."

Trant's chin was down as he lowered his mouth to his chest to call Mac. The girl stood sullenly staring at me. She was a small, slim girl, not much over twenty, it seemed; black hair piled on her head, held with Spanish shell combs, and with a little round black toreador hat on top. A low-class, Italian-American, was my guess. Certainly she was a handsome type, with all the cosmetician's art to enhance her youthfully vivid Latin beauty. She could have been a restaurant window dancer, by the look of her.

Trant was telling Mac about her. I said, more gently this time,

"You were out here as a lookout, weren't you? The men who did these killings and abducted Mr. Carter—how is it you didn't leave with them?"

A queer look swept her face; I couldn't fathom it. She said sullenly, "I have done nothing. You let me go. I—the police came so queek—I could not get away from here."

I CHUCKLED AT that; it was probably the only true thing she had said. Whatever her motive, she had been lurking here, and the sudden arrival of the alarm squad, surrounding the grounds, with guards at the gates, had trapped her.

Trant said, "Mac wants us to bring her right in. He'll make her talk."

I was staring at her, and suddenly I got a flash of memory. That memo of the Crime Prevention Bureau about Arturo Giorni, who had almost wrecked the Midland Airways freighter, had carried notation of Giorni's identification type which was available. I had sent for the type as a matter of routine, and had projected it on our office machine. It showed a scene of Giorni in the hospital room and carried his voice as he proclaimed his innocence in the tower episode. And as I stared at ths girl now it seemed that her face was familiar. Abruptly I realized that she looked like Giorni.

I whispered it to Trant and he told it to Mac.

The chief said, "Oh, she does?" He thought a moment. "Well, you get her out of there," he told us. "Don't let the Alarm men stop you—tell 'em I say this is S.S. private business. I'll inquire further into Giorni—I guess he's still at the hospital. Take her a few blocks away and call me again."

We did that. The Alarm men at the gate were disgruntled that we had a prisoner, but they let us pass. All the streets of the neighborhood were thronged with pedestrians and vehicles attracted by the turmoil of the Alarm Squad. An abnormal number of private cars and taxis were hovering in the lower lanes overhead—a dangerous congestion, and the traffic directors already were warning them away with purple flashes luridly illuminating the gathering fog.

We shoved the girl through the crowd for a few blocks, and then, in a dim arcade entrance, Trant stood apart with her while I called Mac for further instructions. The Chief quite evidently had made up his mind on a course of action. And it surprised us, to say the least. He ordered us now to turn the girl loose—or to let her think she escaped us, which would be better.

"Can you do that?" he asked.

"Why not?" I demanded. "What's the plan?"

"You two follow her. Trant gives me the idea she's no skilled criminal—she perhaps won't realize you're with her. I want to find out what she'll do."

"If anything," I said dubiously. "Besides, she's had a good look at us. It isn't easy—"

"I'm sending Glutz of the B.D. to join you," Mac said briefly. "He'll disguise you neatly. Hurry up—don't talk so much. Turn her loose."

We contrived it. We didn't know if the girl was convinced she had escaped or not. Probably she did think so, because certainly she was no professional criminal wise in the ways of official trackers. We got ourselves tangled up in a pedestrian jam, and she found herself free of us. Whatever her purpose, she went right after it. We saw her gaze around

in bewilderment and, not seeing us, she darted for an escalator and onto a southbound moving sidewalk. We were
there. It wasn't hard to anticipate her movements—and
anticipation is the best method of tailing. I was off that
sidewalk ahead of her and Trant was fairly close behind
her. I imagine it was five minutes after we cut her loose
before she was hurrying into a public audiphone booth,
with Trant and me planted outside.

I focused the eavesdropper on the booth, while Trant
called Mac to tell him where we were so that Gultz, of the
Bureau of Disguises, could make a rush and try and join
us here.

EAVESDROPPING ON THAT booth from fifty feet away
was simple enough. I heard her call a New York City hospital—the hospital where Arturo Giorni was an inmate.
There was some delay in the connection—which was a help
for us; it gave Glutz more time to get here.

Then the connection was made. The girl said:

"Arturo? This is Santa." She spoke softly, swiftly—and
certainly she was agitated. Trant was listening with me
now. We could hear Giorni's micro-phonic voice:

"Santa? What is it?"

He spoke in Italian, which discouraged Trant; but I am
Italian descent—it comes easy to me. The girl said:

"I know what it means now, Arturo. Oh, please believe
whatever happens I tried to do what was best."

"Santa—"

It seemed that there was desperation in both their voice
tones. And suddenly, when he would not let her shut him
off, the girl began talking in code. Now I am fairly expe-
rienced in vocal codes; we have one in the Shadow Squad

which is exceptionally good and we are all very fluent with it. The general public, I know, uses codes very little; they are difficult to master. But the Italians like them; lovers seem to find romance in having their own secret way of talking. I imagine I could make a stab at understanding a good many codes, but this one, in Italian, had me balked.

And Trant also, of course. And Mac was exasperated. The chief already had connected with the hospital. An official there had trained an eavesdropper upon Giorni's bed, and Giorni's end of the conversation was relayed to Mac at Desk No. 4. But the Italian code had us all balked.

Mac murmured, "Damnation! I've tried to locate an Italian coder—to relay him in, but, dammit, we can't find him. To miss this—"

We certainly did miss it. For maybe five minutes that accursed code conversation went on. Giorni seemed to be pleading with the girl, and she was stalling on telling him something. Or he was trying to dissuade her from doing something....

The effeminate, perfumed little Glutz arrived beside us, carrying his black case.

"'Eello, *messieurs*—I come hurrying. How you wish to look?"

"Shut up," Trant growled. "We're in a jam."

The code dialogue seemed about to terminate. Mac's voice said abruptly,

"You, Trant, cut away from there. Get a taxi for Harris-burg. Call me when you're in the air. Go now!"

Trant shut off his instruments and swung on me. "I'm away, Jac—good luck to us, whatever it is." He flipped with his finger the waxen mustache of little Glutz, slapped me on the back and jumped through the pedestrian crowd, hurrying for a taxi take-off ramp.

Mac murmured hurriedly, "She's finished! Look out for yourself, Lombard! You and Glutz stick to her. Have Glutz make you up soon as he has a chance, then you'll be freer to keep close to her. Send Glutz back when he's finished. Call me later."

I shut Mac off. The girl, pallid and grim, was coming out of the booth. Glutz and I darted away. That little Glutz was like a rabbit. He was no trouble to me. We kept the hurrying girl in sight but suddenly, fairly without warning, she jumped into a rolling taxi. Glutz had another taxi stopped even quicker than I could have done it. The pilot grinned at the excited, dandified Glutz.

"Sure I saw yer girl," he declared. "We'll roll or fly right with her."

WE SPED INTO the ramp traffic, chasing that other taxi. And our pilot's eyes fairly popped when I showed him my S.S. insignia; and Glutz snapped open the bag, snatched out a suit of workman's shabby clothes for me and began manipulating his hypodermics and skin wax. Glutz was, and still is, the best man in the Bureau of Disguises.

I don't like the feeling of the wax disguise process-it's disagreeable, but it doesn't hurt much. And Glutz never fumbles; he makes short work of it. Within five minutes he had my nose puffed out, my cheek bones apparently raised, and my lips thickened. That in itself made me look years older and many units less intelligent... I finished with scraggling bushy eyebrows, smarting, bloodshot eyes and my naturally curly black hair straightened, greasy and stringy.

"There you are," Glutz said. "Now the voice—open your mouth—you know Glutz never hurts you, Monsieur Lombard."

Skillfully he stuck that damned hypodermic needle down into my throat. You get the feeling of choking to death when the astringent begins to shrink the throat tissues; and when you go to talk your voice certainly is—well, different, to say the least.

"Now, practice it, *monsieur*. Make it sound natural. I have gif you enough for twenty hours effect."

For twenty hours I was doomed to feel this icy clutch inside my throat. But you get so you forget it. I talked at the pop-eyed pilot until I could master a natural-sounding speech.

"Beautiful," Glutz admired. "I shall make you Lucian Fauré—a good name, *monsieur?*"

He painted out the name on my forearm, and inscribed the other. But you of the public can't do it and make it look real. Anyway, don't try or we'll lock you up for a term of years. Glutz had every skin pore natural as life....

A total of ten minutes, maybe, and I was arrayed in the shabby working clothes.... Meanwhile we had taken to the air, skimming southwest.

That chase was a brief flight, but I'll remember it for quite a while. Our pilot was willing enough—excited at being plunged into a S.S. affair. But the fog had thickened tremendously. The warning flares were up—long slanting purple-red beams through the murk. We were flying lightless now so that the other taxi might not be aware that we were after it. Mac warned the Ground Directors of our identity and not to challenge us. But it was dangerous business. You'd think that people on pleasure rides would stay grounded on a night like this. But they don't. They dash through the lowest lanes, blind-flying with only the traffic-tower radio-beams to guide them; and some of them are alcoholite fools who couldn't ride a beam even when sober.

We lost the taxi ahead pretty promptly, of course. But fortunately it was flying low, and ground observers spotted it, reported to Mac, and he directed us.

We were, by direction, heading for Harrisburg. We were about half way there. But it was almost blind flying now. Our pilot said dubiously:

"Well, I dunno. Never did this before. I can ride a beam as well as the next one, but any minute we might bump into somebody who can't. I guess maybe we better land at Reading."

That was entirely up to Mac, but already I had my ideas on where the girl might be going. Then Mac told us that the girl's taxi was ascending, and in another minute it was lost to everybody.

Glutz breathed a sigh of relief. He didn't like fog flying any better than our pilot. I didn't either, as a matter of fact. Traffic lanes are nasty places in a fog like this. You couldn't see the signal headlights of any passing plane, and one or two whizzed too close for comfort—much too close. And every minute the fog seemed thickening—solid soup from the ground up.

THE GIRL'S AERO was gone. But Mac had the specifications of its last sighting. I told Mac my guess, and it seemed reasonable. That lonely fog tower forty miles or so this side of Harrisburg....

"Try it," Mac agreed. "She may have gone there. Use your wits, Lombard."

Probably it would be a false trail; almost everything we tackle leads to a blank wall, of course. But it seemed the best chance. Trant, as it turned out, had a wasted evening. Nothing at all happened at Harrisburg....

Our pilot was really adept at beam-riding. We came presently within the scope of the designated tower. It controlled everything from ground to stratosphere ceiling, in a circle of thirty mile radius, itself as the center. As we rode its invisible radiations, I had a vague uneasy sense of speculation—wondering if the code-beams were guiding us correctly. It seemed so. Or at all events, our pilot sensed nothing wrong; and with our helicopter propeller we presently dropped down into a mountainside field. I will say we all three breathed a sigh of relief when it was safely done. By the way the fog looked now, in another ten minutes we might not have managed it. And landing a taxi is simple. I had a premonitory vision then of what it means to pilot a big high-speeder through the traffic on a night like this, with no helicopters and a landing speed of thirty to forty miles an hour. Most particularly an unwieldy freighter, which flies low of necessity and so has to encounter the heaviest traffic.

I climbed from the taxi. Glutz stayed in it. The taxi rose and in a few seconds was swallowed by the fog. But it wouldn't have any particular trouble landing in the New York area.

I stood alone in the blank foggy darkness of that mountainside. It's a queerly weird feeling to be in empty darkness after the blare of the tremendous city of New York. There were, of course, lights down in the little valley below me, and maybe a few houses around here, but the fog hid everything. The rise was more a hill than a mountain. I judged I was a few hundred feet from its summit. At the edge of the field I found a path.

4

THE DIM SPOT of light which was the fog-tower was presently ahead of me. It was hardly a tower—a little round glassite trurret perched on a broad flat rock, with a few iron steps leading up to it, and the fog swirling around it. The radio-beam spreaders were ranged side by side around the circumference of its roof. The tower was obviously in normal operation. The spreaders glowed faintly violet. The insulator-bars which gave the beams their distinguishing break like the notes of a scale oscillated back and forth, all of dissimilar rhythm. And at two second intervals the signal puff of lavender light-flare shot vertically upward, ejecting its undulating horizontal streamers like flashing swords.

I couldn't see inside the little circular room when first I reached the summit, nor hear anything. And that was a weird helpless feeling—having no instruments. I had, of necessity for my disguise, left my instrument belt with Glutz. I carried now only a Banning gun and a knife like a dirk in the side of my heavy jacket and Mac's microphone with its alarm band hidden under my shirt.

Had the girl come here? The lone operator, I knew, would be a young fellow named Jones. I had no report on his record—knew nothing about him.

It was eleven fifty-five now. In seven minutes that

Midland freighter would be leaving Harrisburg for New York.

I crept close enough to see through the glassite tower walls into the tube-lit interior. The young operator was there—and I was just in time to see his white-jacketed figure stand and shove at something down on the floor by the pyramid-bracket of power-tubes which occupied the center of the room. From my angle only his head and shoulders were visible. Accursed helplessness of being without instruments! With a curve-light beam I could have seen at once what he was doing. Was he warning the girl to hide down there? Was he, then, aware of my presence?

He rose in a moment. I had moved closer. I saw him as a fair-haired, pleasant-faced young fellow, slim and dapper, with black trousers and white jacket. He sat down at his control table, watching his sender-dials and with his headphones clapped to his ears.

I must say that, as events transpired, this was an affair when my disguise proved a disadvantage. I did not get killed—naturally you know that, since I am here to write of the experience. But I didn't miss death by much. If I had been thoroughly equipped with instruments, I think I should have remained watching and listening at a distance from that fog-tower. And without disguise I would not have wanted to encounter the girl, knowing she would have recognized me at once.

However that may be, we are only human. I was disgusted; and I reasoned that the best thing I could do was join this fellow Jones, give him some glib story, and find out if the girl was here.

I was no sooner within the circle of light that illumined all the fog-swept rock surface around the tower than Jones leaped to his feet. He stood in the doorway.

"Who are you?" he demanded sharply. "Stand where you are. It's against orders to come into a signal tower on a fog night."

One of his hands was in his jacket pocket.

"My name is Lucien Fauré," I said. I made a gesture toward my forearm and took another step forward. "Want to see it?"

"No, I don't. Stand where you are, I tell you."

CERTAINLY I DIDN'T like the look of that hand in his pocket. I could see past his legs now into a portion of the room. Something was there on the floor. If only I could get another few feet forward and to the left....

"What do you want?" he demanded.

I smiled. "I was in a taxi making for New York. Something went wrong with our power receivers—we dropped in a field down below. Fearful night—"

His hand came suddenly out of his pocket with a gun leveled at me. He said,

"Well you go back down. It's against orders for you to be here."

I turned aside, as though startled by his weapon, but as I moved, I went to the left. I said:

"All right, but please put in a reserve call. We want another taxi."

I waved my arms with a gesture. I would have liked to have gotten a hand into my own pocket, but I didn't dare. "Call one yourself," he said.

"We can't. Our audiphone went dead."

I could see more of the floor now. A human foot; the cuff of a man's trouser leg. Not the girl hidden here. A man. It suggested a corpse, shoved down there partly behind the power tubes.

I said dubiously, "Well—goodbye—"

And as I turned my back on him and his gun, suddenly I pretended to be stricken. I stiffened. Gasped with a low cry and then faced him with my feet planted wide and arms outstretched like a grotesque effigy.

"Why—why—" I gasped thickly. "A paralyzer. Somebody—" That got him. He knew of course that he hadn't flung a paralyzing ray at me, and he must have had visions of someone attacking me from outside. Instinctively his gaze swept the fogswirling darkness. His gun muzzle wavered. And in that second I had him covered.

I said sharply, "Lower your gun!"

He was startled afresh as he turned and saw me alert, with weapon on him.

That was a nasty crisis. I didn't want to kill him off-hand; and in his startled confusion he might have flung a shot at me, even though I drilled him simultaneously.

But he was not so confused as that. He lowered his gun and in another instant I was beside him in the doorway, wrenching the weapon from him.

"S.S. man," I said. "Know what that is? I just came to see what was going on here."

He stood with his back to the control table. I never saw such alert eyes—dark eyes, incongrously dark with his fair hair and smooth, pink-white complexion. Then he smiled. He said:

"I was only trying to obey orders, keeping you out of here."

A man lay on the floor by the power tubes. But he wasn't dead. Unconscious evidently, lying with closed eyes and laboriously panting breath.

I kept my gaze on the fellow by the table.

"Who's that on the floor?" I demanded. "What's wrong with him?"

"Jones," he said readily. "He's the regular operator. I'm relief man. He was taken sick almost as soon as I got here—frightened or something. Then I guess he fainted. I reported it. A doctor is coming."

Frightened? Giorni was on duty here a week ago and he got unaccountably frightened....

The fellow spoke with a ready frankness. It almost deceived me. But not enough to make me relax.

"Put up your hands," I said. "I want to see what other weapons you might have about you."

HIS HANDS WENT up obediently. But one of them brushed the outside of his jacket on the way up. And in that second the accursed thing struck at me. I felt a wild thrill of fear. Panic. Terror. Words can't describe it. My heart jumped into my throat and down to my stomach. Then it tightened as though an icy hand had gripped it, trying to hold its wild lunges.

The tube-lit room wavered before me. I flailed my arms. The gun clattered to the floor.

Thoughts are instant things. I knew then what had struck me—and Giorni, here a week ago. The cardiac deranger—damnable little vibrator whose soundless, invisible beam attacks the nodal tissue of the heart. Mac and I had suspected it had been used on Giorni, but the fellow had a chronic heart lesion, so that the doctors could not be sure.

My heart is perfect. That, and my realization that this was not fear, saved me from unconsciousness now. When you think you're frightened, the heart disorder aggravates itself. I wavered and fell. But the fall was partly voluntary, and I lay writhing, fighting with all my mind and will to quiet that wildly jumping heart. My hand and arm were shaking, palsied, as I fumbled for my own gun in my pocket.

The man at the table gave a low chuckle. Undoubtedly he thought that I had lost consciousness. He turned, and suddenly I was aware that he had switched off all the tower mechanisms. The fog tower was dead; its overhead light-beam was extinguished; all its guiding radio paths out there in the fog of the traffic lanes, had vanished. And that Midland freighter had left Harrisburg by now....

Words are too slow a medium to describe instant action. I was still gasping, writhing on the floor, struggling not to lose consciousness, trying to grasp my gun with a hand which barely could hold it. And I heard a wild scream. A woman's voice. Dimly I saw her come in the door, rushing past me. My antagonist gasped.

"Santa!"

I saw her leaping at him; and that second of his own surprise as he recognized her, caused his death. The knife in her hand flashed, stabbed into his chest. He reeled and fell beside me, rolled to his back and lay still with the gleaming metal knife handle standing like a little monument of death over his heart.

The cardiac vibrations of the mechanism he had in his

pocket were shut off. I tried to struggle to my feet. The girl ignored me, flung herself down on the body of the man she had killed, sobbing wildly... I suppose it was half a minute before I got from the floor to the control table, and flashed on the main switch. Thirty seconds of traffic flying blind over the fogbound mountains. But there had been no disaster....

The girl was sobbing, "Oh, and I loved you so much! Why wouldn't you love me—Carrington dear—"

Carrington? This was Carrington Carter! His motive was clear enough now. We found later that he had been a young science student, and then a gentleman adventurer with a companionate marriage to young Giorni's sister. He had tossed her aside and married Editha Baker. He had killed his wife and her father when it became evident to him that Editha could read his guilty mind. He would inherit a majority of the Central Railroad. And this plot to crash the aeros of the Midland Freighters would give the railroad back its lost contracts.

And Santa? She recognized Carter's disguise; he had used it when he was married to her. You never can tell what a wildly jealous woman will do. And she had the added incentive of realizing that he was a murderer. I think perhaps that she was trying all this evening in her own way to prevent him from killing; I think she never really worked herself into the determination to stab him until just at the last when she was in a frenzy of horror, seeing that fog tower go blank, realizing that in a minute or two other innocent victims would die....

At all events, that's the argument I put up when I testified at her trial, and the Referee acquitted her....

THE BANDITS OF PONTOON 9

*Eighty Thousand Feet Up in the Stratosphere
That Strange Murder Was Done—And
Down to Their Hide-Out in the Fathomless
Ocean Depths Flee Five Conspirators*

1

IT SEEMS TO me that there is almost nothing in our complex modern world more awe-inspiring than flying in the stratosphere. From long before my birth low-altitude navigation was a commonplace; but once you go above the forty thousand foot lane with its one-way roaring winds the entire mechanics of flying are changed. You might think you were about to take a voyage into space—which indeed ought to be possible within a few generations now. Our high-altitude air liners, with their pressure devices, seem efficient enough for a call on the moon.

"Riding the Purple Twilight," as the newscasters habitually call it, is a wonderful experience for anyone, for anything less than a flight of a thousand miles or so, it's hardly practical to climb into the stratosphere. No local or private traffic ever gets there. Trant and I had made a few voyages in the big transcontinental and transoceanic flyers, but still the stratosphere was a novelty to us that evening last August when we left Tokyohama on the Pacific non-stop flight for San Francisco.

The case which I call "The Bandits of Pontoon 9" began on that stratosphere flight—and ended, all in an hour or two. It was, in a way, the biggest affair into which we have ever been plunged. Biggest, certainly, in its potentiality

*His body crashed down
almost upon us.*

of evil, for with a different ending the United States and Japan might conceivably have been drawn into war.

And it was a big case for Trant and me personally. It has brought us surprising publicity: not the petty blare of newscasters, for to them it was a routine Shadow Squad job. But we got applause from big officials at Washington, and from the Japanese government. And an unexpected government reward of a decimar each. That was pleasing, to say the least; an approximate ten thousand gold-dollars, even in this day and age of wabbling platinum currency, is a nice air-fall for a Shadow Man.

Trant and I had been taking a semi-vacation week-end in the Orient. For all the American public's dislike and distrust of the Oriental Federation, Trant and I both enjoy the quaint, romantic islands of Nippon. We left Tokyo-hama on a hot evening in mid-August, about sundown. The flight would land us in San Francisco by dawn there, and we were due back with Macfarlan at City Night Desk 4 in New York that night.

The huge banked-cabin plane climbed from the Tokyo-hama ramp and was in the eighty thousand foot lane within an hour. The deep, silent, purple twilight was around us; blazing stars above; and far down, a stretch of clouds like a vast gray blanket hiding the sea. The plane was alone up here. We seemed to be floating; almost vibrationless for all the ten radiac engines, and their whirring deep-pitch fore and aft propellers.

I realize that some who read this have not yet made a stratosphere flight, and would be interested in my detailed impressions. But I am not writing a travelogue. I suggest you try riding the purple twilight. That is better than read-ing of it.

Trant and I seem immune to pressure sickness. Indeed, the pressure, temperature and quality of the interior air are so evenly maintained on all the high-altitude liners of every nation that even the susceptible passengers should not suffer.

Trant and I spent the whole of that evening in the narrow corridor-deck of one of the two-hundred-foot wings, gazing through a side bull's-eye at the brilliant firmament of stars. We met a few of the passengers. There were about a hundred in all—Orientals and Americans.

I need only mention three as important to this affair: Robert Blair, a handsome, dark-haired, smooth-shaven young fellow in his mid-twenties. We chatted with him for quite a while that evening. He was the present owner of the huge Blair Munition Industries; his father, now dead, had been, as everyone knows, the greatest inventor of war devices of the modern world.

"To be as great as my father," Blair told us, "that's my ambition."

And there was gray-haired, kindly-faced Auguste Fraille, Manager of California. I think that no State Manager in America ever was so universally popular. I can understand that now. Young Blair had all the poise and reserve of commanding youth—a great industrial-ist, perhaps destined to be a genius like his father. But August Fraille was only the gentle embodiment of human kindness. He seemed extremely interested in Trant and me; our problems, our exploits, our triumphs and disap-pointments.

He said once, "I think I shall have renewed respect for the Shadow Squad now that I've met you." Flattery or not, we liked it.

THE OTHER MEMBER of our group was one Sato Koji. He was listed as a Japanese importer, bound for New York. American in garb; educated; with a perfect flow of English. Beyond that, how shall I describe him? A small, slim fellow of perhaps forty. Sleek, smooth-shaven, lean; a high cheek-boned face. Dynamic in his every movement, like most

Nipponese. He, too, seemed interested in hearing about the Shadow Squad; but when he joined our group, Trant and I very promptly shut up. That seemed to amuse this fellow Koji. He said suavely:

"You Americans are a very suspicious people. In Nippon we catch criminals, too, you know."

The group presently broke up. Young Blair wandered away to watch a card game; Manager Fraille said he was going to his cabin to bed.

What actually happened to Fraille and Blair, and Sato Koji, during that next hour no one will ever know. It was, I think, shortly after midnight by the plane's corrected time, when a commotion broke out on board. We were still over Japanese-mandated ocean, perhaps an hour's flight to the west of Midway Island, and still in the eighty thousand-foot lane. Trant and I were sitting out near the end of the left wing deck-corridor. Most of the passengers had retired to their cabins.

This plane in its bulging middle section has a triple-banked cabin space. We heard a commotion; a shouting voice; running footsteps.

"Well—" Trant gasped.

I own I was startled. You can think of many things that might go wrong when you're sealed in a pressure ship, riding the frigid, rarified air at eighty thousand feet. We dashed into the upper hull corridor and followed the chief pilot and several half-dressed passengers down to the hull bottom.

The cause of the commotion was instantly apparent. A door here led downward into one of the cigar-shaped pontoons of the ocean landing-gear. The space down there was a pressure chamber—an exit port for emergencies. The corridor door should have been open. The pressure chamber should have been filled with the plane's normal air. But the door was closed. We stared through its glassite pane, down into the dimness of the vault and saw that its outer door was open. The pressure chamber held only the rarified air of the stratosphere.

And lying on the floor down there, was one of the plane's mechanics. Blood was on him. His white jumper was crimson, and torn, as though he had been in a fight and been stabbed. But not killed by a knife, for death obviously had come when the outer door had opened and the air had rushed out, leaving him to freeze and strangle. He lay now contorted, with frozen hands clutching at his throat.

The chief pilot gasped, "Murdered! That's Larsen—my mechanic! Murdered—somebody escaped out of here— one of the emergency cars is gone!"

The little sealed-cylinder helicopter-gliders for emergency descent were racked around the pressure-chamber walls. One of them was missing. The chief pilot slid closed the outer door; pumped air into the pressure chamber. It was a job of maybe five minutes. Meanwhile the plane was being searched. Three Japanese members of the crew were missing. And young Robert Blair, Manager Fraille, and Sato Koji.

The chief pilot climbed down into the pressure chamber, and Trant and I after him. Larsen was dead—murdered— no argument on that. And beside him we found a scrawled bit of paper:

The American government will of course be glad to pay

for the safety of Robert Blair and Manager Fraille. We will communicate later. Do not land your plane short of San Francisco or we will be forced to kill our prisoners.

Koji.

2

I THINK IT was our liking for kindly old Manager Fraille which made Trant and me so eager to plunge into this thing. That, and the fact that by all Shadow Squad training our instinct was for instant action. S.S. men have proven so many times that a leap in the dark promptly made works out better than slow and carefully made plans.

The plane's chief pilot was somewhat confused as to what he should do, as well he might have been. It was obvious that Koji and three Japanese members of the crew had kidnaped Fraille and Blair, and murdered Mechanic Larsen, who doubtless had tried to prevent their escape. How long ago had it occurred? Five minutes? Ten minutes? We could not check on it; but certainly it was not very long. That volplane descent-car could hardly be more than down to the ocean surface by now.

The pilot gave our present position. Latitude 39°50' North and near the International Boundary at 180° Longitude. Midway Island, extreme western outpost of the United States in the mid-Pacific, lay over five hundred miles to the south. We called Midway. Reported the affair. The weather down there was calm; a dark, humid night of heavy clouds. The sea was placid.

The excited Midway operator demanded:

"What shall I do? Send out search-planes? We have

very little passing traffic—the west-bound low-altitude mail-plane stopped here an hour ago. Nobody has reported anything—"

We called Pontoon 9. Huge floating raft, one of the chain of emergency landing fields which every two hundred miles follow the 40th parallel across the Pacific. Pontoon 9 is the most westward under American jurisdiction. From there on to the west, they are Japanese. It lies at 40°N. just east of the boundary.

The operator at Pontoon 9 said he had had no report of anything amiss. The weather down there was substantially the same as at Midway—dark, windless; a glassy ocean. He said:

"What shall I do? Send out a search-plane? I'm short-handed here tonight—only have Robson and Allen besides myself."

We saw his face on the mirror-grid—pale and grim with apprehension. A blond, curly-haired young fellow named Jacks. He said:

"If anything landed within a few miles I'd see it now. I've got the whole damn ocean flaring."

"You better not let search-planes go out," I said to our chief pilot. I had been engaged in several cases where hostages were involved. They are always difficult—you can't act normally for fear of precipitating the death of the people you are trying to rescue.

Our chief pilot saw the point at once; he was, indeed, afraid to do anything. We radiophoned the line officials and the police of San Francisco. Then Trant and I, on the public short-Wave, called Mac at City Night Desk 4 in

New York. Mac had already heard about the case from Midway Island.

"Came through the Federal Alarm Agency," Mac said hurriedly. "I think they're going to assign us to it. I'll know in a minute or two. Call me back. If only you fellows had your instrument equipment—"

But we didn't. We had no private wireless with Mac; our apparatus wasn't designed for such long range work anyway. On this semi-vacation jaunt to the Orient we had taken nothing save our smallest personal-protection heat-guns, which we always carried. Though what good instrument-equipment would do us in an affair like this I couldn't exactly see. This was a novel environment for us—the lonely purple twilight and the barren surface of the mid-Pacific.

I suppose some ten minutes had gone by since we had discovered the abduction of young Blair and Manager Fraille. The line officials in San Francisco had issued hasty orders for our plane not to leave the general locality, pending decision by the Federal Bureau of what we should do.

Our chief pilot, still at eighty thousand feet, had us now swinging a circular course. The speed of the plane at this altitude was some 740 miles per hour. You can't bank and turn at such a speed, particularly in the stratosphere; the tangental thrust is too great. And if you could, you'd rip everything to pieces, including all the blood vessels of your body. Nor can you retard a big stratosphere liner very readily. We were still full-speed, swinging on a circle several hundred miles in circumference, northward and back around Pontoon 9.

I presently got the public-wave again to Mac. He was jubilant.

"Just came through," he said. "Listen to this bulletin:

> In view of the fortunate proximity of your officers, Trant and Lombard, we assign S.S. Use your best judgment to cooperate with Pacific Air Patrol.

"How's that? Something for us, eh?" Mac gloated.

AND MAC HAD word of other developments. The Pacific air patrol was under instant orders from San Francisco; and with the beloved Manager of California in jeopardy, San Francisco was very alert indeed. The air patrol was ordered to keep away; Midway Island and Pontoon 9 were ordered to do nothing; our own liner was directed to reassume its course for San Francisco.

"The theory is," Mac said, "that these damned bandits will demand money payment for the safety of their hostages. If they're chased they'll kill Fraille and Blair. Everybody's ordered to hold off except us. We're assigned—an' I can't find a damned bulletin that tells us we mustn't act. Now you're on the scene—what do you suggest?"

I had an inspiration then. You couldn't call it anything else. No conscious plan—just luck. Good luck, as things turned out. But all I reasoned was that this plane was ordered on to San Francisco—and down under us somewhere were these escaping bandits.

"Where are we now?" I demanded of our pilot.

We were somewhere over Pontoon 9. Very much over it, literally, something more than fifteen miles above it with a solid reach of clouds like a blanket thirteen or fourteen miles below us, hiding the sea.

I murmured to Trant, "You think we could manage one of those descent volplanes?"

That startled him. He grinned. "Absolutely. You tell Mac. I'll get it ready."

Mac said, "Try it. Call me when you can. Call me from Pontoon 9."

"Of course," I promised.

Call him from Pontoon 9! I thought then that we would; but we certainly never did—until the affair was all over.

Trant had gotten the general workings of the volplane descender from our pilot. As a matter of fact the things are simplicity itself—practically foolproof. This one was a sealed globe big enough for ten or fifteen occupants, mounted on a catamaran pontoon. It had an overhead helicopter blade—not much more than a descent checker; and a small water-screw for taxiing on the ocean surface. Because the craft was essentially an emergency apparatus, it did not use the public airpower, but was equipped with its own little radiac engine.

As we climbed in, ready to seal the door bull's eye, Trant said to the plane pilot:

"Don't send out any bulletins regarding us—to Midway, Pontoon 9, nor the air patrol. Say nothing."

"Why not?" the pilot demanded. "If anything goes wrong with you—"

"The Shadow Squad doesn't advertise what it does," I said. "Just a matter of policy."

We sealed up. The pilot rolled us to the take-off slide, waved goodby and left the pressure chamber. We could see his face through the glassite pane of the closed door. There was no need to pump air out of the pressure chamber; the outer door slid open and the air went out with a rush. It fairly blew us out; we rolled over the brink, and dropped.

That was a fall. It still gives me a queer feeling, just thinking of it. I imagine we turned over a few times—I had a blurred glimpse through the bull's-eye of the big plane seeming to swoop overhead and then fading, dwindling away into the blurred purple distance.

Trant murmured, "Something wrong about this—"

There wasn't anything wrong, except that we hadn't started the helicopter. When we did, the overhead blade whirred promptly. But it wasn't designed, against the thinness of the stratosphere, to do more than hold us upright. And that it did nicely; the canopy of stars steadied above us.

WHAT VELOCITY WE reached you can figure for yourself. It was almost a free fall—something like sixteen feet the first second, thirty-two feet the next, and so on. That adds up. And it didn't take long, though it seemed an eternity. The helicopter blade, whirling in reverse, began slowing, laboring a bit as it struck the more solid air. We were retarding, though you couldn't have guessed it. And the air-friction began heating us up. Like an oven—

I said, "A few minutes more of this we'll smother!"

Trant's face was looking purple; but he grinned. "We can open up pretty soon." The altimeter showed us nearing forty thousand feet. Then thirty thousand. And I thank the Gods of the Airways, that needle-swoop was visibly retarding. And then we plunged into the solid clouds.

"Well, I wouldn't want to drop through traffic like this," Trant commented.

Certainly we were helpless enough. But the clouds cooled us off; and then in a moment we cautiously opened the bull's-eye a trifle. That was dank, but blessed cold air.

At some five thousand feet we came into the clear darkness of the tropic night, with the sea a blurred expanse under us. There were no lights; seemingly nothing in the air, or on the sea.

The reversed helicopter might presently have completely checked our descent, but we slowed the engine. We were drifting downward now with full control of our movement.

Trant said, "Very queer that Pontoon 9 isn't glaring. We should have seen it. That fellow Jacks said he had the ocean lighted."

It was queer. The stratosphere plane, according to its pilot, had been very nearly over the pontoon when we dropped. Then suddenly we made out a tiny blurred radiance of lights off by the dark western horizon. We were close to the surface now; those little lights couldn't be more than a few miles away.

We settled to the oily, glassy surface, which was barely rippled, heaving gently with a long swell. The water-screw taxied us forward at a fair rate, thirty or forty miles an hour, I imagine. We certainly were a queer-looking surface craft, lifting, skimming pontoons with the alumite globe like a great bug perched on top.

The glow separated into several small light-spots; and presently we could make out the outlines of the huge pontoon. It is a platform of alumite sheets some two hundred feet square. The pontoons raise it forty feet above the surface. At one end is the low repair shed, with its overhead aerial senders and a big magnetic loading crane. And near by, the little metal bungalow where Jacks and his two assisting mechanics lived. A tiny area of soil—a little garden of shrubs and flowers, languishing in the salt air— surrounded the bungalow.

There were normal lights about the piers. When we were a hundred feet or so away, Jacks came out of his instrument room and stood watching us, and then shouted with electrical megaphone:

"You land off there at the left."

I swung up to the dock rack. It wasn't much of a landing; I never handled a surface craft before in my life, nor had Trant. We all but crashed.

The forty-foot cliff of the pontoon side loomed above us. Jacks stood there, gazing down. Hindsight is so easy! I suddenly recalled now the image of his face on the mirror-grid when we had talked with him from the stratosphere— how queerly pale and tense he had looked—what a queer quaver was in his voice. I thought of all that now, because I saw him staring down at us, looking like that. And the quaver was in his voice now as he suddenly said:

"Jump—"

He got no further with his warning. From behind him, up on the pontoon a stab of heat drilled him. His body tumbled forward, crashed down almost upon Trant and me.

Ignominious for two S.S. men, but it certainly did happen. Three figures rose up in the darkness of the dock beside us—Nipponese men leaping upon us.

3

WE NEVER EVEN were able to draw our little weapons. We knew at least when we were beaten.

I shouted, "They've got us, Georg—"

It quieted Trant, who had fallen and was struggling to heave two of them off him. The third man had his gun against my chest. I saw that he was Sato Koji.

"You've got us," I said. "Tell your men not to hurt him."

Koji seemed ironically amused; it was the same sly smile he had given me earlier in the evening when I so abruptly stopped talking about our S.S. activities. He said:

"You do very surely take quick action? Do not be afraid, we are not American criminals—we want to hurt no one." And as my glance went to poor Jacks, drilled, crumpled here at our feet, Koji added, "That is unfortunate. He should have obeyed orders—he had been very good about that."

Trant and I, stripped of our guns, were herded up to the pontoon. The four of Koji's men were there, with the gun with which he had drilled Jacks in his hand.

I understood now that tense look on Jacks' face when we had called him by audiphone. The bandits had dropped, carefully timing their escape when the big plane was almost over Pontoon 9. Jacks and his two men had been taken by surprise; they put up a fight too late.

The mechanics were killed—we found the bodies later, in the repair house here. And Jacks, with a heatgun on him, had answered the audiophone calls, trying to act natural, knowing that a false word would mean death. And it had brought him death. Seeing Trant and me walk so unsuspectingly into the trap, impulsively he had tried to warn us.

We were taken to the little metal bungalow. I saw as we passed the repair shed, that the descent-car which Koji had stolen had been raised by the magnetic crane and was hidden inside the shed.

In the front room of the bungalow—Jacks' tiny instrument room—were the two hostages. They were seated in two chairs, with ankles and wrists lashed by lengths of wire. Pale and nervous, but obviously unharmed. Young Blair said tremulously:

"Well, where did you come from?" Manager Fraille sat silent. Then as he met my gaze, he said, "That boy Jacks— was he killed?"

I nodded. And Fraille just seemed to shrivel up inside those coils of wire binding him. I realize now that there never could be a man more revolted by violence. I have read, since this occurrence, some of his political speeches against war. But for all that, he is no watery milk-drinker. His eyes suddenly flashed at Koji. He said:

"You assured me no one would be killed. And now, another death—"

Koji shrugged. "I am sorry. It was necessary."

Blair said, "He'll probably kill us all, before he's finished. The honor of a bandit—what good is that?"

Koji only flung a look of irony.

"You better shut up, Blair," Trant said. "If there's any way of getting us killed, you're taking it."

The audiphone was buzzing insistently. There was no Jacks here to answer it and pretend that all was well at Pontoon 9. That presently would cause a public alarm—the Pacific air patrol would know, or at least suspect, that the bandits with their prisoners were here.

My speculations were all wrong. Koji very calmly stepped to the audiphone and gave visual connection.

"Midway? Ah, yes, this is Koji at Pontoon 9," he said.

In the silence we could hear the Midway operator's voice. "I am instructed to tell you that the coin is ready. The government vaults haven't got just what you ordered, but near enough."

"That is good," Koji smiled. "You are sending it now?"

"Yes. They are loading it. A one-man plane as you ordered. I can see you in my mirror, but no one else. I am instructed—"

"And I have two more prisoners now," Koji said suavely. "They are how you call them—Shadow Squad men. They are not harmed. I shall let you see them."

Trant and I had not been wired, we had been shoved against the wall, with two of the bandits covering us. We moved forward now at Koji's gesture so that the Midway operator could see us.

"Important officials," Koji said with bland irony. "I shall give them back to you when the coin safely arrives. You have no air patrol near here?"

"Federal orders keep it away," the operator said. "But I am instructed to see Manager Fraille and Mr. Blair—"

"Of course," Koji agreed.

Fraille's and Blair's ankles were freed and they came forward before the mirror-grid.

"Correct," the Midway operator said. "The coin will start now. I am instructed to tell you that if Manager Fraille and Mr. Blair are even slightly harmed, the Japanese and American governments will hunt you forever."

They would anyway—the American government, certainly. But that was just as well left unsaid.

"When the coin arrives," Koji was telling Midway, "I shall depart with my men. In thirty miuntes after your money-plane gets back to Midway, the air patrol may come. You will find all four prisoners safely marooned here."

It was a brief, low-altitude flight from Midway. All four of us were taken outside to await the coming of the plane. The night remained dark. Low-hanging, solid clouds; breathless, oppressive air. Glassy, dark, empty ocean. Empty lower airlanes. There never was much traffic out here, and it had all been ordered away now, of course. But I could imagine that not more than two or three miles above us, the Pacific air patrol was circling.

WE STOOD IN a diffused area of blue tube lights, out at the edge of the pontoon, beside the repair house. The big magnetic crane was operated from here—a metal switch-box with a double bank of controls. The ocean was forty feet below us, over this brink.

Young Blair and Fraille stood with free ankles, but with wrists lashed behind them. Trant and I were free. But our four captors stood at a little distance with weapons covering us. I saw that Koji was wearing an instrument belt now. Several weapons and instruments pouched or dangling there. They fascinated me. And Trant noticed my gaze. He whispered:

"Don't chance anything too desperate, Jac."

There seemed, certainly, no chance for anything. I wondered how Koji and his men planned to get safely away from here.

"It comes," Koji said at last. He hung his listener back on his belt. And in a moment or two we heard the thrum of the Midway money-plane; then it came with a swoop, circled low with a huge white streamer of fabric flying behind it; and landed.

"Keep away," Koji shouted.

There seemed only one man in it. I was sure the authorities would try no tricks. They could have killed these bandits easily enough, but certainly not without bringing death to Fraille and Blair.

The lone pilot shouted, "Shall I land the money box here?"

"And then you go," Koji retorted.

The platinum, gold and silver coins were packed in a huge metal case. It looked like a tremendous coffin. I never did learn its weight—a ton or two at the least. It had tiny rollers. The pilot slid it down his landing rack onto the pontoon. And in a moment he had taken to the air and was gone. We watched him circle, with his white flag streamer flying. In a moment he had dwindled in the gloom toward Midway. For a time the popping thrum of his radiac motor persisted, then it died into the distant silence.

Koji relaxed. "Very good," he said. And added smilingly to Manager Fraille, "You shall not be harmed."

Our three other captors stood some twenty feet away

from us, unrelaxed, with leveled weapons. Koji went to
the money case; raised its cover; triumphantly inspected
its contents. He was smiling as he closed it and came back
to us. He said:

"Your government is wise. All is correct." He added to
me, "One must be skilled in a trade like mine. With this
crane we can handle this money very nicely."

"To do what with it?" I said. I moved a little closer to
him, but very promptly he waved me back. He stood at
the control box of the crane. The big prehensile arm of
the crane swung smoothly out over the pontoon field; the
electrodes fastened upon the metal case, lifted it, swung it
neatly and smoothly and deposited it here at the pontoon
edge beside us.

I had not seen Koji give any signal; but undoubtedly
he had flashed one. And now on the glassy ocean surface,
an oncoming line of bubbles appeared. An Erentz subsea
speedster. It came to the surface almost at once—a fragile,
tiny craft no more than forty feet wide made of gleaming
white alumite, like a silver-wrapped cigar.*

---

* Because the Erentz subsea speeder has no important commercial use, and is cost-
ly to build, boats of this type are somewhat of a rarity. Millionaire sportsmen like
them; oceanographers have found them indispensable. But you who read this may
never have voyaged in one; and so a very brief explanation of the principles involved
might be interesting here.
Two recently perfected scientific principles are involved. The electrolysis engine, sep-
arating water into its component hydrogen and oxygen, ejecting the gasses through
stern-pipes of the hull bottom, gives a small, light craft the highest surface or underwater speed which has yet been attained.
The second principle—the Erentz pressure-equalizing system—is far more intricate. I cannot attempt to detail here the principle of the conversion of pressure into
kinetic energy. Any modern textbook explains it fully. This Erentz boat had a dou-
ble-shelled hull with a thin sheet of rapidly circulating liquid, which by natural law
absorbs latent pressure from the outer wall, preventing the pressure-energy from
crossing to the inner wall.
By the use of this Erentz system, the great ocean deeps were first probed. This small
Erentz boat used by the bandits might readily have borne Koji and his men to safety.
No subsea freighter can submerge to more than a few fathoms. But that little Er-

4

THE LITTLE ERENTZ craft, fragile and light as an eggshell for all its power of withstanding the tremendous ocean pressures at great depths, came speeding up to the pontoon. It seemed to carry only a single operator—another of Koji's countrymen. With a skilful flourish he whirled up and reversed gas-streams, glided to the little landing of the pontoon bottom, directly under us.

Koji turned and grinned at me—as though he were reading my surprise at his resourcefulness.

I said, "That's a handsome little Erentz boat." I took a few casual steps toward him. He didn't seem to notice this time. He had turned to manipulate the crane controls; he lowered the electro-grippers again to contact the money-case; raised it a few feet. Then, with a curt command, he ordered two of his men down the ladder into the boat to help stow away the huge, heavy box.

That left, momentarily, but one man up here to cover us prisoners. With bound arms, young Blair and Fraille stood side by side, and Trant was with them. The guard was well beyond their reach, with a leveled spreader Banning gun covering them. With a ten-foot range like that its blast

---

entz boat could dive a thousand fathoms or more. Its rising bubbles of gas-exhaust, coming up from such a depth would dissipate and give no clue to its course. Nothing could have followed it.

would have dropped all three of them at once—very prob-ably have mortally burned them.

But I had edged a bit to the side. And at that instant I wasn't more than a step or two from Koji. I saw Trant furtively watching me. We didn't need words—when you've worked together as long as Trant and I have, you get so you can almost anticipate the other's thoughts.

Koji, with the crane, swung the box out over the boat where, forty feet below, his three men were waiting to load it.

Now what Trant and I suddenly did at that instant deserves nothing but censure. It worked out all right, so we have gotten applause. I took a most horrible chance, without any conscious reasoning. In fact, it was more like a temptation. I envisaged Koji and his band making a successful escape. It wasn't the loss of the specie; the American government wouldn't miss it. Nor the escape of a few bandits.

But I saw that this affair might readily bring a national disaster, far beyond the value of the lives of any of us here on the pontoon. Everyone knows that fifty or sixty years ago, no public wanted war. Conflict between nations was always born of greedy, ambitious interests. The reverse is admittedly true now. I saw what indignation would sweep our public at this "Japanese outrage." And the Japanese public is short-tempered, too. They don't like being reviled.

At all events, that heavy money chest swaying in midair over the Erentz boat, and the instrument belt Koji was wearing, tempted me. With a sudden leap I was beside him. My right hand seized the fragile glass globe of a little darkness bomb and ripped it from his belt. And all in one motion I flung it into the face of the man with the Banning gun.

So many things happened simultaneously! The bomb exploded; its light-absorbing gas enveloped us with a sudden shroud of blackness. I heard the hiss of that Banning spreader. But the splintering bomb in the man's face sent the shot harmlessly upward.

I struggled with Koji. He had me by the throat, but I reached past him, fumbling at the crane levers. I pulled all of them I could grip. The crane's electro-magnetism went dead. That two-ton coin chest fell forty feet; it must have crashed through the fragile little Erentz boat as though the boat were glass.

We never recovered the chest, the bodies of the men, nor any portion of the boat. Dimly I was aware of the splintering crash and the splash of water.

I was much bigger and stronger than Koji. My hand came back from the control box with a huge chunk of glassite insulator which I had ripped from its rubber base. And I brought that chunk of glassite down upon the back of Koji's skull. His grip on me loosened; his flailing hand, with the gun he had snatched from his belt, struck me a glancing harmless blow in the face as he wilted and sank at my feet.

FOR AN INSTANT I stood panting in the darkness of the darkness-gas. Certainly no more than ten seconds had passed. It seemed that I heard another heat-gun sizzle. And a cry of pain. And through the blackness now came stabs of white glare. My wrecking of the crane controls automatically had lighted the alarm lights of the pontoon. The field, and the ocean for a mile or so around, was bathed in a dazzling white. It stabbed through our gas-darkness. And the gas, every second, was dissipating.

Then I saw struggling figures near me on the pontoon floor. Two were lying motionless, and two rolling together, fighting. Trant, when I flung the bomb, had jumped for the guard; had caught him when still he was dazed by the bomb. And Trant had felled him with a fist.

Then Trant heard the hiss of the second heat-shot—and a cry of agony from Fraille. The white pontoon glare showed Trant the stumbling, falling figure of Fraille, stabbed by the shot. And young Blair, with wrists miraculously freed, had the still-smoking gun in his hand!

I heard Trant's startled shout, "Why—why, what—"

Then Blair whirled and leaped at him. But Trant dove headlong under the leveling gun; caught his antagonist by the ankles, brought him down so that they rolled, locked together, with Trant gripping Blair's wrist to hold off the gun.

And now I heard Trant's shout:

"Get him, Jac! This scoundrel—" He was indeed, all of that. Youthful scion of an otherwise honorable family of great industrialists. He had said, "My ambition is to be as great as my father."

This was his way of doing it—plotting with these Japanese bandits. Koji wanted only the money; Blair wanted war for the profits and the glory to himself, to be a youthful and gigantic captain of industry, owning and managing the Blair munition factories in wartime.

Doubtless he had planned from the first to be left marooned here with Fraille. Then he would have murdered Fraille, and be rescued alone. Manager Fraille, murdered by the "dastardly Japanese." That would be something indeed to cause an international brawl. And Blair must have thought his choice of Fraille for a victim doubly clever—Fraille's persuasive voice stilled when war was brewing.

The gas-darkness was almost dissipated. Trant and Blair were fighting, rolling close to the brink of the pontoon edge. In the blinding glare of the white beacons I stumbled to help Trant. But it was unnecessary. The giant brawn of Trant, and his amazing aptitude for any rough and tumble encounter, make him a formidable adversary for anyone. Blair had lost his gun. Trant had maneuvered them to the brink; and suddenly I saw Blair go over the edge and Trant lunge back to safety.

There was a splash as Blair hit the water. Trant and I stood by the brink, peering down at the glaring surface. Blair had sunk. He never came up. Perhaps he was stunned. Perhaps a shark got him. Trant or I would have had taken a forty-foot dive into that shark-infested ocean to find out which. We didn't. It didn't matter. Blair's death minimized the scandal.

Everyone knows now that the affair of Pontoon 9 brought no international complications. Koji and one of his men lived to be swiftly and summarily executed by the Japanese authorities. The American public was quite appeased—especially since its own criminal was much the most dastardly of them all.

And Manager Fraille did not die, though he had a hard time of it, due to his advanced years. He is still the beloved Manager of California; and he is mighty appreciative of Trant and me. I sometimes think that secretly he had quite a bit to do with that decimar reward the Japanese and American governments gave us.

WRECK OF THE SUB-SEA FREIGHTER

*Even the Depths of New York Harbor
Could Not Hide the Crime—Down
into the Ooze Plunged Jac Lombard
and Trant to Find the Sinister Plot*

1

DEATH IN THE MIRROR

IT WAS ONLY a few days after our return to New York from the brief but tumultuous affair on Pontoon 9 when Macfarlan, of City Night Desk 4, received a bulletin from the Crime Prevention Bureau. Trant and I arrived for duty at about eight o'clock that evening, and Mac tossed us the bulletin.

"Simple, routine job," he said.

But it wasn't. That's a peculiarity of Shadow Squad work. You never can tell to what the smallest thing may lead. This Crime Prevention Bulletin listed an affair which had occurred that afternoon during the unloading of the sub-sea freighter Nautilus, at its surface dock in the Hudson River. John Magnus, American owner of International Freighters Inc.—a small, newly organized concern, with the Nautilus its only ship—had abruptly changed the entire personnel of his employees. The Nautilus plied on a weekly return-trip basis between New York and Lisbon. It had arrived and been unloaded that day by Spanish labor— parole immigrants who were shortly to be deported.

The ire of the American dock workers caused the fighting, a minor riot at the dock. Several men were injured.

"Crime Prevention wants us to investigate Magnus,"

Mac said. "There'll be a riot every time the Nautilus gets in."

John Magnus arrived soon afterward in answer to Mac's summons. He was a bachelor. A man of about forty—tall, solidly built; smooth-shaven; black hair graying at the temples. A good-looking fellow. Crisp, brusque of manner. The sort of man accustomed to command.

He was willing enough to answer our questions. He said:

"I did not know I had done anything illegal. I employ the most efficient labor I can get—for the least money." He smiled lugubriously. "That's business. With me it's a necessity. The Nautilus, so far, is a losing proposition."

Our financial reports showed that this was true. The two hundred foot sub-sea freighter had been discarded from the New York-London service, and bought cheaply by Magnus. But to my way of thinking there is no future in submarines. Aerial transportation already is too menacing a competition.

Magnus claimed he didn't want to do anything illegal. As a matter of fact, he hadn't… With him now was the Spanish Consul General of the Port of New York. A slim, dark-haired, middle-aged Spaniard named José Gonzales y Agila. He was immaculately dressed. His eyeglass hung on a black ribbon down his shirt front. His tiny black and gray mustache was waxed and uptilted. A smell of pomade enveloped him.

He was not lugubrious; he was militantly angry. He said:

"It ees not illegal to employ my countrymen. You have them on the Immigration Parole. If they cannot find work to support themselves, then you send them back home.

*We saw a plunging shape
coming at us head first.*

And when they find work your American laborers assault them. How is the sense to that?"

"We're only trying to prevent crime," Mac said. "A riot is a crime. Don't you think you had better not employ—"

"Wouldn't it be better to tell the American Laborite Association to stop making riots?" Magnus said. "It's not only the money involved. The principle of the thing is pretty big—"

"It ees indeed!" Agila exclaimed. "My government will protest if your own laws are helpless to protect our Spanish people who live here—"

THE ARGUMENT WENT on like that for an hour. During it, a third visitor arrived. He was Willard Robinson, chief navigator of the Nautilus. He had very little to say—just sat and listened to us. For all his rank as a senior sub-sea pilot he was a young fellow—not over thirty; tall, athletic, with the military look of the government school where he was educated still clinging to him.

We gathered during the conversation that Robinson had piloted the Nautilus only on its last two voyages. Magnus himself, in his younger days, had had a master's sub-sea license. He had been employed on the New York-London run. When he bought the Nautilus he had piloted her himself; and then recently had employed Robinson.

By Mac's bland, cherubic face you can never even approximate his thoughts. He said suddenly:

"You, Captain Robinson—you're the only American-born officer of the Nautilus now?"

"Yes," Robinson agreed. "That is so."

Magnus said: "I had to employ a Spanish crew and officers. Our laws will not let me reduce Americans' wages."

It seemed to me that Robinson looked very queer. A look of uneasiness. And he kept staring at Trant and me. A little later he said to us, aside:

"You are the fellows who killed young Blair on Pontoon 9?"

"I did," Trant said aggressively. "What of it?"

But Robinson's attention had gone to Magnus. The Nautilius' owner was saying:

"I'm not going to retreat from my position. As Señor Agila says, it's the principle of the thing."

"It ees indeed," the consul agreed.

Mac said, "The Nautilus sails tonight?"

"Yes—somewhat after midnight. But you need not worry about a riot. My Spanish loaders are not working."

"Who is?" Mac demanded.

Magnus gestured deprecatingly. "No one. The Nautilus will sail with Captain Robinson and my Spanish crew. But we're taking no cargo."

Queer, that! Why sail a freighter with no cargo? It seemed as though Robinson was about to speak, but he did not. Magnus evidently felt it needed an explanation. He added, "I am having my scheduled freight transshipped by the London line. It will mean a big loss to me, but I'll accept no more freight until this labor affair is settled."

"Then why sail at all?" Mac said.

"Because of the cargo coming back," Magnus explained readily. "By the time I get it here we'll have settled this dispute."

He and Agila and Captain Robinson left us presently. I recall that during the remainder of the interview it had seemed that Robinson's gaze was constantly, though furtively, on Trant and me. Did it hold something of menace? It seemed so. I found myself speculating on whether or not this fellow might have had some personal connection with Robert Blair, of the U.S. Munitions.

Did he hold a grudge against us for having killed Blair?

Certainly neither Mac, Trant nor myself had the remotest intimation now of any plot underlying this labor dispute. It only seemed strange that Magnus should be such a crusader for the labor rights of a foreign nation.

"Well, that's that," Mac said, when we were again alone. "If he chooses to sail without American cargo there'll be no more dock riots. That'll satisfy the Crime Prevention Desk. I guess we can file this case closed."

But we certainly couldn't. Within an hour a federal memorandum came to us from Washington. It was a repeat-bulletin from the Crime Prevention Bureau of Madrid. It read:

> Madrid C.P. advises: John Magnus recently deposited considerable sum here in Madrid to his personal account. His personal safety vault not accessible to us without lengthy legal action, but we have reason to believe he is hoarding several thousand pounds British sterling. Believe New Spain plotters have financed him. We hope this answers your inquiry.

Magnus financed by the anti-government party of Spain! Magnus with newly-acquired personal riches! Another federal bulletin arrived:

> Madrid Crime Prevention Desk suggests your Shadow Squad consult Señor Jose Agila, Consul General of the Port of New York. Work with him in locating Miguel Toreno, leader of anti-government party, now thought to be in America. Señor Agila has Toreno's description. He is being instructed to give every assistance. We are warning him against gullible friendship for Magnus. We believe Magnus, acting for Toreno, may be trying to learn government secrets. Suggest you also privately warn Señor Agila.

WELL, THAT CERTAINLY gave us food for thought! Was Magnus so smooth a scoundrel that he was using this labor dispute as a means of winning the confidence of the fiery little Spanish consul, and thus worm from him information? Was Magnus selling this information to the anti-government plotter, Toreno?

We were still digesting this new aspect of the case when a personal audiphone call for me came to Desk 4. Mac answered the buzzer.

"Shadow Squad City Night Desk 4. Jac Lombard? Yes, he's here."

We got visual connection. On the mirror-grid I saw the face of a stranger; a thin, studious-looking young fellow. The dial indicated that he was calling from a public booth in midtown New York.

He said, "Jac Lombard? You don't know me, but I know of you and Georg Trant. Heard of you from that Pontoon 9 affair."

He spoke hurriedly, breathlessly; and now I saw that his eyes were frightened.

"I've been engaged by U.S. Munitions since the death of Robert Blair. I'm Thomas Allen—certified accountant," he said. "I've been going over the company books—checking against factory production of the last few months. Something very queer—"

Blair's villainy living after him! The accountant seemed to run out of breath. "I—I was coming to see you tonight," he gasped. "I haven't turned in a report yet. And now I find—I think I'm being followed. Somebody—"

He got no further. I saw an expression of agonized terror sweep his face. Mac and Trant were crowding me, all of us peering breathless at that little television mirror. Young Allen's words were choking in his throat. We saw him turn as though trying to look behind him. There may have been the vague hiss of a heat-flash audible to us. I don't remember; we heard only that ghastly rattle in Allen's throat. Then his arms flailed wildly up; his head and shoulders spun and sank out of sight.

He lay murdered in the audiphone booth.

2

THE UNDER WATER SHADOW

MAC SPRANG INSTANTLY into action. For ten minutes or so we all kept busy sending out a score of routine investigation orders. We kept it within the Shadow Squad, of course, though a general police alarm for the vicinity of that audiphone booth was sounded. Mac put me to analyze the bank of mirrors which recorded the neighboring street scenes under the actinic glare of the alarm lights.

The police caught no fugitive. They made half a dozen arrests on suspicion, but as it afterward turned out, all were false trails. I thought once, in the milling crowds, I saw a darting figure vaguely familiar. Four newscasting observers almost simultaneously kept Trant busy receiving the tips they frantically audiphoned in, suggesting we chase what seemed that same fleeing man.

But it was too illusive. I fired alarm lights along an escalator to an overhead ramp. But you can't create a city turmoil like that over too wide an area without disaster. I caused two minor traffic accidents, and then gave it up.

And then a new bomb struck us. A call came in for Trant. Not from a stranger this time; the televisor disclosed the grim face of Willard Robinson, youthful navigator of the Nautilus.

"Trant—"

"You see me," Trant said. "What is it?"

"I—why, I have something to tell you." He seemed somewhat disconcerted by Trant's gruffness.

Out of the tail of my eye I saw Mac turn aside; saw him plug an audiphone to call midtown police.

Trant said, "All right, what is it?"

"I—you heard that a fellow named Thomas Allen was just murdered?"

I said into the speaker, as I leaned over Trant's shoulder, "Oh, yes—we heard it. Not far from where you are now, wasn't it?"

The dial showed that Robinson now was in a public booth only a quarter of a mile or so west of the one in which Allen had been killed.

Robinson said, "Near here—was it? I don't know—I didn't notice. I saw some of the scenes of the news-mirrors a few minutes ago. I wanted to tell you and Jac Lombard—wanted to arrange—"

He stopped as he saw the image of Mac leaning down over Trant.

"Where's Señor Agila and Magnus? You left with them," Mac said.

"That was over an hour ago," Robinson answered. A growing agitation seemed sweeping him. He turned to gaze out the booth window; it seemed by the movement of his shoulders that he might be reaching toward a weapon in his pocket.

"I left them almost as soon as we left your office," he said. "Señor Agila was going to his apartment in the Diplomatic

Club. Mr. Magnus said he'd meet me on the Nautilus. I guess he's—"

"He isn't," Mac said. "Our men have Hudson Pier 8 under surveillance. And Agila didn't go to his club—"

"I don't know," said Robinson. "I don't want to stand here now. I called to ask Mr. Trant—"

"And where did you go?" Mac demanded.

"I—had a little business." He lowered his voice. "I can't discuss it over the air from here—you never can tell—electric eavesdroppers are—"

I saw terror leap suddenly into his eyes. The same look that poor Allen had had, talking to us from the other booth! And Robinson, too, swung around with a wild look. There was a thump from the receiver; the image blurred, then cleared again. Robinson was struggling in the booth, but all we could see of his assailant was the hand that gripped Robinson's throat!

It flashed to me that here was another murder; but at my elbow I heard Mac chuckle.

"Got him!"

From the receiver came a policeman's voice:

"Take it easy, fellow—you'll get hurt... Desk 4? Macfarlan? Here I am. I got him."

"Bring him to me," Macfarlan said.

But the traffic officer who had throttled Robinson demurred. "Well, I dunno—I'm on post—"

Robinson now was protesting violently. "Macfarlan, don't bring me in. I wanted to tell you—and Lombard and Trant—"

"You can tell it when you get here," Mac interrupted.

"I can't. There—there isn't time—I don't want to leave

here. I'll tell you something now if you'll send this police-man away. It's Shadow Squad business—"

I whispered to Mac, "Let him have his say. Give him rope, maybe we'll hang him."

Mac ordered the traffic officer off; and with a swift code sentence told him to watch the booth from a distance. And through another instrument I ordered a police tail-man who was posted in that neighborhood to connect Robinson and secretly stay with him.

Robinson perhaps thought he was alone now.

"Well, go ahead," Trant said. "Out with it—we won't interrupt you again."

"I WANTED YOU and Lombard to come out and meet me," Robinson said promptly. "I'm not far from the Hudson River here." He lowered his voice still further. "I've been down to that old pier, 6a. You know it, I guess. The Nautilus used it up to a few months ago, when Magnus engaged Pier 8."

"We know it," Trant agreed. "What of it?"

"I was down there a while ago—alone. Just about the time young Allen was killed, I guess."

Did he think this was a clever, natural-sounding alibi? He added:

"I had reason to think I'd find something down there. I did. I want to show you and Lombard. There's only room for three—and not much time before the Nautilus sails."

Trant said, "You talk riddles—"

"I can't help it. If you'll come, I'll meet you—river end of Pier 6a. Out by the little steps that go down into the water."

"Well, he must think I'm a loon—sending you out there

so he and his men, wherever they are, can murder you!"
Mac was murmuring to me.

"Let us try it, Chief," I whispered. "Seems like the quickest way to dig into this. That police tailer will be there. We'll join him. Maybe we can trap Robinson—and whoever's with him—instead of his trapping us."

Robinson was saying to Trant:

"You've got under-water equipment, haven't you? Enough for a few fathoms? I want to take you under the water, and a bit northward. I've got my own underwater suit hidden there on the pier. I'll meet you right away—"

Again he was looking nervously behind him in the booth. And he said:

"I'll go now."

The mirror went dark as unceremoniously he disconnected. Trant and I made a rush for our equipment.

"My Gawd, that fellow thinks I'm a loon." Mac said, "Look here, you two—this may be a way of digging into the thing in a hurry, but don't be fools. You contact that police tailer. I'll order an Alarm Squad ready—"

"You keep the Alarm Squad out of it," Trant said. "Chief, don't weaken on every S.S. tradition we've got. Let Jac and me alone. We'll use our heads."

We were ready within five minutes. The underwater suits and helmets made a sizable square handcase for each of us. We didn't burden ourselves with other equipment—just Banning guns in our pockets, and the hooks and knives of the sub-sea suits.

It wasn't more than fifteen minutes later when we were crossing under the Hudson Traffic Ramp beside the river on foot. It was a fairly dark night, with a threat of rain. The elevated airplane landing stages loomed like ghosts around us, their lights high up. The docks mostly were dark. The whole area down on the ground level here seemed abnormally silent and dim in contrast to the lighted, roaring traffic of the ramp, and the buzz and throb of lights in the lower air-lanes.

The Hudson River must once have been fairly well dotted with the old-fashioned surface craft, but that was many years ago. There wasn't a light on it now. We turned south, traversed a little metal alley between two warehouses, and came to the front of old Pier 6a. Once it must have been an impressive structure. But it was a rusting, broken relic of the past now—one of the many which some wise city administration will do well to tear down and replace with fountains and lawns and flowers, like the riverfront further north.

There seemed no one around here. The big, square arcade entrance of the pier gaped with a black yawn.

Then the police tailer, like a shadow, was beside us.

"Well," Trant whispered, "here you are! Did Robinson go on the pier? Macfarlan didn't order an Alarm Squad, did he? How many of you fellows are around here?"

The tailer was embarrassed. "I didn't see nobody," he murmured. "I been waitin' here for you."

"Where's Robinson?" I demanded. "You've had your instruments on him?"

What would you expect from a police tailer? Well, that's what we got. He said:

"I couldn't help it. You told me—"

"You lost him," Trant said. "You don't know if he's on the pier or not. Well, go ahead home—"

"Listen, if you need me—"

"We don't," I said. "Disconnect yourself—switch off—"

"I don't know if the Alarm Squad is around here or not."

"Well, good-by," Trant said. "Thanks for the help. Forget you were ever here—that ought to be easy."

The disgruntled tailer slid into the shadows and vanished. **TRANT AND I** followed a line of blackness and got to the door-opening of the pier. Robinson had said he would meet us out by its end, where steps went down into the water. We had our chest microphones. I was about to call Mac, but Trant at once started into the darkness.

With heat guns alert we moved forward, along the eight hundred foot length of that eerie, littered interior. I will say that I more than half expected some sort of attack, but none came. We reached the open space at the end of the pier. It was a little brighter out here. Broken, old-fashioned staunchions were at the edge, where they used to wind ropes for surface ships. A broken electric loader—used when the Nautilus docked here—stood against the wall.

We stood peering and listening. Nobody here.

"That fool police tailer must have scared him off," Trant whispered.

The little ladder steps that Robinson had mentioned leading down into the water were here before us. Trant and I gazed at each other.

I said, "He had something to show us. Or at least, that's what he said. Something only big enough for three—north of here."

We stood beside the little cases of our sub-sea suits and peered down at the black, sullen river surface. The tide was running out—quite a strong southward current. What was down there? Was it a trap to get us under water?

Maybe you think we were brash fools. I do, myself. We didn't call Mac, because we both knew he would order us not to go. The chest microphone couldn't be used with the sub-sea suit, and the cursed thing turns in our alarm to Mac so easily that we discarded the apparatus now. No use giving Mac an alarm signal. If things got that bad we'd be dead anyway.

We laid our apparatus and our guns in a little pile beside the broken electric loader and donned the water suits. The air-renewers sat like a hunchback's lump on the back of our shoulders; the round goggled helmets, and the suits, bloated now with interior air, made us look grotesque, like strange animals of the deep.

With my gloved, metal-tipped fingers I touched the metal plate on Trant's shoulder for audiphone contact.

"All ready?"

"Sure."

Through the flexible glassite visor his face, faintly illumined momentarily by my belt torch, showed his grin.

"We must keep together," I said. "Quite a strong current down there." Our hooks, scimiter hatchets, and a long stiletto-blade hung at our belts.

"Keep the knife handy," Trant said. "If anybody comes at us, plunge head first. Don't try to stab him—rip the suit." Trant's smile had gone now. He added, "And don't wait to argue. The one who rips first wins."

It sounded gruesome. Certainly it was new to us, the possibility of underwater combat....

Clutching the stilettoes, we cautiously lowered ourselves into the depths of the river.

3

WHO RIPS FIRST, WINS!

IT WASN'T FAR to the bottom; we stood with weighted shoes pressing into the ooze. The current pulled at us, so that we had to lean diagonally into it. Everything was black and soundless down here; only the whir of the air-renewers in my ears; and out through the visor a blurred, black emptiness. At my belt the little torch sent out its wavering beam. Even in the spreading yellow blur of light I could hardly see twenty feet. The ooze sloped downward toward the river middle. Shoreward, up the slope, the rotting barnacled posts of the dock were a tangle. More than half of them were eaten through, broken, lying askew. A shambles; you'd hardly believe that pier would keep from falling when you saw the wreck of what was supporting it.

I touched Trant. "Northward," he said. "Let's go."

We pressed forward, side by side, with the little beams of our belt-lights preceding us. It was slow going against that current. We came into open water beyond the dock. Nothing here but the blurred blackness over the undulating slope of the bottom ooze.

"I don't like this," Trant said tensely. "Our lights might as well be a signal. Here we come!"

We snapped off the lights, stood swaying, clinging

together in a solid darkness. I felt, rather than saw, something flip past my visor-pane. A fish….

The accursed thing was nerve-straining. You feel so helpless; impeded, with every gesture, every footstep an effort. Trant was gripping my shoulder.

"No good. Too rotten dark," he said.

We snapped on our lights again… We may have gone fifty feet; I don't know, you pretty well lose your sense of distance under water. But the direction was fairly obvious from the slope. Nothing here. Ahead of us now fishes darted through our beams; they seemed little puffs of fire as the light glinted on their scales when they flipped away….

Another fifty feet. We passed the tangled, rusted, barnacled remains of some old-fashioned mechanism—an automobile which had fallen in here years ago. It was almost buried by the river-silt.

I suddenly swung my arm out to grip Trant. We saw the thing simultaneously, up the slope, shoreward. The end of a small broken, sunken dock lay tangled in the ooze. Fastened to it was a twenty-foot, cigar-shaped cylinder, resting on the river bottom, swaying in the current.

We stood peering. There was no movement; nothing human around here.

"Come on," Trant murmured. "Let's get closer. A sub-sea boat—"

It was indeed. A submarine speeder—a little sport-ship. Within twenty feet of it our lights gleamed on its alumite hull… Tiny vessel, moored here, equipped and ready. It obviously was of an old-fashioned type. Not built for more than shallow diving; no Erentz pressure-equalizers.

Trant murmured, "It's in use—ready now."

The old-fashioned stem propeller, hung between verti-cal and horizontal rudders, showed in our lights—and the propeller was very slowly revolving. There were several little ports along the hull; an interior glow showed behind them. And there was a tiny waterchamber entrance-port standing open.

Trant murmured, "If we dared get up close enough to look inside—"

Was anyone on board? Was this what Robinson had discovered, and wanted to show us? He had said, "Only room for three."

We moved slowly forward. Eerie business; but there was one consoling factor: Down here under water no heat-flash could stab us; none of the ordinary long-range electric weapons could attack us. Trant voiced it:

"No need to fear anything but a knife thrust. Damned if we can't be as quick at that as anybody!"

We swayed up the slope until presently the alumite hull was beside us. Its bulging middle loomed a little higher than our heads. Through a bull's-eye pane we saw one of the hull-division rooms—a tiny cubicle, with a waist-high bulkhead door forward, and another aft. A single small tube-light was glowing, disclosing a bank of levers and dials, old-fashioned transformers, motor-coils, and a square electro-dynamic storage battery.

It was the engine control room of the little electrical-ly-driven vessel… No one here. But the engine was slowly running, and my hand, pressing the convex bulge of the hull, felt the vibration….

ABRUPTLY WE WERE assailed… I know now that the bloated figure came from the little water-chamber opening, some six feet aft of this bull's-eye window through which we were peering. I felt Trant make a swaying turn. We saw a plunging shape coming at us head first. A hand outstretched with a knife blade.

I sank to the ooze. The shape went over me, but it struck Trant.

Eerie combat, but it was brief enough. I recall my flash of thought that this was Robinson… I saw beside me the two bloated shapes, locked together, each with a knife and holding each other's wrists. Then they stumbled and sank down, rolling with grotesque slowness in the ooze.

I shoved toward them, my belt-light bathing them… Thoughts are instant things. I wondered how many other lurking enemies might be around here. And I recall as I leaned into the river current, shoving forward toward the rolling figures, that I was triumphant. Robinson was having all he could do to fight Trant; one plunge of my knife would finish him. I saw a knife-hand jerk loose; the knife swayed up, came down and struck harmlessly against the metal helmet of the other man.

I was close over them now with knife ready. But suddenly I paused. In the blurred confusion I could not tell which was Trant! I think I backed away, swept my light, expecting to see other assailants. There was nothing but the blurred watery blackness, a leaping frightened fish, and the glow from the little vessel's ports.…

The figures were erect now. One of them lunged his knife—ripped his adversary's suit. Gruesome deflation. Silent, eerie death. There was an upward rush of bubbles… A flat, goggled figure sank to the ooze.…

Seldom have I felt a more horrified shock than the

emotion which swept me at that instant. Trant dead? Then this was Robinson swaying at me… I took a step backward, alert, with poised knife. But the figure's left hand swayed at my shoulder, struck my contact-plate.

Trant's voice, "Got him, Jac. I guess he's Robinson—"

But it wasn't Robinson. The drowning man had been struggling, but he was motionless now. Our lights showed the contorted face, with gaping mouth. The face of a stranger, a Spaniard.

Trant's voice panted, "Got to watch out—not get attacked like that again—others around here—"

We snapped off our lights. There still was nothing in the blur but the dimly-lighted ports of the boat.

"Trant—look—"

We stood stiffened. At one of the forward ports a face had appeared. Robinson! We were only ten feet away. We recognized him.

Trant murmured, "Good Lord, look at him!"

He had seen our lights, but he could not see us now. His face was pallid, blood-smeared; his eyes wildly staring; his mouth gasping. And then he sank down out of sight.

Two or three lunges took us to the window. Robinson lay on the floor, in the tiny forward steering room. He was alone, garbed in an underwater suit, with his helmet discarded. Tragic sight! The little cubby was a shambles with his blood. He lay dying from several stab wounds.

Trant gripped me. "That fellow I killed—he must have just come out—" We were more cautious this time. We circled the little boat, peering into all its bull's-eyes. There seemed no one else on board.

At the entrance port we cautiously flashed our lights.

The water-filled cubby was just about large enough for the two of us to squeeze in. A hand-lever operated the door-slide, and there was a switch for the electric water pump. IT TOOK HARDLY a couple of minutes for us to close the outer door and pump the water from that tiny chamber. Then we slid open the inner door and squeezed through. I closed and locked that inner slide. I don't know what made me do it. Just instinct.

With helmets turned back we stooped in a narrow passage. The vaulted ceiling was too low for us to stand upright… Silence, save for the slow throb of the idling engine. A bulkhead opening, waist-high, led to the engine room. We went through and came to the forward cubby where Robinson lay dying.

We bent over him. His eyes opened; glazing eyes, but they recognized us.

He gasped, "Oh—you—I didn't—think you were coming. I found—what we needed."

He was sprawled face down. One of his outstretched hands gripped a crumpled chart of the rivers, harbor, and lower bay of New York. He tried to raise it toward us, but he had not the strength.

"Don't talk," Trant said gently. "Just lie quiet."

Blood was welling from his mouth.

"I—might as well," Robinson choked. "That chart— shows the place. This—Toreno's boat. He is—you look out—men coming from—the Nautilus near here—"

And suddenly he was dead. Trant's face was white; I guess mine was, too. You'd never get used to seeing a man die like that.

We spread out the bloodstained chart. A little cross was

marked on it, indicating a spot just out beyond where the Narrows widen into the lower bay. It was near the Brooklyn shore; the depth was indicated at nine fathoms.

Whatever it could mean we had no time to guess. No doubt it would have been a valuable clue if we'd ever had time to use it... I chanced to glance up. This little steering cubby had two bull's-eyes on each side, and a glassite pane in front. Blurred submarine darkness had been out there—but now I saw moving lights! Upright figures. And abruptly at each of the ports goggled eyes were peering at us.

Men from the Nautilus! She was moored at her surface dock only about a hundred yards north of here, we knew.

Trant and I were on our feet. Trapped!

I saw a gloved hand with metal-tipped fingers come up to one of the bull's-eyes. The fingers tapped on the pane.

Trant gasped, "Make contact. Talk to them—something I want to do—"

He scrambled aft. I flung on my helmet; touched the metal rim of the bull's-eye. The audiphone voice from outside said:

"Let us in—we have you caught." A Spanish voice.

I said, "Go to the devil."

"Then we will keel you."

Trant came dashing back. "You locked that inner pressure door?"

"Sure I did."

"Thank the Lord for that! They've opened the outer door. Two of them are in the water-filled chamber."

We could hear them pounding on the inner slide. The

man at the window was tapping again. And we heard a queer scraping, rattling outside.

Trant stared at me. "What's that?"

It sounded like chains rattling on the hull plates. And suddenly I guessed it.

"They've unmoored us! They've cast us loose!"

"What fools! Jac, you steer us! I'll start the engine! We'll shake them off—or carry them down the river, and to the surface. Watch yourself, Jac—I'm going full speed ahead."

But they weren't fools. I found the switch and darkened the cubby so that I could see to steer. I heard the engine start, but it only raced wildly for a moment. Then Trant shut it off. The little boat hadn't budged.

Trant was grim when he came back to me.

"No use. They've disconnected the propeller."

Rats, submerged in a trap. The helmeted faces had left the ports; but we saw the glow of the lights.

And suddenly we were aware that we were moving! We felt a little bump. The glow outside showed a broken, barnacled post moving slowly backward.

The men had lifted us. As though we were a stalled taxi, they were sliding us down the slope of ooze bottom, out toward the center of the river.

4

THE RIDDLE OF THE OOZE

WE DID NOT see the underwater signal, but undoubtedly our captors flashed one. The hour for the Nautilus's sailing had arrived. We felt our little craft rolling, with a sudden heave of the water. Only a few minutes passed when we saw the lights of the comparatively huge Nautilus as she came sinking down to the bottom a hundred feet from us. A water-port yawned open. Bloated figures emerged, and then our little boat was slowly turned, shoved forward, lifted and pushed until the water-port engulfed us.

We were aboard the Nautilus. We heard her engines start. Pumps emptied the water out of the big pressure chamber in which our boat was resting. The men doffed their helmets. Other men—the Nautilus's Spanish crew— came through the inner door.

They were pounding on our hull. And we could hear their voices now. A face came to one of our windows. The voice shouted:

"Ave Maria, what fools! When we smash in, we will keel you."

"That," Trant said, "is absolutely true. We'd better go out, Jac."

The water was gone from our tiny pressure-cubby. We

opened the inner slide. The men rushed in on us. Babbling Spanish, they seized us, stripped off our suits, searched us for weapons.

"Easy," I protested. "You might as well kill us as handle us like this. Who's in charge of the Nautilus? You killed Robinson—who's the boss here now?"

"He ees at the wheel," somebody said. "He cannot leave—"

"You take us to him," Trant insisted.

That was their intention. The Nautilus was under way; submerged beneath the Narrows by this time, I guessed. A group of the men shoved us forward along a metal corridor.

Now it happens that I speak Spanish fluently. And from the excited, babbling around us I picked up a significant fact or two—not much, but a little. The Nautilus would stop presently in about nine fathoms, near the Brooklyn shore... The chief would come aboard there... Robinson had discovered too much... The chief had always intended to kill him on this voyage anyway... And young Thomas Allen, the accountant who had been murdered in the audiphone booth, the chief had trailed and had killed him... He also had discovered too much....

The loose ends were beginning to weave together.

The men shoved us into the big steering control room, under the turret of the bow-peak. The man at the wheel was John Magnus.

He looked us over sardonically. "So the Shadow Squad got after me, did it?"

He turned away, intent on steering. We were running slowly. The bow beam showed the undulating bottom close under us, and the green depths of the water sliding past.

"Yes,"Trant said. "And now what? If you murder us you'll have the police of the world after you for the rest of your life."

He shrugged. "That will be immaterial. We will all vanish after this voyage. The Nautilus's work will be finished. She will sink off the coast of Spain and the police of the world will think that John Magnus and all the rest of us were lost. We have only to land this last cargo in Spain."

Cargo? The Nautilus had sailed empty, as Magnus had told us she would! But here was the cargo now before us— in the water, sunk on the bottom of the harbor, *outside* the submarine!

The vessel slowed, sank to the bottom, and stopped. Blurred lights were out there, also two or three helmeted figures and a tiny speeder like the one in which we had been trapped. And around them, in the ooze, lay a hundred or more metal cases of various sizes, cached here, half buried.

Blair's villainy was living after him! The Brooklyn factory of the Blair Munition Industries was on shore not more than a mile away. One by one these cases had been smuggled out and cached here. How long it had taken I could only guess. Months, probably.

Munitions for the New Spain anti-government party. Munitions that would make Toreno the new master of the Spanish Empire. For the secrets of modern warfare are very closely guarded. You of the general public who read this can have only the vaguest realization of the diabolic potentialities of war in this year, 2000.

One of the giant ray-projectors, operated by a single man, is capable of wrecking a city. Spreading Banning heat-beams, so gigantic that a single airplane bearing one could burn a countryside… Disease bombs… Darkness bombs; and light bombs so powerful that a million people could be blinded by them… and weapons with dastardly import the nature of which no law would permit me to name here. A hundred cases of such mechanisms lay there in the ooze. Enough, in modern warfare, to equip the largest army.

A carefully laid plot indeed! Since the war of 1967 munition laws in every country prohibited the movement of any war device from one country to another. Laws for the transgression of which the penalty was death. By no possibility, in his own land or abroad, could Toreno's party lawfully secure these mechanisms. But he had them here, now. Young Allen, the accountant, checking against production, the legal sales and deliveries of the Blair factories to the U.S. War Department, had discovered a leakage. He had tried to inform me—and had paid with his life.

"OUR CARGO," MAGNUS said with a chuckle. "You wondered why I would sail the Nautilus empty, didn't you? Or why I would be such a fool as to run a sub-sea freighter at all? This will bring me command of a great nation. Toreno and I will rule New Spain. But you won't live to see it."

Trant and I at that moment felt that he spoke the truth.

"We will turn them over to the Chief, Captain Magnus?" somebody said.

"Yes," Magnus said indifferently.

"He'll be aboard presently."

The interior of the freighter was a turmoil of confusion now. The cases were being loaded in a water-chamber, similar to the one in which we had arrived, but on the other side of the vessel. Magnus left the control room presently, but four of his armed men stood guard over us.

Trant murmured, "Wonder why they didn't kill us and be done with it?"

"That's up to the Chief, I guess. Toreno—"

One of our guards said abruptly, "Señor Toreno—he ees arrive—"

The man who entered was Agila. Consul General at the Port of New York for the government he was plotting to overthrow!

Agila—or Toreno, to give him his true name—barely glanced at us. We kept silent. If we forced ourselves on his attention the chances were he'd kill us out of hand. For an hour, perhaps, we were there in the control room, watching the bloated, helmeted figures out in the dark blur of water as they carried in the boxes. We could hear the pumps going at intervals as the loaded water-chamber was emptied, so that the cases could be stowed away on board.

Toreno swung on us once. "Interesting, is it not? Your Shadow Squad Chief would like to know of this? Too bad."

He was very pleased with himself. That's a queer trait, but I have often observed it—a criminal who thinks he has a winning hand always likes to gloat.

"Yes," I said. "So you are the great Toreno. Well, you fooled your government."

"All governments are easy to fool," he said. "The American government, the easiest."

Someone drew his attention away from us. The loading went on. Trant and I occasionally eyed each other. We were both thinking the same thing—how to get out of here alive. You can think of many weird things under the lash of complete desperation. I was thinking of one now. I found a chance to whisper it to Trant. He nodded. Looking back on it I realize we were drowning men clutching at a straw. But that at least seems better than nothing, when you're drowning. And Trant murmured:

"At the worst, we die—but these munitions won't get to Spain."

I WAS THINKING of that, too. A million innocent victims would be the price of a revolution in Spain. But Trant and I don't want to pose as noble self-sacrificing heroes. Nothing like that. We desperately hoped to come through alive. That, really, was what we were thinking of most.

I watched our chance. I got myself beside Toreno. "That's the last case they're bringing in? Are you sure?" I said. "I thought I saw others, out there to the left. The light was brighter on them a while ago."

"The last," he said. But luck was with us. It made him decide to consult the man in charge of the loading. As he started out of the control room we moved with him.

"I think there are others," Trant said.

He let us follow him. There were armed men everywhere about the ship. We were unarmed. I grinned at the men who had brought us to the control room, and when we left with their chief they did not follow us.

We passed the engine room doorway. Just across from it, with a narrow grid passage between, was the heavy glassite door-slide of the big water-chamber.

Trant said ingratiatingly, "Señor Agila—or should I call you Señor Toreno?—I think you'll find by the time this voyage is over that we're pretty good fellows. Underpaid

S.S. men. I think, in Spain, we might be of more help than you realize. We know the inside of our government."

He let his voice trail away. I flashed him a significant look. There were two or three other men near us, and one or two in the engine room. I stood with Toreno at the door slide. Through it the lighted blur of the water-filled chamber was visible. Two helmeted men were just closing the outer slide. A dozen or more cases were in the room. The men started the pumps… Close beside me, just over Toreno's shoulder, was a little glassite lever which operated the inner slide.

My heart was racing. Trant caught the quick signal of my hand—and in the midst of his ingratiating words he suddenly seized Toreno by the throat, lifted his slight form bodily, and flung him at the nearest men in the passage.

In that same second I pulled the glassite lever; and with a jerk snapped it off. The door slid open. The cascade from the water-chamber came surging upon us….

I have no words to describe the chaos. For a few seconds Trant and I managed to cling to the passage rail. We were under water as the torrent engulfed us; but we clung. Toreno and the men in the passage were swept backward along it. The water surged into the engine room….

A few seconds. Then Trant and I emerged to breathe again as the cascade died away. It was pouring through the inner doorway only knee deep now. The whole interior of the vessel was ringing with startled shouts. There came a hissing splutter from the engine room; a short circuit there from the flood. Leaping electric bolts—a surge of acrid fumes—

All in certainly no more than ten or twenty seconds. And

of everyone on the ship Trant and I were the only ones who knew what had happened. Trant floundered knee deep in water and reached my side.

"Now for it! In, Jac!"

We splashed into the now nearly empty pressure room. One of the goggled men had been pinned down by a big metal case that had fallen, shifting upon him. The other man was picking himself up near the inner door where the flood had flung him. He had no time to get off his heavy underwater suit. Trant's agile bulk floundered to him, struck him down.

"Come on!" I shouted. I was at the outer door slide. The green-black blur of the bay was outside, nine fathoms deep. I opened the slide to a crack—just wide enough for my body edgewise. An amazing, four-foot high jet of water poured in.

"You first!" Trant gasped at me. That was like him.

"No—you. I'm smaller—easier for me. I'll shove you. Lie down. Go head first."

Behind us the hissing of the engine room sounded even above the roaring of the incoming cascade.

"We can't make it!" Trant gasped. "Jac, we can't get through there! The pressure's too great!"

Whether it was or not we never had a chance to find out. From the engine room behind us came the roar of an explosion. It must have blown outward the other way; we were conscious only of a surging impact of fume-laden air.

THAT WAS THE end of the Nautilus. The hull was ripped on the other side. The water came with a roar, mingled with the screams of men, the hissing of quenched electric fires. Within a few seconds water was pouring in on us from the corridor doorway. It rose above us, waist-high, shoulder-high. The cascade from the outer door-slit became an under-water current, one pressure neutralizing against the other.

In the last seconds of chaos I cannot say that Trant and I were conscious of much of anything save the need to squeeze through and dive out that door-opening. Whether we shoved the slide wider, or which one of us dove first, I never knew. I was aware only of suddenly being under water, frantically pulling myself past that casement, kicking, lunging with an agony of terror that I was trapped. And then I knew I was swimming, free under water, rising with a surge of upflung current and great masses of air bubbles.

It seemed an eternity until at last I broke the surface, swimming with a few fragments of litter floating around me... Another eternity. Then I found Trant, swimming, too.

Passing aircraft in the lower lane had already spotted the turmoil. Trant and I swam together until the swiftly arriving air harbor-patrol came and swooped, picked us out with their lights, poised and scooped us like floundering fish into the life nets.

THE MAN WHO DIED TWICE

*The Fantastic Case of the Corpse
in the Ice Box—the Man Who Had
Died but Was Murdered Again*

1

I THINK THAT probably the weirdest affair in which Trant and I were engaged is one that occurred in September of last year. I call it "The Man Who Died Twice." The records of the Shadow Squad, so far as I know, contain nothing else like it—the murder of a man who already had died temporarily.

The case began about 9 o'clock on the evening of September 14th, 2000, when Jonathan Gregg's nephew came to City Desk 4. His name was Robert Gregg. He had been to the license bureau, applying for permission to carry a Banning heat gun. They had sent him to the Crime Prevention Desk, and C.P. had sent him on to us. He was somewhat disgruntled by the time he reached us.

"Do I have to interview all the officials in New York?" he said. "I feel that my life is in danger—can't I protect myself?"

"Ordinarily, yes," Mac smiled. "But it seems that your affairs—well, they involve elements somewhat weird and unusual, to say the least. Our interest in you is only for your protection—"

"I realize that, of course," young Robert Gregg agreed. He was a good looking fellow; thirty-three years old, according to the records. Tall, blond, smooth-shaven, with the aspect of a trained athlete, he seemed much younger than his age.

"I don't want to seem a coward," he said. "I can protect myself—but it breaks your nerve when you get imagining you're in danger. I guess it's what you say—my affairs are so unusual."

Weird conditions indeed! This Robert Gregg had only one living relative, his uncle, Jonathan. Back in 1940 Jonathan Gregg had been an adventurous fellow of thirty-five. He was a bachelor; fairly well off financially, with only one relative, a younger brother. He was interested in science, and a wild scheme had occurred to him. That is to say, it was wild then; though now, of course, it is usual enough. Scientists had succeeded in suspending the animation of warm-blooded animals by 1935. Five years later, Jonathan Gregg offered himself as a human guinea pig.

All of us at the City Desk, had of course heard of the suspended animation of Jonathan Gregg. His was the first, the most widely publicized case. There are now many other "modern Rip Van Winkles," "sleeping" the years away, awaiting the appointed time to "awaken." But this was the first suspicion of crime connected with such a case.

No matter how matter of fact science may be, to me the thing is weird. Jonathan Gregg actually died in 1940. And, according to the directions he left, he was to be revivified on September 15th, 2000, at noon. That was tomorrow.

"It is all new to me," young Gregg was saying. "It is only in the last six months I found out he is my uncle."

THE PERSONAL HISTORY was rather commonplace. Jonathan Gregg, in 1940, had left his moderate fortune in a trust fund, held by the Consolidated Bankers Trust Co.,

The alarm squad men rose up like ghosts from behind the tombstones.

of New York. His younger brother had been provided for by the trust company, had grown up, and in 1966, had gone to the Yellow War. The records showed he was killed in Japan. He had married there in 1966—married an American girl—and a son was born shortly after his death.

This posthumous son was the Robert Gregg now before us. He had been traveling in the Orient; had only recently come to America.

"You think your life is in danger?" Mac said suddenly.

"Yes," Gregg said. "My appearance in the affair was—well, a surprise to the trust fund administrator. My father—a soldier—didn't bother to notify the administrator of his impulsive marriage. And he had told my mother very little of himself. You know how that sort of thing was. She was a romantic girl. She hardly knew him."

"She's dead now?"

"Yes. She died when I was a child. I've always shifted for

myself. There were papers my father left in a Japanese bank. I never knew they existed until recently. The Consolidated Bankers Trust has them now."

I said, "Who's the administrator?"

"His name is George Franklin. He inherited the administration from his father. You see, my uncle's estate has grown pretty big now—"

Even in these days of gigantic wealth, Jonathan Gregg's fortune now was in the first rank. Sixty years of growth at compound interest had increased the original sum sixteen times.

"Who has the body in charge?" Trant asked. "It seems to me I've heard—"

"Dr. Olin Jared. He also inherited it—from his father, the famous Rollins Jared."

"Did Jonathan Gregg leave a will in case the revivification was not a success and he died without an heir?" Mac asked.

"That," said Gregg, "frankly is what frightens me, I think. The will has always been on file with the trust company. It leaves a portion to charity, but divides the bulk equally between George Franklin, the administrator, and Dr. Jared."

A faint smile flickered on Macfarlan's cherubic moon-face. He turned and reached for his audiphone.

"I've been a rolling stone—I never had any money," young Gregg went on, to Trant and me. "It startles me now to realize that there are people who would profit tremendously by my death."

Mac swung toward us. "And by the death of Jonathan Gregg!"

An expression of startled surprise swept young Gregg's handsome face.

"Good Lord!" he exclaimed. "And I never, honestly, thought of that! I've been so busy worrying about myself—"

Mac was saying into his audiphone, "Bankers' Club? Connect me George Franklin if he's there."

We presently saw the administrator's face on our televisor. A prematurely gray-haired, strong-featured man of forty odd.

"This is City Night Desk 4—Shadow Squad—Macfarlan talking," Mac said. "Crime Prevention Investigation requires you here. Come at once."

When you get a formula-order like that, take my advice and don't argue. George Franklin knew the law.

"I'll be there in twenty minutes," he said.

Mac slammed up the connection and grabbed a police instrument.

"I want nearest police tailer to the Bankers' Club.... Hello—Macfarlan speaking, S.S. City Night Desk 4... You're Tailer X45? George Franklin is at the Bankers' Club.... Yes, Franklin, administrator of the estate of one Jonathan Gregg.... You don't know him by sight? Well, call the Bureau of Identifications—he's prominent enough, they'll have his moving picture type. Or if they haven't, you can call any newscasting bureau. They'll show you what he looks like. Connect him when he comes out of the club— tail him here to me. If he does anything but come directly here, call me at once."

Again Mac slammed up and swung back to young Gregg. I have often heard it said that Macfarlan has for ten years been extremely valuable in crime prevention work,

though of course it is only an adjunct to our S.S. activities. Mac can smell a crime almost before the criminals
have finished planning it. He has one major principle—he
always suspects the worst. It's a somewhat sad commen-
tary on human affairs that when you do that, you're nearly
always right.

"Where would this Dr. Jared be now?" Mac demanded
of Gregg.

"I suppose at his home," Gregg said. "His home, laboratory, where my uncle's body is kept. He and two assistants guard it all the time. The place is really more like a
mausoleum—"

"Where is it?"

"In the Fordham district, near the old Woodlawn Cemetery."

Mac was again at the audiphone. "Jared Mausoleum,
Woodlawn Cemetery—"

2

THE TELEVISOR GLOWED presently with Jared's image. Trant and I leaned over Mac's shoulder. A portion of a small, dimly lit room was visible, and the head and shoulders of Dr. Jared—a man who might have been fifty, with shoulders wide and thin; a lean, smooth-shaven face, deeply character-lined; sunken dark eyes under bushy brows. And a leonine mane of wavy iron-gray hair.

"This is Shadow Squad City Night Desk 4," Macfarlan said crisply. "Your immediate presence is required here for investigation by the crime prevention bureau. Come at once."

But the formula-order didn't work so well in this case. Jared looked startled.

"I'm ordered to leave here now?"

"Yes."

"But I cannot!"

"Why not?" Mac demanded.

"Because I am alone here this evening. My two assistants are off duty—they won't be back until midnight. I can come then—"

Mac's voice nearly always is emotionless. He said:

"You are guarding the body of Jonathan Gregg. He is to be revivified at noon tomorrow, and will claim his huge estate. And this, the last night of your trust, you let your assisting guards go away?"

That swift bland statement unquestionably startled Jared. We heard him suck in his breath.

"Is there some thought of crime?" he said. "I didn't know—"

"There is always thought of crime," Mac retorted, "when large money is involved. It does seem queer that you would unguard—"

"I am here," Jared said. His voice was deeply guttural; ponderous; and it rose now with his defense of himself. "I am armed—on guard always. I told you I cannot leave here before midnight, no matter what your orders."

Mac smiled. "I won't force my orders under the circumstances. Stay where you are. I have two of my young men operators here. You see them behind me—Jac Lombard and Georg Trant. Within an hour or so I'll be sending them to you. They'll conduct the investigation."

He peremptorily disconnected. I said, "You're sending us in an hour, Chief?"

"Hour be damned! You're going right away. Get your equipment!"

"Investigate him? About what?" Trant said.

Mac chuckled at that. "All you're to do is go there and help him guard the body. You get there as quick as you can and stay with the body till it's revivified tomorrow."

Trant and I were already gathering our instrument equipment. Young Gregg sat staring with astonishment at the sudden activity. Mac was using a police audiphone again.

"Give me Alarm Squad, Central Office... Hello—

Macfarlan, Desk 4, talking. Send Alarm Squad immediately to Jared Mausoleum, Woodlawn Cemetery. Surround the premises secretly. Let no one in or out.... Shut up, will you? I haven't time to answer questions. Have your squad captain contact me every thirty minutes."

He slammed up. Within five minutes now Jared's place would be surrounded by the lurking, unseen alarm squad. I give these activities of Mac's in detail because I want his celerity and efficiency clearly pictured. He was working now, of course, with only one idea in mind—crime prevention. And the fact that, despite him, Jonathan Gregg was murdered, certainly was not Mac's fault.

Mac was still putting through his orders. Audiphone eavesdroppers were prepared to relay to him any air-conversation of Jared's. And he trained a street lens-eye on the entrance of the Bankers' Club. I stopped gathering my equipment long enough to glance at the televised image; and across the street I spotted the lurking Police Tailer, X45. A moment later George Franklin came out of the club, started for an escalator-ramp, with the tailer after him.

Young Gregg said, "You fellows certainly work fast. I didn't really expect to start so much action. I suppose I've been an alarmist—"

"You wouldn't see these activities if you didn't happen to be here," Mac said. "But they go on all the time—routine work... I won't need you here any longer, Mr. Gregg. Where are you planning to spend the night?"

"Why, in my hotel room." He named a residential hotel in southern Westchester.

"You're going directly there from here?"

"Yes, that was my plan. Can I have the heat-gun?"

"Don't worry," Mac grinned. "You can't get a license tonight, but you'll be protected. You won't know it, but you'll have a bodyguard."

Young Gregg left the office a minute or two before Trant and I were ready. He was no sooner on the street than two police tailers were after him.

"Well," said Mac, "that's all I can do." Trant and I were ready, so he added, "Take your car. Connect me immediately you get into the air."

OUR LITTLE NONDESCRIPT-LOOKING Police airplane was racked on the roof of the S.S. Building. We slid up into the lower northbound lane with the yellow glare of the city spread beneath us. And Trant at once called Mac on the car's police-wave audiphone.

"Here we are, Chief. Any new development?"

There was indeed. Mac had just gotten a city-street alarm. A traffic officer had fired an actinic light on an upper pedestrian ramp. Young Gregg had gone no more than a few hundred yards from the door of the S.S. Building, when a heat-flash from an unknown assailant had stabbed at him. Fortunately the shot had gone wild; he was unhurt.

The police tailers had been only a hundred feet behind him; they had rushed immediately to him.

Mac was saying hurriedly, "The assailant seems to have gotten away. Those fool tailers—take a look—I'll connect you in."

Our televisor switched to the street image, lighted by the dazzling alarm glare. But we couldn't see much—a tangle of excited pedestrians—an ascending incline up to a traffic ramp where the vehicular traffic was disorganized by the excitement.

Then Mac's voice said sharply:

"Circle back! Drop lower—might need you—"

And then in another few seconds he added, "The assailant got away in a parked Wasp! Tan and brown—you'll see it—they've got a searchbeam on it. Get after it, you two! Catch it! Bring it down!"

We hadn't gone far, and already I had swung back in a crescent and dropped lower. Down through our floor-visor we could see the blurred little glare-spot of the alarm-light. And northward of us now a tiny brown blob was rising, heading in a slant with the police light from the ramp-edge clinging to it.

Mac was saying, "What the hell! You're the nearest armed car to it—bring it down! I'll order off the traffic—"

Trant was connecting our long-range radiac-gun—a device that had been invented by 1935. Under us, down in the city turmoil, we heard the whining electrical scream of the alarm siren; the red-beam signal lights were flashing—crimson swords in the sky. The crowded air-traffic of this lower lane began scattering before us as we plunged like a fire-fighter with our own siren screaming.

In a long ascending slant we followed the fugitive bandit airplane northward into the starlight.

"Give me the controls," Trant said. "You're better at getting range measurements than I am. Are we gaining on him? Doesn't look so. Here are the glasses."

I yielded the controls. We were at two thousand feet, just about over Woodlawn now. With binoculars we spotted the Jared Mausoleum; a low rambling stone affair—two small buildings connected by a stone corridor, the whole surrounded by a little garden with the white headstones of the old graveyard off to one side.

"Wonder if the alarm squad is there?" Trant murmured.

Mac was listening in on us. "It's there," he said. "The place is surrounded. All's quiet. Are you gaining on that fellow?"

We were doing three hundred and ten. That's all you can do in our type Police Wasp at low altitudes. The fugitive car was a few hundred feet higher than us, and two or three miles ahead. We had no trouble keeping it identified.

I put on the telescopic range-finder eye-glasses. As Trant said, I'm better at range-sighting calculations than he is, not that it takes any particular brains; more a knack of coordinating your sight with instant pressure of your split-second watch. The telescopic image of our quarry showed me a tan modern-type Wasp. It was certainly traveling fast for such a car. I caught a glimpse of what seemed a youngish man with shoulders humped tensely over the controls.

"Guess he's alone, Georg. Can't see anybody else."

"We're making three-ten—I can't get the damn thing to go any faster. What's his speed?"

I measured the visual size of the other car's image; waited sixty seconds; then measured it again. I did that three times. The car's image was enlarging on my finder. I took the average of my three measurements, and looked it up on our tables of figures for the sixty-second interval. We were overtaking the other car by about ten per cent.

"Good enough," Trant chuckled. "How far away is he? We'll have him in a few minutes. My guess is he's two and a quarter miles, and I wouldn't take a chance on this gun over two miles flat."

Our radiac projector was supposed to be effective at two and a half miles. But they're not. Why the government doesn't give us bigger ones, when the War Department, as everybody knows, has them up to thirty miles—well, that's one of the mysteries of officialdom—

I measured the distance of our quarry. My directed sound-beam shot, after a few tries, struck the car ahead and echoed back to my eavesdropper. The time-interval for the return trip of the sound was twenty-two seconds. With sound traveling at some 1,050 feet a second, it was only mental arithmetic to determine the distance between us as two miles, nine hundred and ninety feet. Approximate, of course, because we were gaining on the other car—and sound at this altitude does not travel exactly ten-fifty.

But it was accurate enough. "Call it 2.2 miles," I said. "We can try a shot pretty soon if you can keep on gaining at this rate."

If the criminal didn't shoot at us first. But, as it turned out, he didn't have a radiac gun, fortunately. Mac's voice said, "Tailer X45 just informed me that George Franklin seems to be coming directly here. He stopped a minute ago to look at a street newsmirror showing the assault on young Gregg.... I just heard from the alarm squad captain outside the Jared Mausoleum. All's quiet.... Young Gregg, with two bodyguard tailers who joined him at the time of the assault, grabbed a car and took after you. The tailers asked permission and I gave it. You'll see their car—it's three or four miles back.... You're gaining on that fellow, aren't you?"

3

I GAVE HIM the calculations. The fugitive car was at some three thousand feet altitude now, with us about the same. It was winging directly northward, trying to outspeed us. The lone criminal, as we presently discovered, had no instruments at all. He clung to the three thousand foot level. Occasionally a ground alarm light from one of the towns would stab up at him and cling briefly. You might wonder why there wouldn't be a ground radiac gun to bring him down as he passed. Don't ask me. I don't know—except that every State Administration has claimed that the installation expense of the vast numbers of guns needed would never be justified by their occasional use.

"That's Gregg and two tailers behind us," I said to Trant.

We could see the car behind—a little dot. We swept over Brewster. Rolling countryside up here—still a sparsely-settled agricultural district for all its proximity to New York.

"Take a shot," Trant said. "We're closer than two miles now."

I sighted the radiac gun. Fired it. A bit of luck, because you can't ordinarily hit and cling to a moving target at that range so readily. But I struck the fugitive car at once.

The beam of soundless, invisible radiac short-wave vibrations began melting out his ignition wires. Usually it takes ten or twenty seconds. This fellow must have been instantly aware of it. As I fired, the other car dove. But I ranged the beam down with it.

"Good enough," Trant murmured. "Got him! Now if he can land ahead of us, I'm a motor-oiler."

It's far easier and quicker to make an emergency landing with a car under engine control than with one disabled. And there's nobody more skillful at it than Trant. The engine of the car ahead had gone dead. It wavered down, and like a swooping albatross we dove after it.

Trant spotted the ploughed dark field on a hillside where the fellow would drop. We not only got there with him, we came down and grounded like a wafting feather fully thirty seconds ahead of him. With Banning guns Trant and I leaped out to the starry darkness. The other car came down like a wounded bird not more than a hundred feet from us.

"Grand," Mac's voice murmured in my ears. "Don't kill him if you can help it—he'll be valuable."

We went at him on the run. He leaped out of his car as its fall crashed his landing gear. A fellow in dark street clothes. He had a gun, but he didn't try to use it. He took one look at us, tossed the gun away, flung up his arms and shouted:

"Don't drill me! Yu' got me!"

He stood docile under our lights—a thick-lipped, big-nosed dumb-looking fellow of about twenty.

"Take him to your car," Mac's voice murmured swiftly. "I want to get a good look at him. Give me his olfactory classification—I'll see if I can identify him. Hurry it up—I want you to get back to the Jared Mausoleum.

We hauled the prisoner over to our car. "What's your name?" Trant demanded.

"I ain't talkin'." He shot us a foxy glance. "That's for you to find."

I stood him in front of our car's televisor. "Here he is, Chief. He won't talk."

Trant applied the bloodhound machine and gave Mac the olfactory classification.

"Right," Mac said. "I'll have him looked up—see if he has any police record.... George Franklin is here with me now—I'll keep him here."

Mac went silent for a few seconds; then he said.

"My plan, Jac, is that if I can identify that prisoner, you will tell him we find nothing against him and turn him loose down in the city. I'll send Trant after him. Police tailers are no good. We'll see what he does for an hour, then Trant can pick him up again and bring him here to me for the night."

"And I go to Jared's?" I asked.

"Yes. You guard the body there." Trant was saying to our prisoner, "So you took a shot at young Mr. Gregg?"

"I did not. Nobody seen me do it."

Trant's earphones had given him Mac's words to me. Trant said:

"Well, maybe you shot at him and maybe you didn't."

The car with the two tailers and young Gregg now dropped down beside us. The three of them came hurrying over.

"You got him!" Gregg exclaimed.

"Maybe so," I said. "Ever seen him before? Is this the fellow who shot at you?"

Gregg couldn't definitely say—and neither could the two tailers.

But Mac's voice came back at us. "Got him identified. He's Tolly Marr, youngest of the Marr triplets. He's served his term—two years a while ago—he's legitimately out.

"So you're Tolly Marr?" I said.

"All right," said the prisoner. "What of it?"

Young Gregg said, "What are you going to do with him?"

"Wait—we'll find out," Trant retorted.

WE HAD HEARD of the Marr triplets, and Mac was now giving us the full layout. This fellow was a dumb halfwit. His older brothers, Roy and Peter, were just the opposite. Both were dangerous killers-at-large; and both were wanted for robbery of the pneumatic mailtubes a few years ago, and wanted for murder. Were they in some plot now to secure the fortune of Jonathan Gregg? Whether or not, to get a line on their whereabouts would be a big thing for Desk 4.

"Turn him loose back in the city," Mac's voice murmured. "You, Trant, tail him. This would be damned important. You, Jac, you go to Jared's. Have those police tailers bring young Gregg to me. I'll take care of him over night."

We told the orders. "Ask him if I can't go with you, Lombard," young Gregg said. "If my life's really in danger—I guess it is, since somebody took a shot at me—I'll be perfectly safe there with you. I want to stay with my uncle's body till it's revivified tomorrow."

"That's all right," Mac agreed. "Take him along."

We left Tolly Marr's smashed car in the field. Trant and the two tailers climbed into the car the tailers had brought and took to the air, heading back to the city. Trant, as it happened, was sent up a blind alley, releasing Tolly Marr and then tailing him.

Tolly roamed around the city, doing nothing of the slightest importance. Then Trant picked him up again and took him to Mac. The whole case was solved by that time. It had, indeed, an astonishingly abrupt termination. Tolly Marr later fully confessed his part in it. He's in for ten years; that's all you can give a halfwit anyway.

Young Gregg and I boarded my car and got away a minute or two later. Gregg was very solemn and he looked somewhat frightened. He really had never impressed me as being a very manly fellow at best, though he looked athletic and courageous enough. Anyway, I certainly couldn't blame him for being perturbed. As many times as I've been shot at, I don't like it, and I'll never get used to it. When a heat-bolt stabs at you, it's anything but a nice feeling.

"I don't understand this at all," Gregg said.

"Nor anybody else," I agreed. "But that was Tolly Marr who tried to kill you. Ever hear of Tolly Marr before?"

"No. I never did."

It was only a brief flight back to Woodlawn. I racked the car on a public elevated stage a block or so away. On foot, young Gregg and I went down the escalator to the ground level and in another minute were in the old fashioned cemetery with the white headstones gleaming ghostly in the starlight and the little quadrangular garden surrounding the Jared buildings close ahead of us. I kept young Gregg immediately beside me. There didn't seem to be a living human here, but I knew there were fifty alarm squad men near by, at the very least.

Mac's voice murmured to me, "I've told them you're coming. They'll pass you through."

There is one point that I should have made clear before.

This alarm squad had not gone into the Jared buildings—
they merely surrounded the place secretly. In the light of
what happened, that was an error. But that's hindsight,
any fool can reason like that. Mac didn't want Dr. Jared to
know that the place was surrounded.

Mac was saying to me now, "If any of those Tolly brothers try to get into there tonight, we'll grab them. But you
watch yourself, inside there—"

If I had known what I was going into!

I never saw anyone so startled as young Gregg, when
now from behind the dark tombstones, some of those
alarm men rose up like ghosts and challenged us. Then he
laughed.

"Good Lord—your methods are surprising."

We walked on along the path when the alarm men
dropped back into the shadows.

"Say nothing of this to Dr. Jared," I warned. "If he has
any ideas of getting his confederates to try anything—"

"Yes. Yes, I understand."

4

I ADMIT THE thing burst on me like a bomb. I had not even a premonition of it. There was no Dr. Jared here to greet us. He was here, of course. How could he be anywhere else? He had been here talking over the audiphone to Mac while the alarm squad was surrounding the place. But his little one-story stone residence was empty. The front door was unlocked. Gregg and I dashed around the three or four dimly lit rooms.

"There's the connecting corridor. The mausoleum," Gregg said.

We dashed through the twenty foot, vaulted passage, came to a dim vaulted stone room, a weird place of medical mechanisms. Dr. Jared's laboratory. There was a single small, grated window, shrouded by a curtain and one oval doorway.

Young Gregg pointed. "That's my uncle's body. Why—why—"

In a recess of the heavy stone room wall, the body of Jonathan Gregg lay refrigerated in a big glass cylinder which rested horizontal on a raised stone dais. The tube-light gleamed on it.

Young Gregg and I stood stricken. The dials and refrigerating tubes on the cylinder-top were smashed. The frozen body was melting!

Beyond revivification now, Jonathan Gregg lay murdered.

I was standing, during that stricken instant, beside a small table on which rested a public-wave audiphone. The mirror-grid on its raised hinged bracket dominated the room. Mac, over the police split-wave from the sender on my chest under my shirt, must have faintly heard my gasping exclamation of horror. His voice sounded in my tiny earphone.

"What is it, Jac? Aren't you inside Jared's yet?"

It brought me to myself. I clicked on the room's audiphone, murmured "S.S. Night Desk 4" to the public wave sorter. Within a few seconds Mac was seeing the room as I saw it. But he used our split-wave for talking. I heard him gasp:

"Good Lord—where's Jared? Hiding there? Watch yourself! Where does that other doorway lead?"

I stood alert with leveled Banning gun. Beside me, young Gregg was still gasping with horror at the sight of the smashed cylinder. Mac was murmuring:

"I'll send in the alarm squad. Then you search the place, and rush the body to Westchester Emergency Hospital. Maybe he can still be saved—"

But events came too fast for any of that. I swung on Gregg. "That other doorway—where does it lead?"

"I never was down there. Underground, I think. A cellar storage room—"

The oval seemed to show descending stairs. I started for them, with young Gregg close after me. And just beyond the threshold, where the stairs went down, a blob moved! I would have fired in another second, but the blob sank back.

It was Dr. Jared, lying there at the top of the stairs with a knife-wound in his chest. I bent over him, and he gasped:

"Finished me—that fellow—an impostor—don't let him fool the administrator—"

The words choked most horribly in his throat. I guess he died right then. I was kneeling over him. Young Gregg had been with me; then he dashed to the window. He called to me:

"The alarm squad is coming. We'd better go out—"

In nearly every inexplicable affair there seems to come an instant when light breaks on you. That came now, with Jared's dying words. At my belt was a tiny black-light projector, with a fluorescent photographic screen. The whole apparatus occupied only a two-inch cube. As I knelt I whipped it out, flashed its tiny invisible black-light beam at the window across the room. It took five seconds, no more. And what amazing revelation!

Young Gregg had turned toward me.

"We'd better go out," he repeated.

On the two-inch fluorescent grid, half shielded into darkness by the tail of my coat, was the glowing, fluorescent image of young Gregg's face. The reverse of the X-ray, my black-light beam was disclosing his tissues and blood-vessels. And I saw an astonishing abnormality of his face. Part of it was without blood vessels. That meant wax—that his skin had been so cleverly built into new contours that none of us had suspected it! Not even Glutz, master of our own bureau of disguises, could have done a more skillful job. But the black-light ray disclosed the artificial skin-padding—the inert, artificial substance—very clearly. Young Gregg's face normally was cadaverous. He was an impostor. Jonathan Gregg had no heir. This was a criminal trying to claim the estate, with a confederate doing the murder. And Dr. Jared and George Franklin were wholly innocent of complicity.

Five seconds; ten, at the most. Then I said:

"Yes—we'll go out." I rose up; leveled the Banning gun. I added, "Toss up your hands. Any other sort of move— you're dead. I've got you."

I TOOK HIM by surprise. He gasped: tensed as though about to spring on me. Then his hands went up.

"What do you mean, got me?" he said. "Don't shoot— you're crazy!"

"Am I? Well, that's a nice disguise you've got. Stand quiet—"

But I didn't have him. For those few seconds I had turned my back on the door-oval where Jared's body was lying.

"Disguised?" Mac's voice asked.

"Yes, Chief. He's really thin-faced. Cadaverous—"

"Roy Marr! Jac, you—"

It was the killer-at-large, Roy Marr. His halfwit brother, Tolly, had been told to shoot at him, and escape. That would divert suspicion from "young Gregg" when he inherited the fortune of the murdered man. Simple enough. The third brother, Peter, had gotten in here somehow, killed Dr. Jared, and smashed the cylinder. That must have occurred just as the alarm squad was arriving outside, so that Peter Marr was trapped in here. How he became aware of the alarm squad's presence, we also never knew. I think I've mentioned before that a police alarm squad isn't always as secret as it ought to be.

Peter Marr had been hiding here in the cellar room.

The few seconds while I stood with gun leveled upon Roy Marr had brought Mac and me a complete understanding of the affair. Mac's voice was saying:

"He's Roy Marr! Jac, you—" His voice rose with an agonized warning. "Behind you—drill him!"

From the stairs behind Jared's body, the shadowed figure of Peter Marr had appeared. Mac in that second saw him from the room's televisor. I whirled; fired as I turned. But in the same instant Roy Marr jumped on me. My heat-bolt stabbed harmlessly up to the ceiling. I went down with Roy on top of me. I felt him snatching at my gun. And Peter Marr came with a leap.

That was a nasty situation for me. But it was also pretty tense for Mac. With sight and hearing and voice he was here in the room. But actually he was sitting miles away at Desk 4, watching me about to get killed, and himself helpless to do anything.

It was only a matter of seconds. The alarm squad was coming from outside on a run. My two assailants were trying to finish me up and then desperately to shoot their way out. Peter Marr couldn't fire; his brother and I struggling on the floor, were too closely tangled. Roy's left fist caught me on the side of the head as I tried, face down, to rise up and heave him off.

His other hand had me by the wrist, twisting at my gun. I can't say it was any skill on my part, but as I jerked at Roy's grip on my wrist, I fired again. The heat-blast slanted upward—and it caught the oncoming Peter full in the chest, drilled its tiny hole through his heart. His leap ended with the crash of his body on Roy and me. But we heaved it off, got erect, still locked together, fighting for my gun.

This Roy Marr was a powerful fellow. I'm a bit under-sized, but pretty wiry. We wrecked the room with a couple of staggering falls, but I still clung to the gun. And then I broke loose, staggered back against the window and as he rushed me, I let him have it.

If you are one of those who complain of how S.S. men ruthlessly kill the poor criminals, you're welcome to your opinion.

The police alarm squad came rushing in. In one small room, Jonathan Gregg was dead; Dr. Jared was dead; Roy and Peter Marr were dead. I was the only one left alive.

And I'm thankful.

THE METAL MURDERER

A Seven-foot Machine of Steel,
Brainless but Geared and Wired to Kill,
Gripped Jac Lombard's Throat....

1

THE STRANGLING MACHINE

THE AFFAIR WHICH I call the "Metal Murderer" came
to its climax during an evening and night of last October.
Like most of the others which I have described, its action
was exceedingly brief. I would not have you think that
every case on which we Shadow Squad men embark, goes
through with a swift, tumultuous rush. Quite the reverse;
we have many assignments during which we follow futile
clues for weeks, and then in the end come upon nothing.

Some affairs do not make very absorbing reading, and
so I omit them. The case of the Metal Murderer was long
and futile, from the police viewpoint. Trant and I only came
in at its climax, but the police had theorized and browsed
for weeks. The fact that Trant and I arrived upon the scene
just at the night of the metal murderer's greatest activity, I
realize now was not a coincidence. Rather it was that our
presence in the little town of Hampton Valley precipitated
those fiendish acts with which the affair so suddenly ended.

It was a weird, unusual case. If it had lasted longer we
would have been enmeshed, undoubtedly, in a complicated
puzzle of human motives, with several suspects, each of
whom seemed to have very good reason for murder. But
the thing never reached that stage. Its climax—for me,

The seven-foot thing carried a human victim.

anyway—could very easily have been my own death. I can still feel, with memory too damnably vivid, those gruesome metal fingers gripping my throat....

On the evening of October 14th, 2000, Georg Trant and I were scheduled to report to Macfarlan at City Night Desk 4, at 10 P.M. But at eight that evening Mac routed me from sleep, with orders to report at once. Trant and I reached the desk at about the same time, Mac looked up from a sheaf of printed reports, and half a dozen teletype cylinders.

"I'm sending you to Hampton Valley," he announced. "This affair of the prowling robot—the metal murderer— the modern Jack the Ripper—" He grinned. "Well, anyhow, that's the way the newscasters have been blaring it. Mostly public hysteria—if it isn't, I'm a motor-oiler. You two heard much about it?"

Trant and I ordinarily are too busy to listen to the newscasters. But we had heard something of the Hampton Valley trouble, of course. Hampton Valley, in case you do not know, is a small manufacturing city some hundred and fifty miles northwest of New York. It is set in a rolling agricultural section, with many farms and the summer homes of wealthy idlers.

About six weeks ago a young married woman, one Annie Gregg, had been found dead on a road near the town. Mac spread the police records before us now. Annie Wilkinson Gregg, twenty-five years; wife of Carter Gregg, thirty years. A twin brother of the dead woman—one Roy Wilkinson. And an uncle, head of the family, Ezra Wilkinson, age seventy.

Annie Gregg was found dead at daybreak. Evidently murdered the previous evening, on her way home from a visit in town. A stab wound.

Mac said, "No weapon found. No alien scent that the olfactory classifier could identify. No apparent motive—a good, pious young woman, devoted to her husband."

Trant said, "I saw that much of the records at the time—thought you might put us on it."

Mac made a grimace. "The police had full charge. And here's what happened since."

The stab wound seemed peculiar—a thin, curving wound down into the heart. And on the throat were abrasions which suggested strangling fingers. Then some bright police official, anxious for personal publicity, told the newscasters that the stab wound looked as though it had been made by the knife-finger of a domestic-servant robot. Also that metal fingers had encircled the throat.

Mac was saying, "Well, that dumb-wit certainly got his publicity. Hampton Valley went into hysterics. A servant robot out of control—running amuck—a lurking fiend of metal... You can't blame people for letting their imaginations run, with an impetus like that. Personally, I wouldn't have one of those damn metal servants in the house."

NOR WOULD I. Robots—pieces of mechanism designed to perform routine tasks—have been in use for a century. A little metal box of coils and photo-electric cells and dials and levers may perform mechanical wonders. There's nothing gruesome about that. Thousands of such devices of every shape and size have their places in industry. A thermostat controls the temperature of your home—and that's a robot. Thousands of them are in use everywhere, of course. The robot, the photo-electric cell, and the wireless motor were the great discoveries of the twentieth century.

But, I think way back in 1920 or '30, someone started making robots in grotesque human shape. It added nothing to their mechanical value; but it certainly captured the popular imagination. Perhaps you who read this have one of the damnable seven-foot things in your own home now—to do with mathematical precision some of the many routine tasks about the house. Maybe, because you've seen it around you so much, you've grown to like it. Many people do. But not I. Especially since the night when I felt those metal fingers gripping my throat....

"If that dumb-wit policeman hadn't suggested a prowling robot as the murderer," Mac was saying, "I don't believe anybody would ever have thought of it. But for six weeks now hardly a night goes by but what somebody thinks she saw a prowling metal shape in the moonlight—or heard the thudding tread of metal feet in the woods—or lurking by the back fence—"

We glanced down the list of what the Hampton Valley people claimed they had seen or heard since that night Annie Gregg was killed. All vague, conflicting things— mostly by lone, uncorroborated witnesses—and almost invariably by hysterical women and young girls.

Mac pushed the list impatiently aside. He said, "Now get this straight; Annie Gregg was killed. Who or what killed her, the police have failed to find out. These subsequent reports of a prowling metal fiend—every one of them has been carefully checked. The verdict is that every one is imagination. Pure imaginative hysteria. Why, if the wind bangs a window slide anywhere in Hampton Valley, somebody will audiophone the police and say they heard the fiend."

I said, "Assume all that, and still it could have been a robot that killed Annie Gregg."

"A robot, remote-controlled by a human murderer," Trant put in.

Mac nodded. "That's one of the many theories. Don't begin theorizing, for heaven's sake—that only tangles you up. The state police have been patrolling Hampton Valley for six weeks. Not one of them ever saw anything of any prowling fiend. Every domestic-servant robot in the district has been disconnected by government order. The state police withdrew today. The newscasters are forbidden to mention the affair.

"That will stop the excitement in a hurry. There remains

now only to solve the murder of Annie Gregg. The State Crime Investigation Bureau has about worn itself out with useless theories—they're ready to let the thing die, and so the Shadow Squad—"

"You mean Jac and me?" Trant said. "We're supposed to solve this murder of Annie Gregg?"

Mac grinned again. "That's about what it amounts to."

All that the case looked like to Mac and Trant and me, as we sat there at the New York desk, was that we were to attempt the solution of a six-weeks-old crime, on which the police had failed. S.S. men do their best work with swift, impulsive action on a hot trail immediately after the crime. This was out of our line completely.

"Well—" Trant began dubiously.

"Federal orders came through this afternoon," Mac said. "Two S.S. men ordered for a month's stay in Hampton Valley. Divisional Chief gave it to Desk 4, and audiphoned the Wilkinson family that you'd be up to interview them this evening."

Trant and I gazed blankly at each other. Our divisional chief, controller of the ten city desks, often did queer things; and this was one of them.

Mac said, "Don't blame me. Of course I'd have sent you up secretly. But anyway, it's a good thing for you to meet the murdered woman's family. You interview them, tell them you can't get any clues, and that you're returning to New York. Then you can prowl around Hampton Valley all you like. Come back in a week and tell me how you're making out."

He turned away and busied himself with another job.

He thought of course that he was wasting two good men for weeks on useless work. And so did we.

If only we had known!

2

CROUCHED IN THE DARK

WE TOOK OFF in our little car from the roof of the S.S. Building, and headed northwest in one of the lower lanes. It was an evening of nearly full moon, low-ceilinged with thick patches of swift-flying clouds, so that the blobs of moonlight and shadow raced over the ground. Gusts of sullen wind were down there; and up here at one thousand feet, a fitful headbreeze out of the north.

It was about ten o'clock when we left New York. Trant said:

"Pretty late, don't you think, to go in and interview that family tonight? Let's just browse around."

You can't change a leopard's spots, as they say. By all tradition and training, Trant and I were Shadow Men. The same thoughts had been in our minds when we gathered our equipment—we took weapons, but beyond them, mostly the several eavesdropping devices. We had no personal audiphone connection with Mac at this hundred and fifty mile distance from the Desk, and for what he thought would be so long-drawn-out an affair he did not desire it. The alarm-bands, and tiny microphones under our shirts, we tuned for mutual contact. It was our idea to rack the plane in the town, and browse around during the night on foot.

The flight to Hampton Valley took us a little over half an hour. I held the controls; Trant studied the police records of the case of the murder of Annie Gregg. On his desk Mac had had the teletypes—motion picture and voice portraits, made for the personal identification files—of the murdered woman's family and various neighbors and people who had hysterically reported the prowling robot. But he had not bothered to show them to Trant and me. The printed records, we found, had small photographs pasted on them: the murdered woman; her husband, Carter Gregg; her twin brother, Roy Wilkinson; and her rich uncle, old Ezra Wilkinson. This family lived in a big old-fashioned house in the open country outside the town.

"The old man is sick," Trant said, reading the record. "Never much but a semi-invalid, he collapsed when his niece was murdered. He's been in bed nearly ever since— got bronchial influenza, it seems—he's just getting better now. A rich old fellow—Annie's husband, and Roy Wilkinson are both his heirs. The husband, this Carter Gregg—he ought to work, but he won't. So ought Roy. They all quarrel more or less—that's the reputation they have, anyway."

Trant tossed the records aside distastefully. "If this old Ezra had gotten murdered we'd have plenty to theorize on. Two good-for-nothing men are his heirs. And he can't disinherit them, according to the new laws. That's the fool thing about these inheritance statutes. I hope I never have any big money—"

Our arrival over Hampton Valley cut short Trant's complaint at the Federal lawmakers... We circled above the little town. It nestled snugly in a valley with green-clad rolling hills around it. Then from the police-record map, we located the Wilkinson place. Queerly old-fashioned, the sort of thing, doubtless, to which old Ezra had been accustomed in his boyhood. You still see a few of them, especially in rural localities, and to me they're very attractive. It was a big three-story wooden house painted white, with a queer, gabled peaked roof; and at the groundlevel a big-roofed veranda.

Ivy and green vines climbed the walls, giving it an age-old look. A few trees clustered around, and the garden was thick with shrubs. The house stood upon a knoll, down which the ground sloped into a cauldron depression. A little brook wound a crooked course through this lowland, with melancholy weeping willows thickly lining it. The grounds were perhaps a hundred acres, with just a low wooden fence outlining them. The whole area, especially down in the low part by the brook, was solid with trees and heavy underbrush.

We circled twice at a thousand feet… Outside the Wilkinson grounds, a tree-lined road wound off to town, which was a mile or so away. There were no near neighbors—just one small metal house about a thousand feet distant on another knoll. This was a more modern place; cubical outbuildings; a mechanic shed; a tiny private landing field.

Trant said, again consulting the records:

"That's the home of one John Blake. He's a radio pilot on the New York-Albany local run. Age fifty-two. No family except a young wife, Glora. Here's her picture—take a look, Jac—if she isn't a beauty, I'm a motor-oiler."

I took a brief look at the photograph of a dizzy-type, artificial blonde.

"Used to be a television dancer before this middle-aged radio-pilot married her," Trant said. "And he's away from home most of the time. There's potential trouble—"

I headed us off to town. We racked in at the local police-field, and showed our credentials.

"Federal men," I told the awed country official. "We're here for a few weeks on night duty, but nobody knows it. So you forget it, too. We'll come back at dawn and you can feed us and hide us out."

We set off on foot down the dark little road toward the Wilkinson place. It was about eleven o'clock. The moon was riding high—a flattened silver ball, now shining clear, now obscured by racing inky patches of cloud. The road wound through the undulating hills, with trees lining it, and small metal fences outlining the cultivated fields. There were many dark metal cubbies standing in the fields where by day the mechanicians directed the radio-operated farming machinery. Occasionally we could see a giant harvester standing idle for the night beside a little mono-rail track which led to some distant shipping shed.

BY DAY THIS would be a scene of bustling activity; but there were no residences along here; the workers were all in town. Overhead, in the lower lane, aircraft occasionally floated by. We saw a blob-cluster of lights passing far up through the clouds—one of the mid-altitude mailflyers; but it was gone in a moment. Down here on the road a car sometimes passed. We drew back always at the warning of the lights, crouching beside a tree or fence until it had flashed by.

"No use listening yet," Trant said, "but I guess we're not far from Wilkinson's and that other place, are we?"

Listening? We had not connected the electronic eaves-droppers; but I own that all this time I had been straining my ears. Listening for what? For the thud of metal feet? There is something gruesome about inanimate machinery that can ape the look and actions of a man. And now as we slowly traversed this silent countryside, all Mac's scoffing had faded from my mind.

Every dark and silent copse by the roadside seemed now by my shuddering fancy to hold that gaunt metal thing. Crouching with bent, jointed legs. Mailed hand, with an index finger which was a knife. Eyes which were only photo-electric cells, peering at us as we passed. A brain, inside the square metal head—a brain of tiny twisted wires, coils and magnets. Could the damnable machinery of that brain have gone amuck? Out of control? What diabolical, fiendish cunning might come to a brain of wires, coils and magnets, once the thing went awry!

An insane mechanism! What would we do with it if we met it? Would a Banning heat-flash stop its murderous rush? I doubted it. A paralyzing beam, which could strike a human murderer into frozen immobility—that would do nothing to a robot. An old-fashioned, explosive-gas-pro-pelled bullet would rebound from its metal chest. A knife-blade would break harmlessly against that metal armor. And the damnable thing, with the leverage of its steel muscles, would have the strength of ten humans.

Gruesome adversary!

I shook myself free of the wild chain of thought.

"There's that Blake house," Trant murmured.

There was a high metal fence here; and beyond a dark garden on a little rise of ground a hundred feet or so away, we could see the dim outlines of the two-story alumite and stonetrimmed building. A blue glow of tubelight showed behind one of the second-story window ovals.

We crouched by a tree at the fence. With tuned eavesdroppers at once we isolated voices. A man and a woman.

"—tired, John?"

"Eight round trips in fourteen hours. I won't stand this run another season. I'll demand a transfer—"

John Blake, the middle-aged radio pilot, and his young wife who had been a television dancer. With naked eye we could see the blobs of them, up in the room. I put on the telescopic glasses. John Blake was sitting on the edge of the bed—a sparse-haired, thin-faced fellow. He was robed for the night; but the woman was fully dressed.

Trant murmured, "What a queer look he gave her!"

She was placing a small tray of food and drink beside his bed. He watched her with a look very strange. Yet not so strange either—a frail, tired middle-aged man gazing at the strong, youthful beauty of his wife. And I saw now her sensuous mouth; mascaraed eyes; that dizzy, artificially pale-gold hair.

Trant said softly, "If he doesn't mistrust her—and with good reason—I'm a motor-oiler."

"Me too," I whispered.

Blake was saying querulously, "Are you not going to bed, Glora?"

"Yes, of course I am. You go to sleep now, John. You're worn out."

He said, like a futile bomb exploding: "You've seen that man today! And every day! I won't have it—"

Suddenly they were wrangling… Then at last she had pacified him. With lies. Of course, with lies… The light went out. The voices went silent; there was only the sound of the woman's rustling movements as she left his room.

But one thing we had very clearly seen; this futile John Blake was not fooled by her lies. She thought he was, but he was not. And when she had left his room, distinctly we heard him leave his bed, move to one of the windows, and then to his bedroom door, standing listening. I tuned to a higher power. I heard the labored panting of his breath. A man wild, desperate with jealousy.

"Maybe so," Trant agreed. "Or maybe we're getting like police trackers—we can imagine too much."

But what possibly could this have to do with the murder of young Annie Gregg by a robot, six weeks ago?

Trant whispered, "I wonder if these Blakes have one of those damned machine-servants? The police record does not say. That's the trouble with the police. When you really want to know anything—"

We crouched by the fence and searched the house. The black-light Zed-ray penetrated the metal walls; we saw on the fluoroscope the blurred outlines of the moving woman; she was downstairs now. But the black-light would not show the metal of a robot… Then I located that one of the lower windows was the kitchen. We took a chance of discovery and projected, just for a brief moment, a tiny white pencil-light of searchbeam.

"There it is," Trant whispered.

On the kitchen floor, against the opposite wall, a seven-foot monster lay on its back. Gruesome, like a giant metal corpse which somebody had murdered and left lying there. The jointed knees were up; the arms were gripping each other across the bulging chest; the head dangled. The accursed thing looked as though it had died in some horrible convulsion.

Trant snapped off our tiny light. "Disconnected," he said. "Well, that's fair enough, so long as it stays disconnected. Let's take a look at the Wilkinson place."

3

TRIPLE QUARREL

WE MOVED AWAY, like shadows down the dark tree-lined road. Again I found myself straining my senses. No wonder, in an affair like this, that the people of Hampton Valley let their imagination run wild! With the listeners off now, I felt suddenly most horribly handicapped; my human senses so totally inadequate, for it seemed that just beyond my hearing there must be the faint clanking of a giant metal thing stalking us....

The Blake grounds evidently adjoined Wilkinson's. Our road descended into the hollow and crossed a small steel viaduct under which the brook flowed. It was black and soundless down here, heavily shadowed by the melancholy drooping trees—soundless with only the low brook murmur and the chirping of tree toads and the crickets.

We stood for a moment on the little viaduct. Downstream, perhaps a hundred yards away, the dim outlines of an old-fashioned wooden pedestrian bridge were visible, with a path under the willows evidently leading from Wilkinsons' home to Blakes'.

Trant plucked at me. "Come on—let's see what the Wilkinsons are doing."

The big frame house on top of the comparatively bare

knoll showed blue tubelight through several of the second-floor windows, and one in the third floor under the eaves. The moon was momentarily shining clear; the grassy knoll of lawn around the house was bathed in moonlight.

"We better not go any closer," I said. "Try it from here."

We trained our instruments from down here in the blackness of a mossy hollow half under the bridge beside the brook. We had no difficulty with the listeners. But at the moment no one in the house was talking. There was a distant third floor wing which seemed servants' quarters. But it was soundless. We learned later that there were no servants in the house this night.

At a higher power we located—in a second-floor room of illumined windows—a labored breathing, doubtless of old Ezra Wilkinson. There was a man in the lighted room adjoining him, and another man upstairs. We heard his breathing, and his occasional movements.

But we had difficulty penetrating with sight. We were down in a hollow. The lighted glassite windows were unshrouded; but we were fully seventy feet below their level. Any direct, normal, straight, light-bearing ray—the search-beam, black-light, or direct telescopic vision—naturally showed us only the ceilings of the rooms or the head of an occupant who chanced to come very close to the window. The black-light Zed-ray could penetrate the walls; but for observations of humans, that at best, is unsatisfactory.

Trant muttered, "Unless somebody will be kind enough to come and sit in a window, we'll see nothing. Let's chance the Benson curve-light."

The curve-light beam is a faint violet glow; really very

faint indeed, and in moonlight hardly noticeable. We decided to risk discovery. The projector hummed a trifle; but we were too far away for anyone in the house normally to hear it.

The pencil-ray of Benson curve-light arched in a crescent over the little knoll. In the moonlight it glistened like a tiny moon-bow. We trained it into one of the lighted windows… On our small hooded fluoroscopic screen the room's entire interior was imaged in miniature.

Ezra Wilkinson. A gaunt, white-haired old man. He lay, wrapped in a night robe, reclining in an easy chair, reading an old-fashioned, printed book. A tall, spare figure. In his youth doubtless he had been a powerful man; but old age had shriveled him, and illness now had drawn his skin like wrinkled parchment over his cheek-bones.

The room adjacent was a small upstairs living room. In it, with a tall glass before him, lounged Carter Gregg; husband of Annie, who had been murdered. We saw him as a handsome, dissolute looking fellow; a little closely-clipped black mustache; sleek black hair; a broad-shouldered, slim-hipped figure, robed now in an Oriental dressing gown. He was not reading; the amusement-televisor beside him stood silent. He merely sat and smoked, sipping occasionally at his glass.

Experience has made Trant and me very close observers. I murmured:

"That fellow isn't relaxed. He's tense—taut as a violin string."

An air of expectancy undoubtedly was upon him—a suppressed excitement. And at once I found myself thinking of Glora Blake in that other house a quarter of a mile from here—she of the slack-lipped beauty, trying now to get her middle-aged, suspicious husband to sleep.

Trant whispered, "Let's take a look at that fellow upstairs."

We swung the curve-light. Roy Wilkinson, twin of the murdered Annie, sat at a work table, puttering over a radio-televisor which he seemed engaged in taking apart. An amateur experimenter—the police records had said something like that. Queerly sinister figure he seemed now, as he sat alone in this third floor workshop. The tube-light painted his massive overlarge head and the hunch-back lump of his misshapen shoulders. He was only twenty-five years old, but his pinched face made him seem older. He stood up suddenly, crossing the room to get a bit of apparatus. At once his misshapen body showed more clearly. A barrel chest, bent, short legs; long gorilla-like arms.

PERHAPS A FELLOW of warped and twisted mind, as well as body. An experimenter with radio. I thought suddenly of Trant's words to Mac, back there at City Desk:

"It could be a robot, remote-controlled—a human murderer."

But why should this Roy Wilkinson have murdered his sister?... And then I thought of John Blake, in that other house; he was a radio man....

No wonder the police puzzle themselves into a quandary when they delve into human motives... Insidious, useless business. I shook myself free of it. Trant was murmuring:

"Queer looking lad—pathetic—to be malformed like that and try and cope with the world—"

Suddenly the eavesdropper was blaring in our ear-phones; the querulous voice of the old man downstairs.

"Roy! Roy, what are you doing?"

"I'm fixing the receiver, uncle."

"Well, you go to bed."

"I thought you were waiting for those Shadow Squad men—"

It made my heart leap. Then I remembered that the chief had told this family that we would call upon them tonight. And now they were still expecting our visit.

Carter Gregg's voice called:

"I guess they won't come tonight, uncle. You'd better go to sleep—I told you that an hour ago."

To Trant and me it sounded like a harmless enough remark. But a smoldering hatred can so easily burst into flaming, unreasonable anger. The old man rasped:

"Who are you to tell me what I shall do, Carter? I've had enough of your damnable impudence."

And abruptly, very much like that other house of the Blakes, these three were wrangling. A tirade of the rich old man at these two drones who lived upon his money and would not work. The three of them, momentarily gathered in the old man's room, futilely wrangling. Anger is often so childish a thing, when you listen to it dispassionately as an outsider.

"You, Carter—damn bloodsucker—married Annie for my money, that's what you did!"

The handsome Carter Gregg stood leaning against the wall, smoking, sardonically amused. Roy stood glowering, like a little gorilla with swinging arms, huge knotted hands dangling to his knees.

The old man blared at him: "And you—you gargoyle— that my brother should have a spawn like you—"

It struck Roy Wilkinson so that now he was gasping, with words of reprisal choking in his throat—his anger so tumultuous that it shook him visibly. An anger like that could very well rise to murderous frenzy.

"Go to bed, uncle," Carter Gregg said smoothly. "You better go to bed also, Roy. Don't pay any attention to him. We all might as well go to bed—those New York policemen aren't coming. Thank God for that—we've had enough trouble over poor Annie's death."

Then they were talking about us, and why we hadn't arrived. Trant whispered to me:

"Fertile soil for murder here. Lord, you can imagine almost anything."

I think that just at this instant the whole affair changed for Trant and me. We had been mere routine eavesdroppers, really anticipating nothing save many futile nights of prowling in Hampton Valley. Abruptly that feeling dropped away. It seemed now that we had come upon an impending climax. A little group of humans here, with all the diversified complexity of human passions—a little turgid lake of seething floodwater about to break its dam. It struck momentarily from my mind all thought of a prowling fiend.

Presently the three of them were each in their own room; Carter Gregg and old Wilkinson on the second floor, and Roy above them, in a bedroom under the eaves. We had snapped off the curve-light; and down in that little hollow by the bridge with the melancholy willows shrouding us, we sat with only the eavesdropper connected.

And presently there was nothing to hear. Midnight came

and passed. The tubelights of the house were all extinguished. Fitful moonlight bathed the scene with silver.

Trant murmured suddenly, "I wonder if that Blake
woman got her husband lulled to sleep?"

We pondered on going back there. That giant metal
thing lying so gruesomely in the Blake kitchen—inert,
disconnected—would it be there now?

Trant added, quite as though he were reading my
thoughts:

"Police report says the Wilkinsons have no servant-ro-
bot. A police search was made—but you can't trust to a
police search."

Suddenly both our hearts were pounding. The eavesdropper was thudding with footsteps. Somebody in the
Wilkinson house was moving cautiously from the second
floor, down the stairs, through the lower hall.... There came
a click as the front door opened.

With naked vision we could see that front door open.
A blob of a figure came to the dim veranda. It stood a
moment, peering into the fitful moonlight. Then it left the
veranda; skulked furtively down a winding path, heading
down here where the willows shrouded the brook and the
little pedestrian bridge led to the Blake grounds.

The willows presently swallowed the moving figure. But
the eavesdropper still could plainly hear the tread of footsteps. And our telescopic eyeglasses had shown us that it
was Carter Gregg.

4

THE TWO VICTIMS

TRANT WHISPERED, "HE'S going over the other bridge. Crouch lower—he won't see us—too dark here."

Shafts of moonlight patterned the little wooden pedestrian bridge. We saw Gregg's tall, stalwart figure cross it. He was walking faster now. The willows on the other side swallowed him again. Then the eavesdropper picked up the woman's low voice as she greeted him.

Midnight clandestine love-tryst. This woman's husband indeed had cause for his suspicion.... Carter and the woman were seated in some mossy copse, under the willows near the brook's edge.

"Carter dear, you came at last—"

"I was waiting for that light-signal in your bedroom."

"I couldn't get him to sleep. He mistrusts us, Carter— we'll have to be more careful—he's not so easy to fool as you think."

With muttered disgust Trant snapped off the eavesdropper. We felt like a pair of matrimonial snoopers whose ugly profession is to uncover things like this.

"To the devil with it," Trant muttered.

They were no more than two or three hundred feet from us. In the night silence, even with normal hearing it seemed that we could just distinguish the low murmur of their voices.

I whispered, "None of our affair, unless that husband comes out and finds them."

That indeed, could very well be our affair. If Blake should come upon this scene now—armed—I could imagine that he would drill Carter Gregg on sight. And I guess you couldn't blame him at that.

Trant was thinking the same thing. He whispered:

"Let's cut over toward Blake's. We can strike the path part way along. They won't see us—the trees are too thick."

A heavy, sullen cloud bank had now wholly obscured the moon. The night was much darker than before. And less silent—just in the last minute or two a wind was rising, rustling the willows. We followed the road for a piece— half way to Blake's perhaps—and then moved up a rise of fairly open ground. We came to the path. The dark outlines of Blake's home showed to our right.

Suddenly we were stricken. From our left, down the path in the tree-shrouded hollow, a scream floated up! A woman's scream. For an instant it transfixed us. A choked scream of terror. Perhaps there were other sounds; we were too startled to analyze them, nor did we try to tune an instrument. The scream floated into silence. No repetition. A deadly, horrible silence.

"Come on!" Trant muttered. With heat-guns ready, we plunged down that path. It was black under the trees. And suddenly something white was coming at us. Like a shadow Trant melted down off the path and dropped into a mossy hollow, with me after him.

The white thing was the woman, running up the path

toward us; running wildly, babbling with terror. Then Trant and I rose up and seized her as she came past. Heaven knows how she stood that shock of our abrupt appearance. But one may be numbed by an extremity of terror, so that nothing can add to it. She did not faint, but stood panting, staring at us, with slack quivering mouth, that dizzy hair tumbling to her shoulders, and all her cheap beauty swept with terror.

"You screamed," Trant said swiftly. He shook her as though to make her understand his words. "You screamed—what happened? Where is Carter Gregg?"

"He—he—that thing killed him—stabbed—its finger like a knife stabbed him—"

That thing! The prowling metal murderer! We had been so engrossed in human intrigue, forgetting the wild tales of a prowling, inanimate fiend.

But the thing now was abroad. For a few seconds, under our breathless prodding questions, the half-hysterical woman babbled it. The truth—she was far past lying. She and Carter had glanced up. A giant seven foot monster— it was carrying a man's dead body under one arm—some previous victim. Then all in that second it pounced, stabbed Carter Gregg—seized him with its other giant arm— fled, bearing the bodies of its two victims, like children, one under each arm. Fled into the tree shadows while the woman, untouched, rose up screaming and wildly ran....

FOR A FEW seconds certainly Trant and I were engulfed by an awed horror. One might face a human rational murderer with no horror such as this. Demented mechanism! A brainless machine, with a fiendish mechanical lust for killing. A thing of diabolic cunning, abroad here now, skulking under these trees.

Stalking us now? It made the roots of my hair tingle as I stood peering into the black tree shadows around us. Then Trant and I found our wits. Trant gasped,

"It made off, you say? Show us where you were sitting. Carter Gregg is gone—"

It was only a hundred feet further along the path. A little mossy dell. Our hand torchlight swept it. A little mossy dell, just built for lovers. The brook was almost beside it.

Nothing here. A little blood on the ferns.

We listened. Nothing. But the damnable thing must be around here, of course. Or had it fled over the open hills, to seek new killings—or to carry the bodies of its victims of tonight to some secret lair where all these weeks it had been hiding?

Wild thoughts for an S.S. Man! I was fumbling to tune the eavesdropper; but the woman now was babbling:

"I want my husband—I want John—I want to go home. Oh, who are you? You let me go home—I want my husband—"

Certainly, in our own confusion, we were putting her through an inhuman and unnecessary stress of terror. This babbling for the protection of her husband suddenly was pathetic. I said:

"Yes—we'll take you home. We're the police. Don't be frightened— we'll protect you—"

Vainglorious words! Never in my life had I felt less able to offer protection than at that instant with those gruesome thoughts flooding me.

Then from the distant darkness came a human voice.

"Glora! Glora, where are you?"

And again—a frightened, anxious man's voice:

"Glora—Glora—"

Her husband, wild-eyed, half-dressed, brandishing a gun, came running along the path from the direction of his home. And the woman flung herself hysterically into his arms, babbling again her wild tale, while Trant and I added who we were and why we were here.

For that moment he stood holding his shuddering wife. "Glora—dear—you're not hurt?"

"No—it—it killed Carter—Oh, John—I've been so wrong—I see it now—forgive me, John—I see now it's only you I love—"

There seemed something of greatness about the futile John Blake as he stood now with his arms protectingly around his wife; and he murmured,

"You're not hurt, Glora. Come home—I'll take you home—"

I found Trant eyeing me. I could have sworn that Blake was sincere—innocent of any knowledge of this thing. But after all, Trant and I are S.S. Men.

Trant said, "Let me have that gun, Blake."

He yielded it readily; he was intent only on his wife. He said, "I'll take her home. She'll be safe there—we must call the town police—"

AGAIN MY THOUGHTS swung widely afield. I knew that Trant was wondering if that inert metal monster was still lying in the Blake kitchen. And abruptly he voiced that thought.

Blake stammered, "Why—why I don't know—I suppose it is. I disconnected it weeks ago—"

"Did you see it just now when you came out?" Trant demanded.

"Why—no—I guess I didn't go to the kitchen—I was worried about Glora—she wasn't in the house—then I heard her scream—"

"I'll wait here," I said to Trant.

He came close to me; he murmured,

"I'll take them home—call the police—and then come back. You watch yourself, Jac. Stay right here. Use the eavesdropper—if that damned thing is around—you'll hear it—you watch yourself—"

The three of them started up the path—vanished. Silence fell upon me—and my thoughts flung afield. We had not made an undue commotion, but the woman's scream surely must have floated up to the Wilkinson house. Old Ezra Wilkinson, and the malformed, gorilla-like Roy, were up there sleeping. No alarm had come from them. Had the scream failed to wake them? And then a gruesome thought struck me. The woman had said that the prowling monster was bearing a victim under one arm—it had stalked off, bearing both that victim, and Carter Gregg. Who was that other victim? Were old Wilkinson and Roy safe, sleeping through all this?

Down there on the path under the willows, I stood motionless for a moment. With listener tuned, I tried to catch some distant tread of metal feet; but there was nothing—only blurred insect sounds—the hum of distant Hampton Valley—and the blaring voices of Trant and the Blakes. They were at the other house now. I switched off the eavesdropper. And suddenly my chest microphone—

permanently tuned with Trant's—gave its calling buzz. Trant's voice said:

"You, Jac?"

"Yes."

"Heard anything?"

"No."

"I'm at Blake's. He's all right—I don't think he's in this. This damned robot here is lying inert in the kitchen. It hasn't stirred. I'll call the police."

"All right," I said. It was unnatural for us to call in the police. But with a metal fiend stalking the countryside, the affair certainly was beyond our control; we had no wish to shoulder the responsibility of what else might happen.

Trant disconnected. I stood another moment peering around me at the blackness under the willows. Then on impulse I crossed the little pedestrian bridge, mounted the other path, up the knoll to where the big rambling Wilkinson house stood dark, wholly lightless and silent. Silent save that now the rising wind plucked at its shutters, whined and moaned around its eaves.

At the front door, in the blackness under the veranda roof, I stood hesitating. Carter Gregg, on his midnight love-tryst, had left this door unlocked. Cautiously I opened it. The faintly tube-lit hall was empty.

I entered, leaving the door open behind me.

5

MURDER BY MACHINE

THE DIM HALL seemed to echo the dulled tread of my footsteps. Slowly, I advanced, straining all my senses; trying indeed to listen and to peer in every direction at once. The interior silence was muffled; oppressive. It seemed like a tangible thing crowding me—a silence blurred by the sounds of the wind outside.

For a moment I stood at the foot of the central ascending staircase—stood tense, alert, swinging the muzzle of the Banning gun at all the distant shadows. But there seemed nothing here. With the eavesdropper I could have searched the house for every alien tiny sound; I started to tune it, but suddenly was aware that it was too absorbing—it took my attention from my gun muzzle. That dim spot of red, down the hall where the shadows were thickest—was that a baleful, gleaming mechanical eye?

Imagination can be a thing most nerve-racking. I gathered my wits. An S.S. Man should prowl a silent house without these shuddering fancies.

Were old Ezra Wilkinson and his nephew Roy sleeping safely upstairs? I slowly mounted the staircase. The upper hall had a single light. I passed the little room in which Carter Gregg had been; it was empty, undisturbed. And next door to it was the old man's bedroom. The door was ajar. I shoved it open with my foot. The glow of tubelight from the hall disclosed the empty, rumpled bed. The old man was gone.

I called softly, "Mr. Wilkinson—where are you? Roy Wilkinson—"

No one here. Undoubtedly no one here—alive… Then swiftly I was up to the third floor. Empty rooms. Roy's bedroom, undisturbed. His work table, littered with radio devices half connected—all of it seemed undisturbed.

I descended, more swiftly now. Searched, with a brief sweep of torchlight, several of the other rooms. I had reached the main lower hall again. The buzzer at my chest sounded its faint call. In my earphone Trant said:

"Jac! Jac, I'm down by the bridge—where are you?"

I murmured, "At Wilkinson's. Nobody here."

"I'm coming right up—watch yourself—come out of that house!"

Trant had so much clearer a premonition of this thing than I, for all my wild imagination!

"I'll meet you on the veranda," I said; and disconnected.

But I did not meet him there. Do not think me a brash fool. I was alert—no one could have been more tense and watchful of his own safety. I stood peering, swaying my gun nozzle. And suddenly I heard a dull, muffled sound. A rhythmic thudding. Under me? It seemed so. A sound mounting from a lower distance. And now, at the back of the hall, under the curveangle of the ascending staircase, my darting light disclosed a little door. It was not quite closed. The sound seemed coming from there. I opened the door; turned away my light. A faint tube-gleam from below showed a steep flight of stone steps. The ascending air was dank and fetid.

A cellar room. The thudding down there was clearer now. The sound of digging! Someone—something—digging in the earth of the cellar floor with steady rhythmic thuds.

Perhaps it was a sudden wild and impelling curiosity. Or perhaps I did really envisage that some human victim of the monster—being buried here now—might not be quite dead. And I was armed; and I might perhaps save a life by instant action.

I did not reason it. On padded shoes, I went down that staircase inch by inch; hardly breathing, with my outstretched gun preceding me. But I must have been heard. I saw a dim earthy floor; and I was still on the steps when the thudding abruptly ceased.

Another instant—from the bottom step, my gaze swept a very dim cellar cubby-room. A sort of old-fashioned wine cellar. It was some thirty feet square; stone and earthen walls; a dirt floor, with planking laid like a little pathway down its middle. And on the walls, musty, old shelves, thick with silt and cobwebs, where rows of old bottles were standing. No windows. No doors. Nothing but this entrance of steep stairs at the bottom of which I was standing.

No one—nothing alive—was here. My darting light swept the place. No litter behind which anything could hide. Nothing alive here—but the swift glance which gave me these details so much quicker than you can read them, showed me the pile of dirt beside a hole in the earthen floor. A grave being dug. And here was the body of Carter

Gregg—a gruesome slashed and crimson thing lying tumbled here in its half-dug grave.

"Jac! Jac, where are you?"

The words so startled me that my heart choked my throat and all my skin was prickling. But it was only Trant's microphonic voice in my ears. And I could hear now the thud of his footsteps in the hall upstairs.

I murmured, "In the cellar. A door under the hall stairs—I'm coming up—don't come down!"

FOR JUST THAT instant, with every horrified instinct in me shouting that I must escape from this damnable place, I think that I stepped to the floor and turned to leap up the stairs. I had a sudden realization of a section of the cellar wall—seemingly so solid—swinging noiselessly outward. A five-foot rectangle of semi-darkness. And in it, a diabolic thing crouching. Springing—

Undoubtedly my every muscle, in that instant, was paralyzed by horror. I did not leap up the stairs. I peered, transfixed, gaping with numbed witless mind… The jointed seven-foot thing had come through the aperture. It was carrying a human victim—a man's body. It dropped the body now as it rose erect. Then it took a single huge step.

A great hinged arm, like a crane came swinging at me—an arm with a hand of long, prehensile fingers and a curving steel knife blade where the thumb should have been. And behind and above it, that square frozen metal face—so monstrous a travesty of humanity. Eyes gleaming dull red-green—eyes which mirrored only the electronic light of an insane mechanical brain.

I fired the Banning gun. Of that I am sure. I recall the splatter of the heat as it struck futilely against that armoured chest. Then the swinging crane-like arm struck me; knocked me aside, off the stairs; hurtled me like a child flung through the air half across the cellar.

My gun went flying into the dimness. I had struck against Carter Gregg's body, and from it I slid into the half-dug grave. Then I was up, scrambling out.

Trapped in here. The giant metal monster crouched at the foot of the stairs. It seemed now that I could hear the whining hum of its mechanisms. Then again it sprang. Like a leopard pouncing—and I, a frightened kitten trying to dart aside.

But it caught me. Crunched me down, so that I was bent backward prone upon the floor with that bulging metal chest and frozen face close over me. And the machine-fingers gripping my throat.

I think that into those few seconds there was compressed for me an ordinary lifetime of horror. That damnable mechanical grip—both its hands squeezing my throat. My breath was shut off. The end of Jac Lombard....

But I struggled—like a puny year-old infant in the grip of a murderous man. A great metal knee held my legs. But my arms were free. I pounded the bulging metal chest. My head was roaring now; my sight blurring. The whirring, whining electronic hum of the accursed machine seemed rising to blot out all my world. I fumbled for the central fuse-plug. It should be here in the center of the chest. If I could pull out that fuse—disconnect the motivating power—

My fingers found the fuse-box. I gripped the plug. With despairing desperate strength I twisted and wrenched at the circular insulated disc. It yielded at last. It came out and I flung it away.

Terrible realization. I had disconnected the damnable thing—but still its grip on my throat did not relax. The humming of its current did not die. It hummed like a panting breath. Or was this a panting human breath I was hearing, mingled with that mechanical whir?

The ridged, frozen face was close over me now. I stared. The metal cheeks and forehead were vaguely luminous. Transparent. A vizor-pane of celluloid. Behind it I now could see the interior of the huge head. Another head in there. A small, human head. Sparse gray hair; an old, shriveled, parchment-like human face frenzied and demoniacal now with murderous human passion.

Old Ezra Wilkinson. It was he who now was inside this metal monster. He, its motivating force—that fuse-plug a mere ornament—the robot a mere shell of ingenious machinery, with steel muscles and huge leverage to augment into the power of a giant, his own puny human strength!

FULL REALIZATION SWEPT me. This rich old man, obsessed that his hated relatives would inherit his wealth. The dead Annie Gregg—he had hated her as well as her handsome husband, and Roy, her brother. The old man, with senile dementia, fearful that he must die first, and they would get his money; then determined not to die first—and to make sure of that— hating them all—he would kill them.

From what secret and illicit source he obtained his robot has never been disclosed. A man of money can easily keep secret a thing like that. This secret door in the wine cellar—

the workmen who built it, naturally will not now come forward and admit complicity… He had killed Annie Gregg. Taken her body abroad, and left it on a distant roadside… Then he had fallen ill of bronchial influenza; taken to his bed, unable to go on with his killings.

The six weeks passed. The excitement over the prowling fiend was dying down. The state police were withdrawn. The old man's sickness was passed. He was ready to finish what he had begun. And tonight seemed his opportunity. Shadow Squad men were coming. Another investigation. But the Shadow men did not come.

He took his opportunity. Seized, with giant metal fingers, the sleeping Roy. One may fancy that in this last lustful prowling, the old man lost what little rationality had remained to him. As though he himself were an insane machine, he bore the body of Roy out into the night; stalked Carter Gregg at the love-tryst and killed him. Fled with the two victims. His work all done. His three hated heirs all dead. Himself—cunning old man—still alive to gloat over his wealth.

Then he must have decided that the safest way to avoid discovery was to bury the bodies. And so he had fled back to his cellar. Had dropped Roy when he saw me, and pounced upon me. And Roy, despite it all, was not quite dead. We rushed him to a hospital later that night—where, after weeks, he recovered to inherit that legal share which the irrational old man had tried to keep from him. But Carter Gregg was dead. Still, thinking of his wife Annie, whom he dishonored—and poor futile John Blake, who loved his own wife and was so thankful tonight to get her safely home—there is no one who greatly will mourn the death of Carter Gregg.

All this came to me in an instant flash of realization, as I stared now through that luminous robot shell into the murderous face of the old man. His panting breath mingled with the hum of the mechanism... All this in so few crowded seconds that still those terrible metal fingers were gripping my throat.

Vaguely I heard Trant's lunge down the stairs; felt the crash of his body as he struck the robot's shoulders. Doubtless this new adversary confused old Wilkinson. Abruptly the fingers on my throat relaxed. The metal shape rose up from me and swayed at Trant. The crane-like metal arms swung and engulfed Trant—

Amazing mechanical combat! A frail, demoniacal old man—a desperate, frenzied puppeteer manipulating his levers to work this monstrous puppet and make it fight. There was a moment or two of chaos, in which it seemed that the threshing monster was mangling Trant and me. But with it all I was aware that Trant's heat-bolt was steadily stabbing at the metal body. The choking Banning fumes mingled with the acrid gas of fusing metal... Then in a corner Trant and I lay pinned, with a great leg mashing us, and the swaying machine, down on one knee, tottering off balance. I shoved at its side. It fell, but scrambled up. Our own muttered oaths mingled now with the angry, frightened squeal of the old man. Then he got the machine fully erect; lunged at us, with Trant's steady heat-bolt again playing on the bulging chest.

And suddenly the heat melted through. The old man gave a choked, wild scream of agony. The machine, out of control, suddenly seemed to wilt. It fell half upon us, but we lunged out from under it and scrambled to our feet. We were torn, bleeding, dazed.

The monster lay twitching. Metal limbs aimlessly jerking, quivering like a monstrous living thing dying in agony. And within its broken smoking hulk, the murderous old man already was dead.

DEATH IN THE FIRE PIT

*With the Pill of Artificial Death on His
Tongue, Jac Lombard Fights the Enemy
Who Can Hide Amid Raging Flame*

1

TRANT AND I were at Desk 4 one evening, with Chief Macfarlan, when the audiphone buzzed. The wave-sorter announced:

"Request for Jac Lombard."

"Here I am," I said.

The image-grid glowed with the face of a smooth-shaven, stoutish young man. There was only a dark background behind him with just a faint tubelight glow. He said, "My name is Robert Green—I've got to talk fast." He seemed breathless; he spoke in a low, swift undertone. "I've heard of you—Federal men—I think I've discovered a Federal crime—reporting it to you direct instead of calling in the local police."

"Where are you?" I demanded.

"Mauch Chunk, Pennsylvania—I thought maybe you and your partner would want to come up here. I could meet you outside. Then I want you to verify the contents of the vault where we store the engravings. I think maybe that tonight—"

He checked himself abruptly. His face vanished. There was only darkness on the image-grid; and then came the click of disconnection.

With Mac and Trant staring at me wordlessly, I buzzed violently for the wave-sorter.

I landed on his back.

"Your caller disconnected," the wave-sorter said.

"Well, buzz them again. Not out of order?"

"No. Just hold a moment, please." Then, after an interval: "There is no answer."

Trant and I, as it happened, had nothing important to do this night.

"Warning us of a Federal crime," Mac said. "Well, it might be a lead worth investigating. You and Trant get ready. I'll find out who this fellow is."

There had been something peculiar about the way that face left the image-grid, just before the disconnection. It seemed to sink down out of sight. We were only a minute or so equipping ourselves. Mac had put through several calls.

"That message came from the Mauch Chunk Branch of the Federal Coin-Scrip Mint. It was evidently Robert Green, production checker."

Mac can smell a real crime like a hound-dog smells a fox. We get lots of calls from alarmists and publicity seekers, but Mac seems to have a sixth sense in weeding them out. He had sprung into swift action now.

"You two fly over there. Make a roof landing. The place is closed for the night—only watchmen on duty. Get going—if anything happened I want you there first. Call me shortly."

We took off in a rush in our small plane from the roof of the Shadow Squad Building. It was about ten P.M.—a dark, sullen evening of September, 2000. A brief enough flight, westward across New Jersey, into Pennsylvania. I called Mac within a minute or two after leaving New York, using the secret split-wave of the tiny microphone fastened to the alarm-band under my shirt.

Mac's voice said, "I've just called one of the watchmen on the main lower floor. There's a conference of some of the officials going on upstairs. Green must have left it to call us from another room. I told the watchman you'd be making a roof landing in a few minutes, to have an interview with Robert Green. When you land, don't make it seem important. Show your credentials to the roof guards, then go inside and find Green. He called us from Room 2-14. That's the second floor—the top floor. The watchman says the officials are having a conference in Room

2-1. That's also top floor, on the other side of the building. You'll probably find Green in Room 2-14—"

HE DIDN'T HAVE to tell us what we'd find; we sensed it. We were only a few minutes making the flight. The industrial and mining city of Mauch Chunk lies in the valley of a mountainous section. The central traffic tower director guided us to the mint building—a small, quadrangular stone and metal structure, two-storied, flat-roofed. It was, we knew, one of the smallest branches of the Coin-Scrip Mints—a little factory where the coins for temporary circulation were minted from government-patent alloy of lead and tin.

Trant said, "Coin-scrip is stamped from an engraved die. That's what that fellow Green mentioned—wanted to verify the contents of the vault where the die engravings are kept... All looks quiet down there."

We were dropping to the roof of the little Federal building. I saw that it was a quadrangle surrounding an interior courtyard. The whole place was dark—a few dim roof-lights, and a light or two in the windows of the upper story.

The two roof-guards racked our plane.

"Federal men," Trant said, and showed our credentials. The guards passed us into a roof-kiosk where stairs led downward.

"What's in the air?" one of them demanded.

"Nothing at all," I said. "We want to go to Room 2-14."

"One flight down—turn left. It's Mr. Green's office."

We closed the roof door, and went swiftly down a dim stairway. The corridor was shadowed and silent, with a double row of dark office doorways.

"Here's Number 2-22," Trant whispered.

The number glowed on the doorpanel. For a moment

we stood listening. No sound. The corridor was about a hundred feet long, with a right angle turn at each end. We started forward, our soft rubber soles silent on the stone flagging of the floor.

Then we came to Room 2-14. The door was wide open, the interior dark. There was a faint sound inside, just as we approached. With Banning guns in hand, we went over the threshold like cats pouncing. Our torches disclosed Robert Green lying on the floor under the audiphone bracket. Dead—the livid face, gaping mouth, made that obvious. Drilled through the back with a heat-flash.

And beside the body, an old gray-haired man was clutching the audiphone. He dropped it as we appeared; and he stood gasping, pallid-faced, dazzled by the actinic light of Trant's torch.

"Got you!" Trant said. "Up with your arms!"

The old fellow stood shaking while Trant searched him.

"No weapon, Jac. See if it's around here."

"I—I didn't kill him," the man protested. "I just came in—found him here—I was phoning for help—"

The magnetic detector showed pretty clearly that no weapon was hidden around here. There was no disorder in the room. It was Green's office-desk, chairs and filing cases. A window overlooking the courtyard; and the corridor door through which we had entered.

Trant said, as I stood up from my brief search:

"This fellow says he's Ezra Peters, the chief engraver. He was in Room 2-1—this floor around on the other side. Three other officials are there now... There goes the damned alarm."

It was bad luck for us. Peters had already gasped into

the audiophone the news of the murder; an electrical siren on the roof of the building was whining. Distant voices were shouting. The officials in conference in that room on the other corridor were coming on the run. And in a few minutes the Mauch Chunk police would be here.

Trant was calling Mac for orders. I snuffed the room with the olfactory classifier—the bloodhound machine, as the newscasters call it. Disappointing. There were too many scents.

Mac was saying, "Don't try to do anything much, unless you get a good lead. Let the police take the routine. But it's a Federal crime all right—murder of a Federal employee. Maybe it'll be assigned to Desk 4, and maybe not."

Excited voices were out in the corridor now. Then two of the watchmen guards burst in, with the three officials behind them. Trant said, "We're Shadow Squad men from New York."

They gaped at us; and then they all stood horrified, gazing at Green's body. It was hardly five minutes before the Mauch Chunk police arrived; and with the turmoil here, Trant and I certainly had no opportunity of accomplishing anything. The three officials were George Carroll, big, florid production manager; Thomas Allen, a small, alert, wiry-looking fellow, who was purchasing agent of supplies, and old John Franklyn, the general manager of the mint. Our first interest went particularly to him—a large, erect, distinguished-looking man of nearly seventy.

Trant and I sent them all to the corridor, where they stood waiting for the police. Their voices were a babble.

"Green was stabbed by a heat-bolt while he was talking to me," I said. "He sank down—he didn't disconnect."

2

IT WAS OBVIOUSLY the murderer who had disconnected the audiphone, so that there would be no "out-of-order" signal. We snuffed at the instrument with the bloodhound machine. If we could get that murderer's scent where he had gripped it—

Again disappointment. The reaction was a blur—Green's scent, and Ezra Peters'. And others—too many to prove anything.

"No use," Trant muttered. "But if this is an inside job, we've got the fellow right here, and we ought to find some way of nabbing him."

Certainly there was no great intricacy or mystery to the case so far. I was convinced that we had already met the criminal. But what was the crime of which Green had been trying to tell us? The police presently would begin delving. Which of these men had left Room 1 at the time of the murder? A myriad details like that... But S.S. men do not work that way.

Trant said, "Close that door. I'll call Mac. No use letting them hear me."

The men in the hall were peering in at us. George Carroll, the production manager, said, "You Federal men certainly got here in a rush—"

"Right," I agreed. "We try to be prompt. We'll be through in a moment."

I banged the door. Mac's voice was saying to Trant, "You've got just one good lead—the vault of engravings. Watch your chance and take a look at it."

The police came, and we turned the affair over to them. The Mauch Chunk police captain was somewhat disgruntled. He said, "How did you Federal men get here ahead of us?"

Trant grinned. "We work fast, Captain."

We stood aside, watching the ponderous litter of instruments which were being dragged into the room. And presently the four officials were being questioned, with blood-pressure testers, cardiac recorders and the black-light ray scanning them for their physical reactions… What a maze of contradictory theories you get into by that system!

"They won't get anywhere," Trant murmured to me. "That conference didn't begin till after the murder. It's the motive we're after, Jac."

The motive was that Green had been killed to keep him from telling us of another crime. That other crime was the important thing. What was it?

The white-haired, handsome John Franklyn was saying, "There's been something queer going on around here for some time, Captain."

"Green knew it," young Allen put in. "He hinted at it, to Mr. Carroll and me. Some crooked work—theft of the coin-scrip maybe. But there has not been any theft."

Carroll said, "I'm the production manager. There has been no theft."

"None," agreed Franklyn. "We're a small plant. I had everything checked today—supplies and minted coins. There is nothing wrong."

What a fool a police investigator can be, tangling himself up in theories like that! Micro-photos of every portion of the room were being made now. The body was being subjected to a dozen tests. But there was nothing to learn, save that somebody had crept in here and drilled Green with a heat-gun. The big police olfactory classifier was baffled, as ours had been.

The police captain was on another tack. "Who discovered the body?"

That brought in Old Man Peters, who commenced a frightened explanation. We watched our chance. We got George Carroll away from the others.

TRANT SAID, "WE'RE interested in the vault where you keep the engravings. Is it near here?"

"Why, yes," Carroll said. "Our stamping rooms are downstairs, but the engraving room and the storage vault are on this upper corridor."

"Let's see the vault," I suggested.

No one seemed to notice us as we moved away. The vault was in a corridor recess. Old Man Peters, Carroll told us, made all the engravings. A dozen of them, for this forthcoming stamping of the October scrip-issue.

We stood before the steel door of the vault. "Who has access to this?" I demanded.

"Why, all of us," Carroll said. He seemed somewhat surprised. He added, "The die-engravings are never particularly guarded—no intrinsic value."

"Twelve engravings are here now?" Trant asked.

"Twelve, yes. We start the October minting tomorrow."

But there were only eleven of the little round dies in the vault. One was missing.

I said, to the startled Carroll, "Can you keep quiet about this?"

"Why, yes, of course."

But Franklyn, Allen, and old Peters were with the police captain in the corridor, coming toward us. Allen called out:

"You learned anything? We saw you leaving."

The captain said, "What is it?" You'd have thought that our movements were the only things he had on his mind—which I guess maybe was so. They all crowded us. Old Man Peters stammered, "What's the matter? These are my engravings—what's wrong with them?"

We told the captain of the missing engraving. I think now that Trant and I were very dumb. To let yourself be annoyed is a bad thing. You lose alertness. Just who handled that row of tiny engravings in that moment of confusion, I don't know.

The police captain said, "Move back, all of you—I'll inspect them."

There were twelve engravings now. It made Trant and me look somewhat foolish; but we withstood the captain's patronizing look and said nothing.

Then Mac suddenly called us; and we escaped to a nearby empty office. "I've got something more tangible," Mac's voice said. "Young fellow out in Des Moines just captured by the police. Tried to escape and they drilled him—he's pretty badly wounded. They are questioning him now—I'll plug you in if you'll call me on one of those office phones."

We were in a dark, empty office, very much like Green's.

An audiphone was here on the desk. We got Mac and he relayed us to the Des Moines Criminal Hospital. The grid glowed with the image of a young man lying in the sterile-white hospital bed, with half a dozen of the police bending over him. He was fully conscious; but he wouldn't talk, save with sullen rejoinders which told nothing.

"What'd he do?" I demanded of Mac. "What's the charge?"

This young fellow had been caught transporting over ten thousand dollars' worth of scrip-coins. Authentic coins—not counterfeit. He wouldn't explain where he got them.

And the coins were earmarked as of this Mauch Chunk mint—a portion of the October stamping.

But that stamping had not yet been made!

3

——

"**THERE'S YOUR CRIME,**" Mac said. "And the scene of it won't be in that factory. You need an outside trail."

An outside trail! Heaven knows, we were soon enough destined to get it. Trant stumbled on it. Poor Trant—I wouldn't want to have gone through what he did in the next hour!

Mac's voice was saying, "They're trying to identify this fellow now, in Washington. We'll have the reports in a minute. His arm signature is disguised, but if he has a criminal record—"

He did have one. The word flashed from Washington. He was named Willie Peters.

"Peters?" I said. "Why, the chief engraver here, an old fellow, is named Ezra Peters—"

I got no further. Behind us, beyond the door of the dark office, there was a gasp. Out in the corridor, Old Man Peters had been listening. He cried:

"Willie—wounded—dying?"

He came a step forward, gripping at his chest, his face ashen, and then he just sank down unconscious. Fainted from shock. I bent over him. He was already showing signs of recovery.

"Guess he's all right," I said to Trant.

But Trant wasn't with me; he stood a few feet down the

corridor. And abruptly he murmured, "Someone else was listening! Got away—I'll go after him!"

He vanished around an angle of the hall... What an amazing set of circumstances were destined to surround us, when next I saw Trant! But I had no premonition of it now. Poor old Peters was pretty ill. He was recovering consciousness, but he was limp, bathed with the sweat of weakness; and then he began sobbing, demanding that we let him talk with his son.

"Wait," Mac's voice said. "They are trying something, out there in Des Moines."

I still had visual connection with the hospital. I saw young Peters in the bed, himself pale as death. One of the policemen out there was saying, "They jus' told your father you was drilled—dying maybe. What was the matter with the old man? Bad heart? He jus' faded away—"

I am not one to criticize or to defend police methods. But that sounded pretty drastic to me. The young fellow in the bed stared.

"My dad—he died?"

"Yeah—" Then suddenly they were all pounding him with questions. How did he get that scrip? Did his father have a bandit stamping machine?

And Willie Peters broke. "My dad wasn't in this—I tell you he wasn't—he never did anything wrong in his whole life. You listen—I'll tell you who's in it with me—"

I guess there wouldn't have been the faintest mystery to this case in another minute. Young Peters was ready to tell what he knew. But fate wouldn't let him. I saw his pallid face go whiter, if anything. And he gasped, "I—I got to get my breath. Wait—be all right—" His eyes closed. He lay panting. There was a doctor bending over the bed, with the Des Moines police. The doctor said:

"You fellows better let up on him for a while. You'll kill him—"

Mac's voice cut in, "That's about the end of the case, Jac. This Peters boy knows everything. Now listen, you and Trant tell that Mauch Chunk captain to hold all those officials."

"All right," I agreed.

Old Man Peters was better now. I got him up onto a chair. "You want a doctor?" I asked him.

"No—I'm all right. My boy Willie—"

"He's all right, too. No danger."

"I—I want to talk to him—"

"You can't, now. Maybe later. What you're going to do now is go home."

I found the Mauch Chunk police captain with the official surgeons in Green's office, still examining the body. The captain looked up at me sharply.

"I've concluded that everyone who was here at the time of the murder is a suspect," he said. "Have you finished questioning them?"

I stared at that. "I haven't been questioning them. Where are they?"

It brought the captain to his feet. He was startled. I was myself. And neither of us was to blame. The building was surrounded by police guards, who had orders to pass no one out. And the roof was guarded.

Old Ezra Peters was here. But John Franklyn, Carroll, Allen and Trant—were vanished!

THE GUARDS ON the roof explained it, and they couldn't

rationally be blamed either. The three officials, and Trant, had come up and climbed into one of the small company planes, taken off, and were gone.

The police captain was speechless. I said, "And you let them go? You had orders to pass no one."

"But they had the Federal man with 'em," the guard defended. "The Federal man told me he had orders to take 'em."

"Where?" demanded the captain.

But Trant hadn't said. "He left a message for his partner," the roof guard added. "He said, 'Tell Jac Lombard to wait here—I'll be back.'"

The Mauch Chunk captain said, "Well, I call this a pretty high-handed proceeding. You Federal men think you can do anything—"

He stalked away. I stood confused, with a miserable sinking sensation inside me. I called Mac; told him what had happened.

"You connected Trant lately?" I demanded.

"No—no, I haven't." I guess Mac felt the same sensation; I never heard his voice so grim, apprehensive.

I said, "I think I'd better take our plane and get into the air. Don't you think so, Chief?"

"Yes."

I rolled out our little Wasp and took off. The traffic director in the Mauch Chunk tower couldn't give me any information. Why should he watch every local plane? He had no orders.

I rose through the lower lanes. There was a little traffic—not very much. The night seemed darker than before. I circled, ascending over the nearby mountains.

Mac called me. His voice was just as grim as before. "I can't raise Trant. He doesn't answer."

"No alarm signal from him?"

"No. Just nothing." Mac's voice suddenly sharpened. "Wait—here's something—"

And then, a second later, Mac got the dreaded red-light message of danger from Trant. It meant that Trant had been assailed; the secret alarmband around his chest had been broken; and the red-bulb signal-light was flashing on Mac's desk!

I held my breath. Then Mac said tensely, "He connected me—he just whispered, all in a rush, 'Landed Summit Hill near escalator top. Jac can trail—they've got me—'"

I sucked in my breath; I couldn't find anything to say. Mac added, "His connection's permanently broken. He must have just had a second to whisper it to me. Then they caught him at it. Found his chest-band and ripped it off him."

I found my voice. "Chief, don't turn in any police alarm. They'll kill him if they think they're chased."

"Yes, I know it. Go after them, Jac. Use your head—"

Summit Hill, near the top of the escalator… The Mauch Chunk tower-man gave me the directions. Summit Hill is the name of a village which used to be on this rounded mountain-top. It is a thousand or fifteen hundred feet above Mauch Chunk—a rolling, plateau-like surface of several square miles, with steel sheer drops to the surrounding valleys. There had been, half a century ago, a thriving community up here. Prosperous coal mines honeycombed the mountain top. But the coal-stratas now have long since been exhausted. The village, with mining its only industry, languished and died—absorbed by the swift growth of Mauch Chunk.

There was up here now only the dark, desolate spread of abandoned coal mines. Their old-fashioned wooden shaft houses were falling into ruin. The shafts, many of them, had caved in.

I made a muffled, lightless landing, dropping like a frightened bird at the top of the pedestrian escalator, which for twenty years now had not been running. I rolled the little car under a tree clump and climbed out.

Queer conditions of industry and science, which would bring desolation to this abandoned little mountain top, so close to the modern bustling activity of Mauch Chunk. There was hardly a light up here. Ahead of me, a rotting wooden shaft house stood in the darkness like a ghost of the past. A mile or so to the left, a tiny spot of tube-lights marked all that remains of the village of Summit Hill. An old-fashioned road wound over the broken ground in that direction. Near me, it forked to the right. And out that way, there was a queer, distant, yellow-red glow.

I murmured to Mac, "I'm here. There's something burning off to the right, maybe half a mile away."

"Burning coal mine," he said. "It's abandoned—been burning half your lifetime." Mac added, "Can you get the trail? They must have landed near there—hidden their plane and taken Trant on foot somewhere."

4

AS A MATTER of fact, we afterward found the small plane hidden within a few hundred feet of where I left mine. But I did not stop to look for it now. I stood with the electrical eavesdropper tuned, but it yielded nothing. Then with the olfactory classifier, I snuffed at the fork of the road. I knew Trant's classification, of course. But the bloodhound machine did not pick it up.

"Nothing yet?" Mac's anxious voice whispered.

"No. I'll try toward the village."

I was losing so much time! I crept past the crumbling ruins of the mine shaft. There was a dark, broken abyss here where for a hundred feet the ground had caved in and fallen to crush the honeycomb of mine tunnels. Still the bloodhound machine yielded nothing. Then at last I caught the trail. It was back beyond the fork, on the road leading to the right—toward that yellow-red glow of the burning mine.

"Got it!" I whispered. "Fairly fresh—they passed here maybe fifteen minutes ago."

"I've got an alarm plane ready down in Mauch Chunk," Mac responded. "They'll come when you want them. Keep contact with me."

I started off through the darkness. I passed several dark, abandoned mines. At intervals little rocky trails branched off from the road, at each of them I had to stop and verify the trail.

"Hurry it," Mac whispered. "But keep your wits—don't walk into an ambush."

Not a pleasant thought. I stood at a place where the road itself had fallen into a mine tunnel. From the overcast, sullen night sky there was just enough light so that I could see the little abyss. It was a littered gully, the bottom of it a tangle of rotting timbers of the old tunnel, with rank vegetation growing over them.

A possible ambush? The trail of Trant's scent skirted the top of the gully. I stood in the darkness, gun in hand, straining my senses to see and listen.

There was nothing. Then the eavesdropper heard something. A man's breathing. I melted down to the dark ground; and I oriented the breathing—a man on the ground, about a hundred yards away....

I had no trouble stalking him. I doubt if he had seen or heard me; he was simply crouching in a rift near the top of the gully, waiting. And within a minute or two, I got around behind him; and I flung a rock far over his head. It landed with a clatter, in the gully. And before he could recover from the surprise of that, with a bound I was on him.

"Toss up your arms or I'll drill you!"

He was on his knees, peering toward where the rock I had thrown was clattering. His arms went up. My light dazzled him. I saw his gun lying on the ground beside him.

He gasped, "Don't drill me—"

It was Thomas Allen, the purchasing agent. As I turned my light away, he recognized me. Relief swept his face.

He was a good actor, this saturnine little fellow. He said, "Oh, it's you. What are you doing up here?" That made me chuckle, for all my anxiety over Trant.

"I guess I'll ask you that," I said. He stood docile while I searched him. He had nothing but the one gun, which I pocketed.

"Me?" he said. "Well, I'll be damned if I know what I'm doing here. Your partner Trant is sure a secretive fellow— brought us up here on some trail he's following, and then he told me to wait here in case you came along. His message is for us to wait here—"

It wasn't much of a story, but it was the best he could manage; and he rattled it off as though of course I ought to believe it. On the ground beside him was a big white bundle.

"What's that?" I demanded.

"Why—why your partner Trant left it here with me."

"Open it up. Let's have a look at it"

I held my gun on him while he unwrapped the bundle. It was a fire-suit, of the modern type the professional fire-fighters use—a thick, shaggy white garment of asbestos metallicoid, with boots and gloves; and a big cylindrical helmet with thick mica panels.*

Now I have no alibi for what happened next. Sometimes I'm clever at handling a situation, and sometimes I guess I'm just plain dumb. This was one of those dumb times. Before I had caught Allen, I had tuned my eavesdropper and located his breathing. If then I had tuned the eaves-dropper in other directions, with different range-tuning,

---

* A fire-suit and helmet, very similar to this, was first commercially manufactured in 1935.

of course, I'd have heard other things. But I hadn't. That was dumb; I admit it. And now, as I stood regarding that fire-suit, Mac's voice in my earplug suddenly whispered, "Jac! Jac! Watch yourself—"

BUT IT WAS too late. There came a sudden numbing flash. Thoughts are instant things. If you've ever heard that electrical growling mumble, you'll never forget it. A spreading paralysis beam. I don't know whether I got its full effect, or not. I recall stiffening; and Allen leaped sidewise and dropped flat on his face. Then something very ponderable, which was no mysterious Horton paralysis-vibration, but a very prosaic chunk of rock, struck me a blow on the back of the head.

My senses faded. I was aware of falling—trying to get up—falling again, like a blob of meteorite through endless centuries of endless space....

But I think it wasn't over five or ten seconds, and I don't believe I ever quite lost consciousness, for there lingered with me a blurred memory of what had happened. Then something came at me... an armed man coming at me; I would be captured or killed now... the sweat of weakness bathed me; I knew I had no strength to move. But I could lift an arm; I fumbled with numbed fingers at a pouch of my belt.

All this in a few seconds. The big shape of a man with a gun in his hand stooped over me. But I had shoved a tiny pellet into my mouth. The "death pill." That's the lurid term the newscasters use. But it isn't that, of course. Damnably unpleasant experience. Never but once before in my professional career had I ever had the desperate need to try it. But I did it now, in frantic haste, without conscious reasoning. The drug, alkaloidal digitalite, is a drastic heart depressant. It drops you almost instantly into something of catalepsy. A "death pill" indeed, so far as you look under casual examination. But it's not dangerous—if your heart is sound.

The damnable shock wafted me instantly off into an abyss of almost soundless blackness. But I fought against it. And as though coming from a great empty distance, I heard a voice say:

"He's dead—"

I sensed rather than, felt the rough hands which were stripping me of my instrument equipment and my weapons. It was a hasty search. Afterward a foot kicked me contemptuously.

Another dim voice said, "Hurry it up—leave him—you can't tell how many more of these damn Federal men might be around here—"

Then, in truth, everything which was me, drifted away into a void....

5

THE "DEATH PILL," to one of my health and strength, isn't effective for more than a few minutes. I came drifting out of the void. The slow coming back is the worst part. I lay, it seems to me now, pondering a phantasmagoria of my childhood—with myself, bodiless, hovering, watching. I thought that a mind demented might always roam in a blur like this, trying helplessly to focus on something real.

Then, like instruments in a silent orchestra one by one starting to play, I became aware of my physical senses. I was conscious of my head—the back of it paining where that rock hit me. Then I could feel my foot, and hear the scrape of it as I squirmed on the ground. And then at last I could see the dim, rocky darkness.

I was alone; left for dead; and these bandits had taken Trant. Taken him where? I lay pondering it, almost too weak to move. But my strength rapidly was coming back. I was not injured, save a ragged scalp wound on the back of my head, which throbbed now with pain and had risen to a lump, with blood matting my hair.

Or had Trant been killed and left here with me? I was presently able to stagger around. No one—nothing here.

The fire-suit was gone. I suddenly remembered that fire-suit. And that there was a burning coal mine near here. The mystery of where they were going was made plain.

I could see the glow now, ahead of me in the darkness. I started forward, stumbling and shaky. Queer how helpless you feel without weapons or instruments! My connection with Mac was broken; my earplug wires had been ripped away. But the chest alarm-band, hidden under the shirt, was intact. I was thankful that Mac had had no red-light signal from me. He would have sent up that police plane, and a squad of blaring police up here would mean the death of Trant.

I can't say that I recall much of the run I must have made toward that distant glow. It proved to be not nearly so far away as I had expected—a quarter of a mile, or perhaps even less. I found a section of the burning mine presently close in front of me. The mine had originally occupied a little hundred foot cone-shaped hill, on the brink of the main mountain top, with a great spread of open valley far down in the distance. The cone was a veritable volcano now in aspect. The fire had eaten its way underground. The broken shaft tunnels were all oozing smoke. At the top of the cone, like a crater, a yellow-red glare mounted.

I stood at the broken, rifted entrance of an old tunnel shaft, which went horizontally into the hill. The timbers had partly fallen, but there seemed room where one might creep under them. I could feel the heat of the interior now—a drift of fetid gas-laden air coming out.

And suddenly I stiffened. There was the faint, blurred and muffled sound of a distant cry. I thought I caught the words, "Don't—do—this—"

I moved slowly forward. The shaft tunnel led gently downward. A deep red glow was ahead; waves of outcoming heat surged against my face. I suppose I went twenty feet, with the utmost caution. The old tunnel passage rounded an angle, opened or broke away to an interior ledge. I crouched by a rock spire, peering.

Weird scene. An interior cavern, which years ago the fire must have eaten out of the coal and rock. It was dim with flickering red-yellow shadows, blurred with smoke-fumes so that I could not guess its size or shape. A tumbled, rifted grotto. And I saw, ten feet below the ledge on which I was crouching, another ledge of the terraced floor. Figures were down there. Beyond them was a long descending ramp-like surface, ending a hundred feet away in what seemed a red abyss.

Familiar figures on the ledge, with the red glare painting them. Trant, and old John Franklyn, the general manager of the mint. They lay like bundles bound with rope—lay with the heat of the accursed place enveloping them. Near them stood two men, both helmeted, shrouded in the gray-white fire-suits. They evidently were just now binding Trant. And abruptly I heard Trant's voice, tense with desperation:

"You don't have to do this. You can spare him—not kill us both."

For all the heat, I stood with a shuddering, numbing chill. Carry them down the smoking ramp? Toss them into the red glare?

Without weapons, I stood helpless. I could not even see a loose chunk of rock which I might throw. I could not move forward a yard without being discovered… Trant, to be killed now.

The helmeted voices were blurred. There was a steady hissing, muttering rumble from the fire-pit down the ramp. The men in the fire-suits were Thomas Allen and George

Carroll, I was sure of that. But I could only tell them apart now by their size. They booth stooped over Trant.

"You first—" Then Carroll straightened. "We were fools to leave that other fellow—his body lying out there. Just as well cremate it, too."

I could only hear fragments of their talk. Allen and Carroll had bandit coin-scrip, hidden here in a burned-out section of the mine. They had come to get it, and then, because the game was up, they would vanish. Some hideout they had prepared in a distant city. The police would think that Trant and I had met death from unknown bandits—and that Franklyn, Carroll and Allen were all victims.

But my body was lying out there where they had left it. That would spoil that scheme.

"… don't want to be suspected of the murder of a Federal man—all hell after us forever—"

Allen was going back now to get my body… I went like a rabbit back through the decrepit tunnel. At the entrance I climbed to the top of a small, overhanging rock. The shapeless, shaggy white figure of Allen came out through the rift. His doffed helmet dangled at the back of his neck.

I LANDED ON his back, dropping from the overhanging rock like a pouncing puma. A brief encounter, and the advantage was all with me. He was a small fellow, and certainly not skilled at rough and tumble fighting. The impact of my body flattened him, and we were both wedged down into the narrow shaft entrance. I was on top of him; he could not reach the knife in his belt. He was trying to get at it, heaving me upward, twisting. The blows of my fists in his face made him mumble suddenly:

"That's enough—I give in—"

Now most distinctly I want it understood that I had no intention of killing this fellow Allen. I would really have preferred to have saved him for the police. He went limp to signify his surrender, and I pulled him up half to his feet. There was in my mind only the desire to get back inside to Trant. I knew I would have to silence this fellow—leave him out here. I'd give him a "death pill." Why not? I was groping to take his knife away from him, when abruptly I saw it in his hand, stabbing at me.

"Got you!" he murmured.

But he didn't have me. I ducked under the knife, and lunged with my head, butting his chest. He fell over backward again, and this time he went wholly limp.

"Come on," I panted, "you can't work the same trick twice."

My hand plucked the knife from his limp fingers, and then I found that he was unconscious. His head had struck violently against a sharp projection of the shaft wall—a ragged gash. I did not stop to examine it. I hauled him three or four feet to the open ground; and stripped him of the fire-suit. He was alive, but the look of the gash in his skull made me have no fear that he would recover consciousness. As a matter of fact, he was dead when later Trant and I came back to him.

For a moment I stood panting, gripping Allen's knife. Would Carroll inside have heard our noise? There was no sound from within the tunnel. Then swiftly I donned the bulky, shaggy garment. Allen was about my size; it fitted me perfectly. My gloved fingers gripped the knife. The flexible visor-helmet encased my head. There was no mechanism for interior air. Merely a nose-clamp and mouth breather of moist chemicalized fabric.

I started back through the tunnel. At the upper ledge I paused, again peering. Not over two or three minutes had passed. The scene had hardly changed. The gray-haired, portly figure of John Franklyn lay bound where he had been before. I saw his gaze swing upward to regard my shaggy form as I appeared on the ledge above him.

And I saw Trant. The big figure of Carroll in the other fire-suit was carrying him down the slope of the ramp. Trant was bound with rope. He lay stiff as the man staggered with him. Already they were fifty feet down that smoking broken surface, with the red glare painting them.

In that second my gaze focused on Trant's face. It was grim and set; red with thick blood suffusing it, and the sweat pouring from it. I suppose the temperature down there was 150°F., or more. Trant, being slowly roasted now as he was carried forward to his death. That glimpse of his tortured face was to me a sight most horrible.

And suddenly a cry broke from him. "Carroll—if you do this to me—you spare that old man—"

There was, we believe now, of all the employees of the Mauch Chunk Scrip-Mint, only Allen and Carroll in this plot. Both had free access to the engravings; and Allen was purchasing agent of supplies, so that he could readily get the necessary lead-tin alloy out of which the coins were stamped. By night they had purloined, one or two at a time, the die engravings. We later found their small bandit stamping mill. It was hidden in a cave, up here in a burned-out area of the burning mine—a cave-recess surrounded now by the smoldering portions of the mine, so that fire-suits were needed to reach it. Allen and Carroll doubtless thought it was a well-hidden place. It was indeed; we found it, with the Mauch Chunk police, after a lengthy search the next day. And also found some fifty thousand dollars of coin-scrip.

Queer banditry! The coins were not counterfeits. They were merely a portion of the government-run, in duplicate, so that once they were in circulation, they could never be identified. Young Willie Peters had been the main outlet for them. He did not die of his police wounds. He has made a full confession. We are still trailing, and already we have caught and convicted, several of the men who were circulating the scrip in many distant cities. Willie, for his aid, and because of his youth, has received a light sentence. I am glad of that, for his old father's sake as well as his own.

I must give a word of explanation of Trant's sudden exit. That night in the mint building, Carroll and Allen found an unexpected net closing suddenly on them. Young Green had discovered something of the banditry—just what, no one will ever know. One of them drilled him, there at the audiphone. Even then they thought they were safe. They hastily replaced the die engraving which they had taken from the vault for use in their bandit plant this night.

And then came the news that Willie Peters was arrested. His confession would be the end for them. They turned desperate. They had already impulsively committed one murder. Their only desire was to get out of the mint building, to get their stored scrip, and vanish. But their only way of getting past the guards was to have Franklyn and Trant with them. Trant came upon them in one of the dark corridors as they had seized the old general manager. A heat-gun was at his chest. A move from Trant, and Franklyn would have been drilled.

You can tell complete murderous desperation when you meet it, and Carroll and Allen were in that mood. Trant yielded, to save Franklyn's life. And Franklyn and Trant both were covered by Carroll's gun, when in the semi-darkness they passed the roofguards and took off in the company plane.

I THINK I have made everything clear… At Trant's cry now, as Carroll carried him down in the glaring suffocating heat of the fiery ramp, I called instantly:

"Carroll!"

He stopped momentarily. The helmet and the wet fabric-breather at my mouth muffled my voice. I waved my arm in gesture, and leaped to the lower ledge. I was within a foot or two of the bound Franklyn.

"Wait!" I called.

Carroll stooped; he lowered Trant to the smoking rocks. And in that instant I had bent down and with a swift knife-slash I cut Franklyn's bonds. He did not move, but only swept me with a startled inquiring glance. With a leap I straightened and went past him. Carroll had not seen me pause—he was rising from where he had put Trant at his feet. He shouted, "What the devil's wrong? Why didn't you go—"

I said, "Listen—something queer—" I ran plunging, half staggering down the ramp toward him. I said, "Something queer—"

I met him, with Trant at our feet. I was gesturing with the knife. I said, "You listen to me—" And I ended the knife-gesture with a stab at his chest. The accursed asbestos metallicoid fabric bent inward, resisting the thrust, and the thin steel knife-blade broke off at the hilt.

Carroll let out a startled oath. Then the fire-glare on my visor showed him my face. He gasped, "You!"

He must have thought I was a corpse come to life. He staggered back. I stumbled forward over Trant; and then Carroll lunged at me, his own knife stabbing at my throat where the helmet flap was thin. But I struck with clenched fist at his wrist. The knife went flying away into the smoke and glare. And then his powerful arms closed around me. We reeled down the slope, locked together.

I think I shall never forget the horrible minute or two of this unarmed combat. I felt the strength of his grip, his bulk, thrusting at me. Quite different from the slim Allen. This fellow Carroll was far stronger than I, a head taller, and half a hundred pounds heavier. Once he picked me up bodily, trying to carry me. Then as I fought and squirmed, he flung me ahead of him down the ramp.

But I was up in a second; more agile than he. I recall leaping over a smoking, red-glaring two-foot crevasse as I came back at him where he stood like an infuriated bull waiting for me. We were thirty or forty feet further down the ramp now. Far above us, I saw that old Franklyn had struggled to his feet; braving the heat he had staggered down to Trant. And then he was stooping, carrying, half dragging Trant up to safety. We'll never cease being grateful to John Franklyn for that. I imagine that in another minute Trant might have died, lying there in the heat and the gas-fumes.

Again I struck at Carroll. We locked; fell; rolling one over the other. And always downward… We came to a brink. For an agonized second I thought that was the end of us both. We went over—but there was a drop of only six or eight feet to another ledge. The fall parted us, but we both jumped erect. Flames were around us now; red-yellow, and bluish little tongues licking at my legs; smoke and gas-fumes choking me for all the protection of the helmet.

A blurred chaos of fire. I reeled through it. The swaying, bull-like figure of Carroll was blurred by the blue flames as he came charging at me. A fused, dull-red glowing chunk of coal seemed loose at my feet. I picked it up with two gloved hands. It was soft with heat. I heaved it at him.

It struck him, but he kept on coming.

And then, as I jumped sidewise, I fell. Carroll caught me; lifted me. I tripped him. Gripping each other we were rolling swiftly downward... A brink here—a red abyss, far down....

With what desperate lunge I squirmed free, I do not know. But with wide-spread legs, and arms out-flung, I found myself flattened at the brink, and Carroll going over me.

I think that just at the last, he screamed....

I lay, that instant, with head beyond the brink. I saw him go like a plummet downward—a tiny, dwindling blob in the blurred red chaos. The blob vanished. There was not even a little added wisp of smoke to mark its cremation.

THE CASE OF THE FRIGHTENED DEATH

Gaunt and Cadaverous Was the Face in the Green-Bronze Wasp—the Bringer of Death!

1

———

I THINK THE affair I call "The Case of the Frightened Death" embodied some of the weirdest, most inherently terrifying elements which in all of my nine years as an operative of New York's Shadow Squad I have ever encountered. The very basis of it was terror—the terror of the Unknown.

It was a brief affair. So far as Trant and I were concerned, it was over within a few hours of the time Mac assigned us to it. Not that I mean we deserve any particular credit for solving it in a rush. Merely that the cards fell that way.

The newscasters began blaring of the thing the previous evening. Mysterious deaths occurring at several different places. A mysterious fiendish murderer roaming New York's streets and terrace levels—a sort of modern "Jack the Ripper."

Trant and I had no expectation that the Federal Shadow Squad would be assigned to it. The thing seemed for the police Alarm Squads who could charge upon the scene of the crime like bulls in a china shop, and either seize the shadowy fiend or not, as the case might be. A maniac, of course, for the killings seemed unrelated and motiveless. Well, he was a maniac, as it turned out—but mostly mad with the lust for power.

THIS DAY OF August 4th, 2003, Trant had spent with me,

in my Westchester cubby apartment. We awoke about 8
P.M., had breakfast and flew my little aero to the roof-stage
of the Shadow Squad building in Mid-Manhattan, ready
for whatever routine job might be ours for the night. We
always worked in pairs and Trant had been my partner
for some seven years—a blond, easy going, good-natured
giant, the perfect contrast to me, for I am small, dark and
swiftmoving. And somewhat short of temper.

Mac was in charge of City Night Desk 4 in his dim elec-
trically insulated office when we reported for duty. A visitor was with him—a short, thickset, foreign-looking man.

"One of my night-teams," Mac explained to the visitor.
"Dr. Levise, meet partners Georg Trant and Jac Lombard."

He was rather a distinguished-looking fellow, this Dr.
Charles Levise—gray-black hair, a small neat mustache
and goatee in the quaint old-fashioned style. He wore a
dark suit, ornately braided with whip-cord; and an eyeglass
ribbon hung across his ruffled white shirt bosom. He
appeared to be an Austrian.

"I'll send you a guard, maybe tonight," Mac told him.

As I fired, I caught a glimpse of his face—and then he was gone.

Dr. Levise picked up his hat and cane. "I thank you, Chief Macfarlane. We are very worried—frightened. That is the damnable part of this thing—" His thick shoulders twitched. "Real or imaginative fear—how can you tell the difference? The thing spreads among my patients. And as I told you—two deaths last week—heart cases, but still it seems mysterious—"

"Yes," Mac nodded. "An investigation order came through, mentioning it. But now the thing has spread so widely—"

"We would appreciate a guard," Dr. Levise said. His smile was lugubrious. "Even so, I do not really think, with any of my patients, that it is more than apprehensive hysteria—"

HE DEPARTED PRESENTLY. Mac explained that he was the owner of a private Sanatorium for nervous cases, in the Tarrytown section. Two of his patients had had heart attacks a few days ago. And now he thought that this outbreak of the frightened death might explain it. Even if not, the newscasters' accounts of the mysterious fiend were causing hysteria among his patients which the presence of a Shadow Squad guard could help to dispel.

"It's damned weird," Mac said. "You can't blame anybody for being alarmed."

Weird indeed. A Tower Traffic Director had slumped at his lightswitch keyboard. A dozen traffic accidents in the crowded local lower air-lane were narrowly avoided. The Traffic Director was dead. Heart failure? Maybe. The autopsy showed nothing. And the Traffic Director, so far as was known, never had had anything the matter with his heart.

That was the first. Then a woman—proprietress of a little public eating place on the Third Level at the 59th Street Circle—had told the cashier that she was frightened. She had looked it, standing there with her face first pallid, then flushed, her breath jerking with terror, her hands clutching at her breast. Terrified at what? Certainly the cashier did not know, nor did the stricken woman. Frightened at her own weird feelings of illness, of impending death? It seemed something like that. She had screamed for a doctor—screamed that she was dying.

Then she had fainted. With merciful unconsciousness, the terror left her; the strain was removed and she did not die. She was in the Federal Hospital now—and the doctors could find nothing the matter with her save nerve-shock, and a terrified apprehension that the thing would happen to her again.

There had been a dozen such incidents, all the others fatal. It was some weird assailant, of course.

"Some rational weapon," Mac was saying. "If it isn't, I'm a motor-oiler."

IN THIS DAY of modern electrical weapons, it is bad enough to have stupid laws so that criminals can use all our own devices against us. But here was a criminal with a weapon unknown, even to us. Diabolical thing, most certainly. Some mental power? Hypnosis? Suggestivity? A learned Professor of the Modern Society of Occult Research already had delivered an aircasted address to that effect. But he did it for the publicity, of course. You could never make Scientific Authorities—or any of us hard-headed S.S. men—believe in the Evil Eye.

"They ought to bar all aircasting on a subject like this," Mac was saying. "The first thing you know we'll have mass hysteria. The panic is spreading. Twenty or thirty reports an hour, an' you know damn well most of them are imagination."

"From women?" I said.

"Yes. Women and young girls. Hysterical stuff—tales of a lurking, fiendish-looking figure—"

Mac shrugged. Our Deck Chief is a rotund little fellow, with a cherubic face and a bald spot. But he can look grim upon occasion. He was lugubrious now, but we knew him well enough to realize that under it he was genuinely worried.

"The Alarm Squads are baffled," he added.

"As always," I said. But Mac didn't grin.

"I had a General Order yesterday for Routine Investigation of those cases at the Levise Sanatorium," he went on. "It was just a Preliminary Question Form to be filled out. I don't have to send a man there now, since Levise has been here. But I'm thinking—"

"You're not thinking of putting us on this, by any chance?" Trant interjected.

"I am," Mac said. "General Orders from the Washington Bureau an hour ago."

"Doing what?" I said. "The Washington Bureau thinks it knows how to do everything—"

Mac fingered a teletype message. "It says—'Roaming Duty.'"

That brought a snort of disgust from Trant. We've been shoved into things like that before. You get stuck on a long-winded, clueless case and you roam around for weeks doing nothing. That's a job for a Precinct Snooper, not the Federal S.S. Even at that, I was afraid of something worse—guarding the Levise place—a gum-shoe idler, putting courage into nervous patients in case the fiend might come.

"If you'll just give us a clue," I suggested. "A starting place. You know we can go pretty fast on a trail—after we start."

"There's a green-brown aero-roller," Mac retorted. "You've heard of it? Last year's Wasp-type Ankro—six wheels—double lateral folding wings. It's been seen three separate times leaving the vicinity of these deaths. That's too many for a normal coincidence."

A green-brown Wasp-type aero-roller. Maybe it was the fiend's vehicle; maybe not. The aircasters had been forbidden to mention it, so that the murderer might not be warned.

"All you have to do," Mac added ironically, "is find that

Wasp-type Ankro. Board it. Seize its occupant—and there you are."

His grin faded as he added, "Have you seen the latest? Dr. Levise and I were watching it here, just before you arrived. The fiend is on his job, right now."

Mac touched a button of his control board. One of the foot-square image-mirrors on the desk glowed fluorescent, and Trant and I crowded forward, peering at the televised image. It came from a lens-finder on the Fifth Level at Park Sixty.

THE AFTERMATH OF the mysterious murderer's latest attack. A dozen actinic alarm glares bathed all the vicinity in dazzling blue-white light. Wheeled traffic had stopped; but every level, ramp and escalator incline was jammed with milling pedestrians.

"The Grantline Screen Theater," Mac was murmuring. "The panic started inside it."

He switched us to a closer viewpoint—the theater entrance. Bodies were being carried out on slabs; the Big Black Mortuary Roller was waiting to receive them. Others, still alive—were coming out on stretchers.

Mac tuned in the auditory connection. Over the confused babble of voices a woman was screaming—heart-rending, and anguished, as she recognized some loved one among the dead.

Mac shut off the mirror... I found my heart pounding. What was this thing? I—Lombard of the S.S.—shuddering over a few deaths in a theater panic! But it was my awe—fear perhaps—of the Unknown. I guess that is instinctive with everyone.

"Good grief," Trant was murmuring. "What happened?"

Mac let us hear a newscaster blaring it. Nothing at all had gone wrong in the theater—except that the audience had gotten frightened. Several people—those with heart afflictions, no doubt—had died even before the main panic had started. Then in a mad rush to get out, many others had been killed....

Mac was staring at us grimly as he clicked off the newscaster's voice.

"You see how it spreads," he said. "Like a stone thrown into a pond—a widening wave of terror. By tomorrow the whole city will be frightened. In a week, the whole nation—"

Nothing is so communicable as fear. An epidemic of terror—spreading far beyond its original, tangible cause—spreading to terrorize the world....

Nerves are damnable things. Certainly mine have never bothered me much, but at that instant, with my shuddering fancy far-flung upon the diabolic possibilities of mass terror, the sharp buzz of one of Mac's audiphones made me jump like a frightened child.

Mac reached and pulled down the swiveled instrument.

"Night Desk 4—Shadow Squad?" It was the incoming wave-sorter of the S.S. Building.

"Macfarlane," Mac said.

"Emergency call. A Madeleine Blair—wants help— fears attack. I have audible and visible—here you are."

The audible and visible connections clicked on. The tiny audiphone mirror-grid glowed with the image of a young girl; a pallid, beautiful face, framed by dark hair. A red scarf was at her throat; a filmy dark dress draped her slim shoulders.

"Shadow Squad Office? Oh—I see you—thank you very much, Sorter."

And then she gasped at Mac: "I'm here alone in the house. I need help—I'm frightened—"

More imaginative hysteria. But something about her seemed to deny it. Her dark eyes were wide with terror. But somehow she didn't look hysterical.

"I've been out and just returned," she said. "A roller was following me—I'm sure of it. A green-bronze Wasp—"

Well that certainly galvanized us. Mac took her address in a rush.

"You think there's an intruder in the house?" he demanded.

"No—no, I really don't. But I was followed here. There's more to it than that anyway. I'm worried over something else—I was coming down to the Shadow Squad Building to consult some official on it—then I thought I'd better wait till tomorrow. And now—now I've just gotten afraid—"

"I'll send two men," Mac said. "See them here—"

She smiled wanly at Trant and me. "Yes, I see them—thank you very much."

IT SEEMED A possible lead—a girl who had been followed by the green-bronze Wasp. Even before Mac had broken connection with her, Trant and I were buckling on our equipment.

"Get right up there," Mac said as he racked the instrument. "Keep your eyes open for that Wasp. Get the girl's story—something worrying her that she was going to consult us about tomorrow. Determine if it has any

connection with this roaming fiend. Call me at intervals
for consultation—"

"Mac!"

It was a startled gasp from Trant. I whirled from buckling on my Banning heat-flash to see Trant standing transfixed. In his hand was the little dial of his eavesdropping
detector. The detector needle had stirred; was swinging
violently around now into the red sector.

An eavesdropping ray, penetrating here into the sanctity
of Mac's office! Ordinarily we are insulated, but tonight
the barrage current chanced not to be on.

Mac stiffened at Trant's impulsive exclamation. Then he
saw my gesture to the little detector and he understood.
For that instant none of us spoke. Then Mac said casually:

"Well, you'd better be going, boys."

The eavesdropper might be here in the building. His
electric vibrations, penetrating the room, were bringing
him our voices. But he couldn't see us. And if he were in the
building, it might be possible to locate him and nab him.

And then I saw the Benson curveray. In most lights it's
difficult to detect; but suddenly now I noticed the faint
pallid sheen of it—a narrow curving beam of light; an arch-
ing crescent, coming in our undraped window, carrying the
image of our room to the eavesdropper who was watching
us as well as listening.

"No use," I said to Mac. "He sees us—"

The faint violet sheen of the curveray abruptly vanished;
Trant's detector needle swung back to normal. All three
of us dashed to the window. We were on the eighth floor
of the S.S. Building; one of the upper traffic ramps of the

terraced street was not far below us. Undoubtedly the Benson ray had come from there.

"Look," Trant murmured. "The Wasp!"

It had evidently been parked in a small alcove of the curving traffic ramp. It was slowly rolling out now, waiting its chance to edge into the traffic.

Mac made an impulsive jump for his instrument panel. He could have flooded the neighborhood down there with the actinic alarm glares; touched off the street alarm siren and summoned the nearest police Alarm Squad. But in the bedlam, doubtless the murderer would have escaped: and anyway, instinctively an S.S. Man avoids those methods. We work in darkness—without trumpet blares.

Mac whirled on us. "I'll split you two, for now. Trant, get to the roof. Take an aero—"

"Mine," I interjected. "It's racked up there."

"All right—his. Fly low—I'll notify the towermen not to challenge you. Keep that Wasp in sight—it'll probably take to the air—nab it when you get the chance. You, Jac, hustle downstairs. Take a car for that girl—we mustn't leave her alone any longer. Keep in touch with me—both of you—for further orders."

We dashed from the room. We were on the trail—two trails in fact.

Trant rushed in an emergency lift for the roof. I hurried down to one of the street levels, grabbed a public meter-roller and sped Northward to the address the girl had given us.

2

IT WAS A small but very high class cubby apartment. The traffic ramp and an upper pedestrian level passed close to its little arcade entrance. I dismissed my roller and stood for a moment surveying the premises. It was now somewhat after ten o'clock—a dark humid summer night. Up past the blue-lit spires of the surrounding apartment buildings I could see the sullen gray of the sky, dotted with the insignia lights of passing aircraft in the lower lane. A traffic guider's beam swung like a silvered sword above them; and high up, dwindled by distance, one of the big liners went by—the Night Mail over the Great Circle Stratosphere route for London.

There was not much traffic here on the ramp—an occasional roller, and only a few people on the pedestrian level. I watched my chance; it seemed that no one saw me as I darted through the arcade entrance which bore the nameplate, *Sir John Blair.*

There was a small inner courtyard. At the oval panels of the door entrance, I found the buzzer and plugged it. My hand flicked to the Banning gun at my belt; this could be a lure. There was a lens-finder in a bracket beside the door. I saw it glow as the current went into it, taking the image of me for the inside occupant.

Then from a small speaker-grid, the girl's microphonic voice said:

"Who is it?"

I smiled at the lens. "Jac Lombard—S.S. Man. You saw me at the office, just a few minutes ago."

"Yes. I recognize you. Just a moment, please."

As I waited, I plugged the tiny portable televisor, and connected Mac.

"I'm here, Chief. She seems all right. I'm just going in."

"Correct," he said. "Trant's after that Wasp. Call me later."

As I dropped the tiny diaphragm back into my belt pouch, the inner fastenings of the heavy door clinked. The panel swung inward. The casement framed the girl; she stood illumined by the soft blue tube-lights of the room's ceiling—a small, slim, black-haired girl. A long dark cape hung from her shoulders; a red silk scarf was wound about her throat. Her face was beautiful, but pale now with apprehension, though she was smiling with relief at sight of me.

"Oh—come in, please."

It was a small, luxurious room. A window with drawn shade faced the front pedestrian walk. The shades of two other windows were drawn. There were two door ovals with closed slides connecting with other rooms.

"You're not so frightened now," I smiled.

"No. I'm not. But I'm worried."

She was a girl about twenty—refined, cultured, undoubtedly wealthy. My impression of her on Mac's image-mirror was renewed. This Madeleine Blair was not the silly, empty-headed type of young female. Whatever she had to tell me, it couldn't be discounted as imaginative hysteria.

"These aircasted stories," she added. "Roving fiend, frightening people to death—" She smiled lugubriously as her slim beautiful shoulders twitched with a shiver. "It makes you imagine almost anything."

"It does," I agreed.

"And tonight—I was rolling back on one of the river ramps from the Tappan section—I thought a car was following me—"

I leaned toward her. "Had you ever heard of a green-bronze Wasp in this thing before?"

"No—but that's what it looked like. Is—is it outside now?"

I shook my head. "How long ago did you get home, Miss Blair?"

"An hour ago. Maybe more."

THERE COULD BE many green-bronze Wasps in the city. This might or might not have been the same car which Trant now was after. If it was, then it had stopped following the girl, had gone perhaps to the Theater over Columbus Circle, and then to the S.S. Building.

Futile reasoning. I may as well state now that to this day, the movements of the guilty Wasp have never been determined. We know that Trant chased the murder car but many of the reports of the "green-bronze Wasp" doubtless had no guilty significance whatever. That condition always exists in every case on which I've ever worked....

"I just got frightened, being here alone," Madeleine Blair was saying. Her gaze, still lugubrious but certainly apprehensive, went to the room's inner door-slides. "I've just been sitting here," she added, "since I audiphoned your chief. Oh I know I'm just silly. I know this roaming fiend has nothing to do with my own personal troubles."

But she had named a green-bronze Wasp. That made, to me, a very clear connection.

"I don't think you need be apprehensive," I said. "Your personal troubles? Are they what you wanted to consult the Shadow Squad about?"

"Yes," she said. "I feel I can trust you—"

"What goes into the S.S. Bureau never comes out," I smiled.

Her father was a titled English financier—a leader in Parliament. A widower. He had come from London six months ago, on business, bringing his only child, Madeleine, and his nephew—a man of thirty, Ruffo Blair. They had rented this cubby apartment. Sir John, overworked, had become ill. Over in London, his life had been threatened many times by political enemies. The strain of it had broken his health. His heart was weak. Ten days ago, Madeleine's cousin, this Ruffo Blair, had persuaded the old man to go to a Sanatorium and rest.

"So Ruffo," she went on, "suggested Dr. Levise's place— What's the matter, Mr. Lombard?"

"Nothing," I replied. Certainly here was another connection. Dr. Levise had feared the frightened death might have already invaded his Sanatorium. At the very time he was discussing it in Mac's office, the weird fiend was attacking a theater full of people at Columbus Circle.... Was Levise justified in his fears? Did the weird roving murderer have some direct connection with the Levise Sanatorium? With this girl and her family?

"Go on," I prompted. "Your cousin Ruffo suggested Dr. Levise's place. Did your father go there?"

"Yes—he's there now."

Another thought rushed at me: two of Levise's patients had died. I hadn't heard their names. Had one of them been Sir John Blair?

"When did you see your father last?" I asked.

"This afternoon. Oh, he's all right—so far. But I'm afraid for him. I—I want to get him back with me. I guess I want to get him back to London."

"Why are you afraid for him?"

She sucked in her breath. Her gaze met mine and she smiled wanly. "Now you're just going to tell me I'm an imaginative fool. But you don't know my cousin Ruffo. I've known him all my life. I—I'm afraid of him—I haven't any tangible reason to be."

"Afraid he'll do what?" I said.

Her gaze swept the room as though now she feared we might be overheard. Her eyes as they came back to my face were dark pools turgid with her nameless terror.

"I don't know," she said. "I'm just afraid of Ruffo, that's all. Father has political enemies who would pay a hundred thousand pounds to have him dead. He's often said so. Ruffo—I've always felt he was unscrupulous. And he and I inherit father's fortune.... I got frightened—I wanted to get father out of that Sanatorium. So I drove up there again tonight. Tomorrow—might be too late."

"You didn't see him tonight?"

"No. They wouldn't let me see him. Dr. Levise wasn't there. The head nurse—" She shuddered. "Her name is Emmeline Gros—she—she turned me away. She said father wasn't quite so well tonight—doctor's orders. So I left. I was coming down to your Shadow Squad to tell all this. Then I thought I'd wait until tomorrow. And a car seemed following me—then—then I was just afraid to stay here alone—or to go out or do anything—"

She ended with an almost incoherent rush and her words had brought a real terror into her eyes so that I put my hand on her arm.

"Take it easy, Miss Blair. We'll report this to my Chief—I guess he'll issue the necessary orders to remove your father, if that's what you want."

She nodded.

"Oh, it is. And I want him guarded with competent guards."

"And guarded from this cousin Ruffo," I said. "I imagine I can fix it." Questions were pounding me. Was this a separate plot into which I had stumbled, which belonged properly with the Crime Prevention Bureau? Or was it interwoven with this maniacal fiend who was roaming the city, wielding the frightened death?

"Where has Ruffo been all day?" I demanded. "Where is he now?"

"I don't know. He left here at noon—said he was busy and wouldn't be back till midnight. I—that's another angle to it—I'm afraid to be here with Ruffo tonight. Last night he—well, I had to lock myself in my room. He apologized this morning—but I dare not—"

HER VOICE SUDDENLY broke. She was staring at me—and abruptly I saw something come into her eyes that had not been there before. An astonishment? And then a dawning horror....

"Why—why—Mr. Lombard—" She no more than murmured it. Then she jumped to her feet and stood with panting breath, her breast heaving.

I was up beside her. "What's the matter with you?"

There had been no sound, no hostile rays that I could determine.

"I—don't know. I feel so queer—"

She collapsed suddenly to her chair, gripping its arms and trying to steady herself. The blood had drained from her face, and now it came back in a wave so that she was abnormally flushed.

"Miss Blair—good—"

She was clutching frantically at her breast. Her mouth was forced open by her laboring, gasping breath.

"I—I guess I'm ill—oh—help me—"

It was a piteous appeal. I've never seen anyone with a severe heart attack, but I imagine this must have resembled it. At all events, I recall that my first startled thoughts were that I ought to call a doctor or this girl would die on my hands. Her eyes had terror in them—terror undoubtedly because she believed every breath she struggled to draw would be her last....

She was slumping in the chair, and as I gripped her with an alarmed exclamation, she slid to the floor, lying in a crumpled heap, unconscious... Or was she dead? The damnable thing was so unexpected, so realistic a simulation of natural illness that for those seconds it had taken me unaware. Then with a rush came realization, that this was the frightened death. The lurking fiend—somewhere here.

I stood stiff, wary, with my gaze sweeping the room. The heavy draperies—the shaded windows—the door-sides. Had the attack come from within the apartment, or outside? This mysterious weapon—diabolic—soundless with its invisible attack—I had no possible idea of its range....

The room was utterly silent. There was only the faint drone of the outside city....

I had whipped out my little Banning gun. My heart was pounding. I confess it. The thrill of combat with an adversary was missing. This was the Unknown, so baffling that I stood motionless, with nothing to attack. Then suddenly, as I peered across the shadowed, silent room, I became aware that one of the door-slides was slowly, soundlessly moving. It seemed to have been ajar. I had not noticed the narrow shadowy slit before—and now the slit was widening.

The sight stung me into action. I fired the Banning gun. The sizzling stab of heat hit the door-slide and I plunged forward, thrusting aside the slide. I had a dim instant vista of another room dark and soundless. Then there was a crash upon my head so that all the world seemed bursting into an inferno of light and sound as I fell.

For a second or two, with fading senses, I was aware of the patter of footsteps.... I just had the strength to pluck at the alarm band around my chest, hidden under my shirt, breaking it to flash the red light of danger on Mac's desk. Then my senses slid away into an empty soundless abyss.

3

I THINK MY first stirring of returning consciousness made me aware of a vast commotion... Screaming women, men's voices shouting frightened questions. The thudding tramp of heavy footsteps, the whining electrical scream of the neighborhood alarm siren.

I was lying in the doorway where I had fallen. I staggered erect. On the floor was a heavy metal ashtray which the marauder had flung. And on the back of my head was a ragged wound, with blood matting my hair.

Then Trant burst in on me. "You're all right, Jac?"

"Yes, I guess so."

"He got away." Trant was panting. "I just caught a glimpse of him—missed with my heat-stab—"

Trant had gotten back to his feet, half blinded by the puff of light, but unhurt. The door of the servant's entrance barred him. He melted through it, found himself in a maze of lower corridors and rooms.... The alarm was bursting around him. Then he found another door, open, leading out to another lower pedestrian level. The fugitive was gone, and Trant rushed back to me.

We found Madeleine Blair lying where she had fallen. Pale as death, but she was stirring. We raised her up and laid her on a couch. The windows glared with the police flare out on the Traffic Ramp. The traffic was halted; pedestrians were shouting; the accursed siren was making the night hideous.

Then the living room was full of men. The Police Alarm Squad.... A bedlam! In the midst of it I stood, weak, shaky, and dizzy, with Trant beside me as we bent over the girl.

"Somebody hurt?" the Squad Chief demanded. "Who is she?"

"Get a doctor," I said. "She may be dying."

"Who are you?" They pounced on Trant and me. "Armed! Both of 'em armed—"

"Don't be a dumb-wit," I said. "S.S. Men—Desk 4—" I showed my insignia, tattooed on my forearm. "Get a doctor, I tell you—"

The agonized Mac hadn't skimped with his Alarm Call. Doctors from the nearest branch of General Hospital were here. They cleared the hubbub away from the girl....

But the rest of the room—and all the neighborhood—continued in a wild turmoil. Trant and I shoved ourselves into a corner, watching the Alarm Squad drag in its cumbersome apparatus to get all the technical clues of the premises.

And suddenly I thought of Mac, apprehensive about me.

"We got to call Mac," I murmured to Trant.

"I've got him on here," Trant responded quietly.

That's Trant for you. My own apparatus was put out of business when I smashed the Alarm band. I leaned over Trant's little diaphragm.

"I'm all correct, Chief."

"Yes. I see you are." The bouyancy was back in Mac's voice. "You two come back here—we'll line this thing up and see what comes next."

But I had my own ideas on that. After all, I was in possession of far more facts concerning this thing than either Mac or Trant. I made an excuse to cut Mac off. I wanted to hear what had happened to Trant.

"What happened to you, Trant?" I asked eagerly. "Did you catch the Wasp? Who—?"

"I got it," Trant said slowly. "But I didn't get him. After you left, I took your aero and followed him from the thousand foot level. I tried to use my electro-binoculars but all I could get was a glimpse of him—enough to tell it was a man.

"He must have guessed that I was following him, for as we reached the Hudson ramp, he charged up the incline and was in the air. Then he made his first mistake. He flipped the Wasp upward and vanished into the clouds. You can probably guess the rest, Jac. I let him have it with the radiac beam, after picking him up with your infrared detector. It was a direct hit, the ignition was disabled and the green-bronze Wasp came sliding out of the clouds.

"I shot your Nomad down and landed, got my gun out and waited. The Wasp floated down near me, but there was no one in it. He had tricked me and bailed out, probably in a tiny volplane glider.

"Mac ordered me to join you and while I was on the way he called me again to tell he had just got a red flash from you. He was almost in a panic... Well, I was at the courtyard within sixty seconds. I was trying to find the entrance when a shadowy figure appeared at the end of the courtyard. I fired, but my heat-flash missed. But I did get a glimpse of him. His hood slipped back and I saw a gaunt, cadaverous face with high cheek bones—a grim slit of a mouth. I was about to fire again when his arm moved in a throwing gesture. There was an explosion, a blinding glare of light. He had missed me but the force of the explosion knocked me down and he escaped.

"Well—you know the rest. I told you how I melted the lock and got in. And that's about all."

He grinned as he finished. That was like Trant; to crowd earth-shaking events into a short narrative, play down his own part in the affair, and then dismiss it with a grin.

"I picked this up back there in the courtyard," he added.

The thing that the fiend had thrown, which had exploded with that blinding puff of white light. It was a small mechanism about the size of one's fist. What it had been originally was not determinable now. A mechanism perhaps of wires, a diaphragm, coils and levers, intricate as a watch. But now it was a fused shapeless wreckage.

"A projector," I murmured.

We stared at it in awe. The projector of the frightened death. We could not doubt it. And the thing undoubtedly was devised so that when thrown it would destroy itself and its secret.

"Well, so much for that," Trant murmured. He dropped it back into his pocket. No one in the room here was paying any attention to us. I heard one of the doctors say:

"She's coming around all right—nerve shock—fainted from fright.... The frightened death—that's what it is—"

The frightened death! Those three diabolic words spread around the room, through the doors, out over the now crowded pedestrian ramp.... The frightened death. Like a fire in prairie grass—I could imagine just those three words of the doctor's might sweep the whole city....

THE ALARM SQUAD CHIEF here knew approximately what had occurred, of course, for Trant had swiftly told him.

"Let's answer his damned questionnaire and get out of here," Trant murmured to me.

But my plan was formulating. I told Trant what the girl had told me—and what we ought to do now.

Trant stared. "If the Chief will let us—"

"I'll argue him," I said. "Just a second. I want to speak to her—"

It was certainly a relief to know that she was recovering. That girl's beauty sort of haunts me even now.

I bent over her, motioning away the doctors. I can be vehement upon occasion. They raised their eyebrows, but they withdrew.

"You're going to General Hospital," I said. "But you're all right now."

"Yes," she murmured. "But my father—"

I bent lower. "That's the idea, Miss Blair—my partner and I are going to get him out of there—"

"Oh—if you could—"

"We will. Secretly. None of this alarm stuff—" That would probably cause his death, but I didn't mention it. "We'll get him out—I'll have him with you in General Hospital—say in two hours."

I was smiling. Heavens knows I had no such optimism.

Her eyes were thanking me. She murmured, "Oh that's what I want—"

"And in the meantime," I whispered, "what happened to us here—you can answer questions on that. Tell it freely. But your personal affairs—"

She mustered a wan smile. I've met a lot of girls in my professional routine, but I will say Madeleine Blair topped them all. She murmured faintly: "What goes into the S.S. Bureau never comes out—that's what you said. So now that it's in there—I can't get it out."

"Correct," I nodded. And as I turned away, I said:

"Two hours—General Hospital—"

Her eyes still were thanking me.

Mac put up quite an argument when we called him. He had had such a shock, getting that disaster call from me. But even apart from any possible danger in which Madeleine Blair's father might be, there was every reason in the world why we should try to plunge this thing through to a swift finish. This alarm here at the Blair cubby already was being broadcasted. Public hysteria—mass terror it had almost grown to be—was swiftly mounting. Evidence of it everywhere was pouring in on Mac's instruments. A woman fainted at the wheel of her roller as she listened to the accursed aircaster. It caused a traffic accident. The crowding pedestrians thought that the fiend of the frightened death was among them. They stampeded. Three women were trampled. A pedestrian towerman lost his wits and stabbed with a heat-flash when the crowd wouldn't obey him. A man was killed....

It couldn't go on. Federal orders choked off that broadcast within a minute or two, but by word of mouth the whole city was terrorizing itself.

"I'll send three teams of you," Mac said.

"No you won't, Chief. You let Trant and me do it—"

Then Mac suddenly yielded, and we shut him off before he could change his mind.

I shoved Trant through the maelstrom of that Alarm Squad routine. They were using the olfactory classifier now—the "Bloodhound Machine" as the aircasters so luridly call it.

Trant had found a fragment of the fugitive's black robe, which had been caught in the slamming door as he escaped. We borrowed one of the smallest, portable classifiers.

"What you want it for?" the alarm man demanded.

"Federal Orders," I said. "You wouldn't interfere with them, would you? We've got a clue in Washington—or maybe it's in Florida. I forget."

We shoved our way out to the ramp, found my Nomad Official, and in another minute were in the air, headed north for the Hudson River Tappan section, where on an incongruously lonely wooded hilltop the Levise Sanatorium was perched.

4

I CONTACTED MAC. "We're on our way, Chief. That girl Madeleine Blair—she may not have left for General Hospital yet. Call her and get a description of her cousin, Ruffo Blair."

The cadaverous face of the tall, gaunt fiend—

Mac's answer came in a minute or two: "Ruffo Blair—age thirty. Dark, stocky—face apparently type three."

Far from cadaverous. "Thanks," I said. "See you shortly, Chief—"

"You watch yourselves, Jac—"

"Sure enough," I promised.

The Levise property had belonged to an eccentric millionaire. He had owned all the hill—one of the few sections here which still was as nature had made it. Flying lightless, silent with totally muffled engine, we circled nearby, inspecting it with the telescopic glasses. It was an eerie looking place—dark save for a few outer spots of dim light and a faint glow from within, shining through the translucent glassite panes.

The hill was half a mile from the river—a steep upward climb of a winding road through the trees. In the distance the valley of the Hudson was visible—clustering lights along its banks. But there was only one house on the hill—a long, low, single-storied, rambling structure, old-fashioned in design, but modern with its many big shaded glassite windows. It was perched on the rock summit, with only a little level space where the road wound around its side and front. And the balconied back hung at the brink of a cliff—a sheer precipitous drop of two hundred feet or so to an inner valley where, a quarter of a mile away, the woods and the suburban city lights were strung in a solid mass.

"Can't land near the summit," Trant murmured.

I wafted vertically down and dropped into a little glade perhaps halfway up the hill, where the trees and heavy vegetation would shroud the Nomad. We climbed out. It was Stygian dark here. Sullen clouds overhead, with a night wind swaying the tree-tops.

It was a brief climb up through the thickets of that dark, rocky slope. Brief, but unpleasant. I've trailed many a bandit through city corridors—assaulted them in squalid cubby rooms. But this was wholly different. It seemed suddenly, that every copse, every black crag was masking the lurking fiend with his eerie, diabolic weapon trained upon us. The damned thought had me jumpy. I was glad enough when in a minute or two we crouched on the brink of the summit, with dark crags around us.

THE SMALL LEVEL open space was here before us—the arriving roller-road, and some fifty feet away, the wall of one side of the building. Its heavy glassite windows were all dark and shaded. A silence brooded here—there was only the sough of the wind in the tree-tops around us.

"Can't get any closer without instruments," Trant murmured. "We could be seen."

Which was true enough. We were still some thirty feet vertically below the building's level, and there were occasional outside tube-lights which shifted a band of illumination on the the open space and the roadway. We had noticed while aloft that this band of illumination encircled the entire building, except the end that overhung the precipice. No one—unaided by instruments—could cross that lighted area without being observed....

Our plan was to determine now as much of the interior conditions as possible; then for me to get inside, locate the girl's father and get him out. With Trant outside to aid my entrance and cover the escape.

I imagine it was intuition mostly which convinced us that the fiend of the frightened death—he of the cadaverous face—was here now. Lurking out here in the woods— or lurking inside the building. We could not guess which.

"Shall we try the classifier now?" Trant whispered. "If we could pick up a trail—"

I hate to admit that my mind was more on the safety of that girl's father than killing the fiend of the frightened death. Crouching beside Trant, here in the windy darkness, I was roving the lightless building with the eavesdropping ray. The interior sounds were mostly so blurred and dim that nothing I heard seemed to mean much. Certainly at the moment there was no one talking in that part of the building. Very slowly I focused upon different sections of it. I came upon heavy breathing and the occasional rustling or slight thumping as someone moved. Once it seemed there was a sequence of blurred footsteps. It went out of focus, I lost it and could not seem to pick it up again... And once I caught the thump of a door closing with a clicking lock.

And then I stiffened. "What is it?" Trant whispered.

I let him share the receiver. From a point down at the

distant, opposite end of the building, we were getting voices.

"I tell you, Ludwig, you're mad—insane...."

It was the voice of Dr. Levise.

Then another voice: "Mad, Charles! Because I have a dream? So many had my dream—Alexander—Napoleon—to conquer petty worlds peopled by ignorant fools. What a different world we have today. Worthy of a master—"

It was a weird voice, throaty and then slipping with the vehemence of emotion almost into falsetto... And weird with a queer wildness as though dominating it were a passion almost uncontrollable.

"Your dream is mad, Ludwig—impossible—"

"Impossible? You dare to say it again? Why—why—"

"I tell you I won't have it. This damnable frightened death—"

"Ah—the frightened death, Charles—they name it well—" There was an eerie gruesome burst of cackling laughter. "The frightened death—and you with your petty plots. This Ruffo Blair—"

"He thinks you are mad, Ludwig. Mad with lust—"

"He—thinks? You—told—him?"

"How could he help knowing?"

There was a sudden silence. I felt Trant gripping me.

"Jac—"

It was a silence most horrible. A second or two of gruesome expectancy, pregnant with murder. Then there was a rustle—a thump—a faint, gasping choked cry that suggested blood rattling in a throat constricted by death....

Grisly tragedy taking place now behind the grim dour

walls which stood before us! In a few seconds it was over. There was only the panting, lusting breath of the victorious murderer; a faint padding step, dying away, blurred as it passed beyond my focus....

For a moment Trant and I crouched in silence.

"I'll go in," I whispered.

"Be careful, Jac," Trant already had put up his argument on being the one to go.

"Oh—sure," I agreed. "Blank me out now."

HE HAD ALREADY connected the small apparatus of the invisible ray; and he projected it upon me. Weird sort of thing—our modern development of the old Roentgen ray, with a vibration rate of some 600 billion per second. I felt nothing, of course—but since the light-rays reflecting from my body were far beyond the frequencies which the human eye can record, I was invisible.

"All correct," Trant murmured. "Direct me now and I'll keep it on you."

We were connected with our tiny split-wave audiphones.

I whispered, "I'll head for that main doorway first— direct line. When I get into the shadows of the walls I won't need you. I want to try the classifier—"

I crossed the band of light. Trying the classifier at the main doorway was a bit of luck. I didn't have to prowl for this trail. The levers of the bloodhound machine were set with the classification of the scent of that bit of torn, black robe—the scent of the fiend of the frightened death—he of the cadaverous face. The classifier is intricate of construction, but certainly simple enough in principle: the mathematical index of the scent which differentiates every individual from every other. A thing so simple that every dog knows it....

And luck was with me. I snuffed the the little vacuum cups along the ground as I walked, and then near the doorway, I hit the trail. The classifier buzzed faintly as the matching scent came in. It was strongest at that main threshold. The fiend of the frightened death quite obviously was no lurking marauder here, for he had entered the building quite openly by the main entrance....

The long concrete and metal wall of the building was shadowed at its foot. "Snap off," I told Trant. "I'm going in that little doorway—looks like a cellar entrance."

"Try and come out the same way," Trant's voice murmured. "I'll be watching—and if you give me a call, I'll be in there in ten seconds—"

"Correct," I said. I edged along the wall, toward a small lower grid door, sunk a few feet below the ground level— seemingly a cellar entrance. Then abruptly I had a chance to use the curve-ray. The window of a projecting wing was open at the top. Trant's voice suddenly suggested it.

"Footsteps in that wing. Try the Benson, Jac—the angle is wrong from here."

I took a chance and very briefly arched the beam into the opening. It disclosed a segment of dimly tube-lit corridor. And abruptly a figure appeared. A woman carrying a tray. She looked like a head nurse. Emmeline Gros. The name popped into my mind with memory of Madeleine Blair's mention of it. The girl had shuddered. Well she might. This woman was fully six feet in height. Gaunt, wide-shoul-dered, angular... A long black dress, pinched at the waist, white ruching at the wrists and throat, gray-black hair, primly parted.

And then, with the angle of her altering as she advanced, I saw her face. Pallid—gaunt—a mouth like a slit, grimly dour—sunken cheeked. The cadaverous face of the fiend of the frightened death.

In a few seconds she had passed beyond my vision.

I reached the little cellar door—a solid metal panel, with a strong interior lock. But nothing like that can withstand an oxyo-electronic heat-torch. Trant, from his place a hundred feet or so away, again flashed his high-frequency ray upon me, to mask the glow of the torch and the fusing door. Within half a minute it yielded… For a moment I stood tense, peering into darkness. Then I went inside.

5

IT WAS THE cellar, thrumming with the low whir of the electrical mechanisms of lighting and heating. I found a corridor, padded cautiously along it, looking for stairs or a catwalk incline that would lead me upward.

I was calm enough now, wary, thoroughly alert. This certainly was in my line. Soundlessly I went a hundred feet or so down that corridor which had dark rooms—storerooms—mechanism rooms and the like—opening from it. I was not bothering with instruments now; my alert senses were enough. My padded-soled shoes were soundless. My clothes, my linen shirt and collar were black, highly absorbent of light. I dropped the black-silk mask-shield over the white flesh of my face, and shielded my hands. My hooded light was reduced to a mere flicker—pallid and elusive as a wisp of moonlight.

I came presently upon a little spiral incline, and in a moment was in the upper main corridor. It had a low vaulted ceiling and the floor was padded. Closed doors showed along it, bedrooms, I had no doubt. For a moment I stood, Banning gun in hand, pressed against the wall in a patch of shadow. A tiny shaded light down the corridor seemed to mark the entrance of a dark reception room. Beyond it there was a foyer. At a night desk a young girl in white sat reading by the light of a small hooded tube.

Should I tackle her? My plan was simple enough—in theory: quietly to seize the first person I encountered—find the location of Sir John's room, and get him out. I had changed the plan now. It was that woman of the cadaverous face I now wanted to locate; make her take me to Sir John.

This corridor branched here close beside me. As I peered down one of its shadowed lengths, the distant dark blob of a figure showed—a prowling shadow like myself. It seemed a man. It was moving away from me, and in a second it had darted across the hallway and was into a yawning black door oval.

I went down that corridor like a loping cat. At the oval casement, where the door slide stood open, I melted flat upon the dim corridor floor, peering with just my eyes beyond the opening.

It was a vaguely lighted, vaulted sitting room. A mute scene of tragedy. The table had a hooded light, with a little circle of illumination casting down upon the body of Dr. Levise, slumped in his chair, head and shoulders sprawled on the table, and in his chest a knife was buried to its hilt, with a crimson stain sodden on his ruffled white shirt.

The murder which Trant and I a few minutes ago had overheard. And here now, with his back to me, a stocky man was standing peering at the body. He didn't hear me when I hitched over the threshold and slid the door panel. At the click as it closed, he whirled, stared into the diaphragm of my gun as I crouched on one knee before him.

"Easy," I murmured. "Any sound and I'll melt through your heart. Lock your hands over your head."

He locked them. He was a young fellow, perhaps thirty. Dark, stocky—face type three.

I backed him against the wall with the dead eyes of Dr. Levise staring at us.

"You're Ruffo Blair?" I asked.

"Yes. How—how—" He was terrified almost beyond speech. "Who—who are you?"

"S.S. Man. Hard luck, eh?"

He gasped, "I didn't kill him—" His locked hands tried to gesture at the slumped body of Dr. Levise. "I swear—I had no idea—"

"Of course," I chuckled. "Ludwig killed him. You know Ludwig, don't you?"

He looked blank.

"The frightened death," I added.

"Frightened death? Emmeline Gros—she—I—I tell you I've got nothing to do with it. You get me out of here—"

I HAD NO trouble making him talk. Madeleine Blair's fear of him certainly was justified. He had plotted the death of Sir John—hired Dr. Levise to cause it with his diabolical weapon so that no trace of murder would be left. A murder house, this Sanatorium. There had been two others, and when the suspicion of the authorities had been aroused enough to cause a routine questionnaire, Dr. Levise had come to us, demanding a guard to throw us off the track.

Young Blair, under my prodding gun, blurted it out. He seemed to have no idea of the real nature of the weapon he had hired to kill his victim. And now that Dr. Levise was dead, and Sir John presumably still alive, the terror-stricken Ruffo seemed fearful that he was in danger of sharing the fate of Dr. Levise, so that he wanted me to get him out.

"Fair enough," I said. "You haven't done much apparently—only plotted murder—"

If Sir John were still alive…. This had been a swift soft colloquy; I had not lingered more than a minute. Ruffo told me now where Sir John's bedroom was located.

"Correct," I said. "You're lessening your penalty with this help—we'll go get him out—"

He suddenly murmured, "Look—the door slide—moving—"

There are not many tricks that in one form or another, I haven't had tried on me. I had to flash a look at the doorslide, just in case it was moving; but the tail of my gaze still observed Ruffo. His hands came down and he made a leap for me. Now most assuredly I did not intend to kill him. I stepped backward and fired the Banning flash down between us to stop his rush, but he stumbled and went down so that he caught it full…. His body only twitched for a moment, then stared up with frozen eyes—mute dead gaze seeming to cross with the stare of the dead Levise….

I had the door-slide softly opened in another second or two. The dim corridor was silent and empty. The bedroom Ruffo had designated as Sir John's was in this wing, not far away. Its window would overlook the roadway.

I padded to the door. I could only hope that Ruffo had not lied. I turned the lever; the door yielded.

The window of the small unlighted bedroom was closed, but not shrouded. The night had cleared a bit; moonlight was streaming in, and by its glow I could make out the room's dim outlines. Metal furniture, a padded easy chair, a huge black velvet portiere apparently shrouding a wardrobe recess. And a small single bed.

I breathed again. The figure of a gray-haired man was recumbent on the bed. In the silence I could hear his regular breathing.

"Sir John—wake up—"

I sat on the bed, gently prodding him. "Please—no outcry—I'm a friend—" I was alert to clap my hand on his mouth if he should try to scream. He stirred, gasped a little, and then he sat up.

"Who are you?"

"An S.S. Man. You're in danger—I came to get you out of here."

"Danger—"

"Your daughter was attacked tonight—not hurt much—"

That quickened his wits. He was trembling, confused and pathetic-looking as he sat in his gray-braided night suit, the mass of his white hair rumpled.

"Madeleine—hurt—"

"Not very much. But she's worried for your safety. I've got to get you out of here—quietly—now— You're to meet her at the General Federal Hospital—"

I got him off the bed and to the window. His dressing gown and slippers were on a chair. I robed him in them.

Then I called Trant.

"You Jac—" his voice murmured. "I've been worried—"

"All correct. I've got him." Trant wasn't more than two hundred feet away from the window now. Then I told Sir John how Trant's ray would make us invisible; I pointed to the shadowed clump of rocks where Trant was crouching across the band of roadway illumination....

"Hurry it," Trant's voice urged.

"Coming," I murmured. "You go first, Sir John. You can make it—"

"Of course I can make it." He had braced up now. I slid him feet first through the window; it was no more than three or four feet above the ground.... He got there safely. For an instant the moonlight illumined him; then he faded ghostlike, a shimmering wraith for a second as Trant's vibrations enveloped him.... Then the vision of him had vanished....

CORRECT. MY HEART was pounding, exultant... I was panting. Queer.

In those seconds I whirled, snatched the Banning gun from my beltclip. The big black portiere across the room's alcove caught my attention; could the damnable vibrations be coming from there? I darted at it, shaking on trembling legs; shoved it aside. The wardrobe recess showed a faint radiance behind the hanging garments.

A secret-panel door-slide. The murderer's entrance to the room of his victim. Staggering, I shoved past the garments, one hand clutching at my throat, the other striving to hold the leveled gun steady. Staggering, I went through the opening. There was a long dark vaulted room, with moon-light straggling in its windows—a dining room of empty tables and chairs. Far across it at another door the moon-light struck on a tense figure, with arm extended; a figure, skirted, tall, gaunt with white ruching at the throat... the woman with the cadaverous face—Emmeline Gros—friend of the frightened death.

There was a startled cackling outcry at my entrance—my leap carrying me to stagger against a table. I fired. The stab of heat hissed wide of the mark and the side portieres went up in a flame.

I must have stabbed another flash as I sagged. The jibing cry from across the long room abruptly ceased....

Then something snapped in me. Bonds breaking. My heart still raced, but there was a relief. I saw as I straightened erect that the distant door oval was empty.

I must have staggered as I ran—but my youth and health and strength quickly steadied me. The corridor beyond the oval was dim and silent save for distant alarmed cries from other parts of the building. Thirty feet away I caught a glimpse of the fleeing figure darting into another oval. My heat-stab missed it as I ran forward; around an angle— through another room—to the back of the building now.

I was barely ten feet behind the running shape as we plunged through a black doorway. I found myself on a twenty foot balcony, with the woman backed against the low rail and the abyss of the valley behind her. The moonlight struck on her weird snarling face; teeth bared like an animal—burning eyes, wide with murderous lust.

With a leap I caught her. "Got you! Give me that damned weapon—"

But suddenly her arms went around me, bony fingers gripping my wrist. I felt the Banning gun wrenched away, heard it drop to the floor.

Amazing, demoniac strength of this adversary! Abruptly I found myself fighting against the knee-high rail—moonlit abyss far below. The twisted face of bared teeth snarled at my throat.

We staggered sidewise, momentarily away from the abyss.... And suddenly as I fought, I saw that my antagonist's primly parted gray hair was askew. A wig. It fell off, disclosing a bullet head of close-cropped black hair.

A man! He towered over me. The Ludwig who had murdered Dr. Levise! The damnable little mechanism was in his hand now. He was trying to thrust it against my chest, but I desperately caught his wrist, twisted until the accursed thing dropped to our feet.

Then again I felt the rail at my knees. I almost went over that time, but somehow I twisted free, and clipped his chin with an uppercut. For just an instant he staggered. Then on the little low rail he seemed hanging…. A second at the brink of eternity, with an eerie scream bursting from him.

Then he was gone. Panting, I gripped the railing and stared down. There was just a rotating blob, dwindling as it fell, and then a crumpled, broken shape far down on the gleaming rocks, with the sound of the thud still echoing in my ears.

6

MAN OF DESTINY. In failure, they are madmen; in success, we call them Conquerers.... We got a few details of this Ludwig Levise from the London Police. He was Dr. Charles Levise's younger brother; wanted in London for petty murder, and political plotting. He had been a research physicist in Austria, some ten years ago.

Enough of him. An unsuccessful Conquerer deserves no more lengthy obituary. Perhaps he had some rational plan for developing his reign of terror into a conquest, but if so, it must forever remain unknown.

I am thinking of a subject more pleasant—the scene that night at Federal Hospital when I took Sir John Blair to his daughter's bedside. My memory will always hold the vision of her eyes thanking me.

And there is one scene more I must record. That little projector of the frightened death which I had wrenched from the murderer's hand, had not exploded. I found it intact. It was the only one of its kind that was found; and the Shadow Squad turned it over to Dr. Georges Martel—a Federal Consultant of Experimental Physics.

I recall that evening about a week later when Trant, Mac and I sat in Dr. Martel's little lecture auditorium. A full hundred scientists and government officials were assembled.

And the white-haired old Dr. Martel addressed us.

"Diabolical," he was saying. "Yet simple in principle. What causes our heart to beat? Have you ever thought of that, gentlemen? The mainspring of life—that inner stimulus so mysterious. The heart is a muscle. Within it, deep down somewhere—there is some mysterious urge—some rhythmic stimulus. The initial impulse. And it is electrical...."

He held the cylindrical little mechanism in his hand.

"This thing fires a ray—call it that—a beam of vibration quite akin to radio waves. A different frequency—there are many frequencies in the band beyond the A, B and C rays, the nature of which we still know very little. And this beam—soundless, invisible, imponderable—deranges that initial impulse. The heart races. And unless he gets relief, the victim will die."

The old scientist was still gazing at the cylinder. He added:

"We could learn much from this diabolical little thing. It is, I can readily believe, the only one of its kind in the world. I could take it apart, study it, construct others. But do you know what I am going to do with it?"

He raised his hand suddenly over his head and flung the cylinder to the floor. It smashed with the roar of an explosion and a blinding puff of white light....

The end of the frightened death. And speaking for myself, I'm glad of it.

WHERE READERS AND EDITORS GET TOGETHER

HAS RAY CUMMINGS got his dates all wrong? His letter on suspended animation, which is a feature in his story "Crimes of the Year 2000," in this week's issue of *Detective Fiction Weekly,* is printed below. As we go to press a violent controversy is raging. One scientist in California claims that he has *already* suspended animation in a monkey, and a human volunteer has offered himself for experimentation, like Jonathan Gregg.

Other doctors say the thing is impossible, and the experiment would be murder.

We wouldn't know. We're only wondering whether the title of Mr. Cummings' unusual stories should be changed to "Crimes of Next Year."

DEAR EDITOR:

Regarding the present-day advancements of science in the direction of suspended animation:

For years experimenters have been able to take certain species of fish, freeze them solid—actually kill them—and then successfully revive them. But with warm-blooded animals, the process is far more complicated. The main difficulty has been that in the blood there exists a chemical called fibrogen. It usually causes coagulation of the blood after death, which of course is fatal to suspended animation.

But that difficulty now has been overcome, according to published reports.

In "The Man Who Died Twice," something like the following happened to Jonathan Gregg:

In the year 1940, sodium citrate was injected into his blood. This destroyed the fibrogen. He was then placed in that sealed glass cylinder, into which oxygen and ether were pumped. When he had lost consciousness, carbon dioxide was pumped into the cylinder—and that killed him.

Then, after dehydration, the body was kept refrigerated for sixty years… and that's the condition Jonathan Gregg was in during the action of the story.

Cordially,

RAY CUMMINGS

www.ingramcontent.com/pod-product-compliance
Lightning Source LLC
Chambersburg PA
CBHW031201020726
47499CB00002B/439